First Edition

RAW MAN

RAW MAN

A Novel by

FRED RIVERA

A Word with You Press*
Publishers and Purveyors of Fine Stories
310 East A Street, Suite B, Moscow, Idaho 83843

www.awordwithyoupress.com

Rivera, Fred
Raw Man

ISBN-10: 0988464632
ISBN-13: 978-0-9884646-3-6

Raw Man is published by:
A Word with You Press
310 East A Street, Suite B, Moscow, Idaho 83843

For information please direct emails to:
info@awordwithyoupress.com or visit our website:
www.awordwithyoupress.com

Book cover designed by Scott Siedman
Book interior design: Teri Rider

First Edition, October 2014
Author's limited edition, August 2014

Printed in the United States of America

10 9 8 7 6 5 4 3 2 1   14 15 16 17 18 19 20 21 22 23

Acknowledgments

I would like to thank the Anti-Social Writers and Creative Misfits meet-up group in Oceanside, California for their encouragement and support. I attended their Wednesday night meetings diligently for a year, and when the pain that the long drive imposed was more than I could tolerate, they came to my home in Murrieta to conduct the meet-up and critique. I will never forget that gesture of support from fellow veterans, Ed Coonce, Dante Puccetti, Russ Shor, and Barry Drucker, and fellow writers David Boyne and Thornton Sully.

Thornton Sully believed that I had a great story to tell, and convinced me I had more talent than I gave myself credit for. With his guidance, love, and belief in me, I was able to tell it. He was to become my mentor and guide on this long journey of creation. He brought along his incredible staff of *A Word with You Press*. My thanks to Billy Holder, chief IT man, for the incredible video and website; Tiffany Monique, a most organized staffer and logistics manager, who told me where to be and when; Teri Rider for thoughtful book design, who helped me to understand that book-design is not just a craft, but an art. I thank associate-editor Kristine Tsatsakos-Starr, who helped develop the story arc and caught every misplaced comma, and period, and gave so much of herself to the betterment of the story.

I thank my best friend Scott Siedman, the most creative force in the universe, for being my word and idea tree. When I was stuck, I only had to reach out and pluck a word or phrase from his bountiful tree of ideas. He also designed the book cover and the T-shirts.

I thank my friend Bob Kahn, the galley editor and writer who told me what to expect from a publisher. His words: "Don't take it personal when they chop thirty pages off the top" helped me to keep on writing when it looked like I had lost all control.

I want also to thank my friends John Fortuna and Lance Goto, who appear in Raw Man and continue to play a big part in my life.

I am grateful for the support from my family, strangers and acquaintances who believed in this project and raised the funds needed through Kickstarter to make this dream a reality.

A special thanks goes out to my cousin and life-long pal, Edward James Olmos. His passionate commitment to social justice opened many doors which would have forever been shut, locked, and bolted to my small voice. My opportunity to work with veterans with PTSD and our struggle against "bad paper" would not have be possible without his help. Thank you TuTu!

I will forever be in the debt of my incredible wife, Lynda, for being by my side as I re-lived some of the most brutal, painful and traumatic experiences of my life. I sat at the keyboard with her loving arms wrapped around my shoulders.

I thank the men I served with, especially those who never made it back, for teaching me what real love is and what an incredible gift it is to open my eyes each morning, take a deep breath, and go out and try to be the best person I can be.

This book is dedicated to the loving memory of my parents, Arthur and Marina Rivera. They loved me unconditionally. They inspired me to write this book by saving every letter I wrote to them from Vietnam. They taught me how to love the same way.

In his own words: Author's Foreword

After my mother passed away, my sister and I were going through Mom's possessions as people do when closing a home. We were trying to figure out what to keep, what to give away, and what belongings were personal to each of us. My sister, Barbara, came across a shoebox filled with letters. We discovered that Mom had kept every letter I had ever written to my family from Vietnam. Chronologically arranged, covered in that red dirt of Vietnam, the letters gave us a few hours of distraction from our grief. When we finished reading them, I took them home and they sat on my shelf for years.

A friend suggested that I type them onto my computer so I could better preserve them. As I typed out each letter, memories flooded my mind as I recalled the truth of every incident that I wrote home about. I realized that I was always trying to shield my parents from the horrors of my existence. The letters are the genesis of the book you are holding in your hands, and they were purposely left unedited with misspellings and grammatical mistakes. They were written by the twenty-year-old Fred, sometimes by torchlight, almost always under duress.

The names have been changed except for a handful of men that I loved. For my surviving brothers: I am happy that you may see your name in this book and it is not on a marble slab in Washington, D.C.

All the battle scenes are as true as my 66-year-old mind can remember them. Because some events and characters are composites, it is more accurate to call Raw Man a novel, rather than a memoir,

but most of the things I write about happened in front of my eyes ...
seared into my heart and for me, 44 years later, are still real.

"My soul," he repeated. "It's gone.
I've been without a soul since the war.
I killed.
I killed a boy. I did wrong.
I can't feel a thing."

"War And The Soul"
Edward Tick, Ph.D

It makes no difference what men think of war. ...
War endures.
As well ask men what they think of stone.
War was always here.
Before man was, war waited for him.

"Blood Meridian"
Cormac McCarthy

Prologue

The sink in the men's restroom at the Long Beach VA hospital took an overdose of Percocet this morning. I was shaking so violently that half the bottle fell in. I salvaged what I could. I only hope those pills help take away any pain the sink might be experiencing today. As for me, they stopped working some time ago.

I am in chronic pain, and spikes like I am having today bring out the worst in me. They insidiously remind me of the time I spent in the jungle of Vietnam.

The VA gives me 100 percent disability for the pain and suffering resulting from me getting blown off my track in 1969, and for 30 years of inescapable, intrusive thoughts of war. PTSD can hit you out of nowhere and it came roaring out today.

My father is dying of cancer and I'm trying to be with him as much as possible. He is surprisingly reflective, considering all the drugs they have him on. My war ended nearly 30 years ago and Dad's more than 50, but I'm discovering psychological wounds linger longer than some physical ones do. Dad still has nightmares from his time in WWII.

After I OD'd the sink, I came struggling out of the bathroom to see Dad's newspaper open to the crossword page. The paper was upside down as I sat at the foot of the bed. Five down was a three-letter word for armed conflict. Transfixed with terror, 27 years after I got on the flight home, I saw that Nam War was *Raw Man* spelled backwards.

I'm pretty raw today.

I
Face Toward Enemy

The rain came five days ago and has not stopped for one minute. No mail has come in or out through this fucking weather. The wind is so strong that the resupply choppers can't make their drops. We have started heating C-rations with what is left of our C4 plastic explosives. No one has shaved or brushed his teeth in a week. Benson and Billy have malaria and we can't dust them off in a medical helicopter. A scorpion bit me last night while I was trying to scrape the mud off my boots. My hand swelled up to the size of a baseball and burned like hell. Doc Sykes, the troop medic, gave me a shot of Soldier's Joy; that's what we call morphine. We all carry ampoules of it.

Doc does the best he can. We all do. Doc has his hands full with broken men. There are worse wounds to tend to than a scorpion bite.

Morale is so low that fights are breaking out within the platoon. Rain sizzles on hot tempers. There is so much rain, it can't just be the weather; maybe God crying His eyes out for what His children are doing to each other down here, or maybe for what He has done to us.

I feel like I'm an octopus living underwater. Two of my tentacles stay busy cleaning my weapon, one swats away mosquitoes, and three stay busy setting up trip-flares and Claymore mines. One tentacle holds a cigarette in my mouth while one rubs my feet. My feet are so swollen from jungle rot that I can barely walk. I have no dry socks. The mud is two feet deep. Last night we got hit with rockets and the damn things didn't explode until they hit solid ground. We were sprayed with mud. This was far superior to catching shrapnel, but annoying as hell.

We've been up along the Cambodian border for more than two weeks and our platoon is shrinking. Vehicles are broken. Machine-gun parts and ammunition are in short supply. Men are dying. Worst of all, we are running out of cigarettes.

I hate this place. I hate the NVA, I hate the Army. I hate everyone and everything.

Well, almost everyone.

There is one guy that I've grown particularly fond of. He is my best friend in this muddy, wicked world. His name is Herman.

It was in the early days of our time in the field. Herman came walking toward me holding a canteen of Kool-Aid, a lit cigarette dangling out the corner of his mouth, and a rucksack full of wires and detonators. He had a big smile on his face and his eyes were wide and happy, and he handled the explosives like a sack of groceries. He ignored the "no smoking" part of the field manual when working with this shit.

"It's Howdy Doody time. It's Howdy Doody time. Come on, let's set some mines. It's Howdy Doody time!"

He still sings that stupid song to me when it's our time to go out at night. What a team we are. Our job is to set up the Claymores and trip-flares. I put up with his shit and he puts up with mine. He tries hard to hide his fear with this cheerful little tune, but I know he is scared. Christ, I am too. This is when I love him the most. Our fear is our bond, thicker than the mud that cakes around our ankles.

The unhurried way he moves and sways with such nonchalant swagger while swinging the bag of death over his shoulder has a certain graceful terror to it. His grin lingers behind him like the Cheshire Cat as he moves about. He is a slim black kid from the streets of Detroit. Just another Jack who was drafted, like me. Both of us hate the Army and make no attempt to do anything more than survive another day. We smoke pot and drink and party in the middle of this fucking jungle while rocket and artillery shells ring off in the distance and the arc lights from B52's cast long shadows in the triple canopy forest.

"Charlie gonna get you, boy," he beams each night. "Mr. Charlie just waitin' on your sad ass."

I love the way he handles himself after years of growing up fatherless in the ghetto. The way he teases me makes me feel warm inside.

Every evening after the platoon clears a landing zone, Herman and I go out into the bush together beyond the perimeter to set traps for the enemy. Claymore mines are concave sheaths of plastic explosives about the size of a quart of Jack Daniels filled with hundreds of small shards of shrapnel. Claymore mines are funny. On one side the inscription says, "Face Toward Enemy." That always struck me as bizarre. As if some junked-out GI would actually face it toward himself? I suppose it has happened. Claymores can wipe out four or five Congs at a time. We set trip-flares across trails, or what we think the route of an enemy soldier might be. It is haphazard at best. What do we know?

Herman just wants to get the shit set up and get back inside the safety of the perimeter as soon as possible. We are alone in the jungle at night and his fear is contagious once you cut in under the masquerade he always wears.

"What was that? Did you hear that? Man, let's get out of here," he would whisper.

We weren't always up here along the Cambodian border with six dead Americans stacked like cordwood 100 meters in front of our track. It was a long, cruel turn of events that brought us to this place.

One summer night we would take part in one of the more bizarre adventures of our young lives in this already strange place called Vietnam.

Thursday May 1, 1969

Dear Mom and Dad,

Well, here I am in Vietnam and it's raining and hot. I was not able to change my MOS (Military Occupational Specialty) yet. Everyone here knows that I'm a professional musician, but they say my MOS is too critical. I'm an Armored Intelligence Specialist which is just a fancy way of saying a Scout. I'm still trying. I just flew in to my Base camp. I'm about 45 miles north of Saigon with the 11th Armored Calvary. We call the Base camp Blackhorse. The Blackhorse is the symbol patch for the 11th Armored Calvary. I don't know what troop I'll be with yet because I have to go through a week of jungle training here with live fire. Don't worry about me-the heat doesn't bother me too much. I'm in no danger yet, I just want you to know I'm all right. I'll write and give you my address and tell you about what I'm doing as soon as I can. I have much to tell you about the people and the country. The people live ten times worse than in TJ.

Suddenly, in the middle of writing this letter, two white guys I didn't know came up behind me and peeked over my shoulder.

"Well, at least he knows how to write in English," the taller of the two said.

"What part of Mexico you from, beaner?" the second one chimed in.

I stared the smaller of the two in the eyes and said, "Fuck off, you little piece of white trash!"

The taller one pushed me to the ground and they both started laughing. Even at that distance I could smell the booze on their breath. I scampered to my feet and now that I realized they were drunk off their asses at ten in the morning, I felt the fear leave my body only to be replaced with anger. I grabbed the shorter one in a headlock and rammed his head into a tent post. A small cut opened on his forehead.

"What ya do dat fer?" he asked, as he wiped the blood out of his eye. "We were just fucking with you."

"Would you have pulled that kind of shit on a white guy? Can't you see I'm in the middle of writing a letter?"

Just then, two black guys, Benson and Olgovey, came walking back from the chow hall. Benson looked at my dirty uniform and the blood on the ofay's head. Benson is close to six feet two and though I hadn't gotten to know him yet, he stopped and asked, "Everything all right here?"

The two white drunks didn't even acknowledge Benson and started walking away.

"Couple crackers," I said to Benson. He gave me a smile, slapped my hand, and he and Olgovey continued on their way. I gathered my writing papers and turned back to my letter.

> *This place stinks like burning sewage. It's weird to be in a foreign country and I can't get used to the fact that I'm in a war so far away from home.*
>
> *So far, the only thing that I've seen or heard of the war was a B52 raid about 25 miles from here last night. The ground shook and the sky lit up. This country has a strange beauty. It's lush and green and the ground has a strong reddish texture that turns into crimson rivulets when it rains. It rains constantly. There are more stars at night than I have ever seen in my life. It will be an interesting experience. I have to go and process in right now so I'll see you later.*
>
> *Love,*
> *Fred*

In the first days and weeks I couldn't sleep because of the heat and the noise. The reality of my life had changed in just a matter of days. On Friday night I was out with my friends cruising down Hollywood Boulevard, looking for girls.

On Tuesday, I was here. On Wednesday I saw my first dead body.

All night long, jets and helicopters fly low on their way to missions. Rain, rain and more rain. Rain makes mud and mud makes misery and misery makes for desperation. The heat is unbearable and the humidity as thick as butter. Changing my clothes is not a top priority. The heat dries me off to some degree, but the humidity leaves me in a state of constant dampness. The smell of mildew permeates everything.

On my second night in country, one of my new acquaintances blew another guy's head off with a shotgun. I saw it. Everyone was jumpy. We were FNG's (Fuckin' New Guys). Anything that moved, we shot. I never knew the dead American soldier's name. There was loud talk to hide the quiet dread. We were homesick babies in a strange land, but at least Herman and I were becoming tight.

We liked the same type of music and listened to The Four Tops and The Temptations for hours on end. We talked about the big things in life. We chuckled at the small shit and for that week in the rear we became inseparable.

We had arrived in country within days of each other. Herman set foot there first and in that situation even four days more experience made him an old-timer in my eyes. He knew the ropes so to speak. He knew where to cop the dope and where we could go to smoke it. We talked for hours about life back home.

"Levi Stubbs is a motherfucker," I said.

"You know about Levi?" Herman was surprised.

"Of course I do. He's the lead singer for the Four Tops," I replied.

"Fred, man, how you know this shit? This ghetto shit."

"I'm a musician, Herman. Been playing blues and R&B all my life." All my life amounted to a scant twenty years. "I've backed up the Coasters and the Drifters and an R&B singer named Peppy Hill. Been hanging with the bloods for years. I know about Otis Williams out of the Temptations. They are both Detroit groups. Tell me you don't know them."

"You a brother from another mother," he smiled. "Damn, Fred, you blow my mind. Let me take you with me to meet the brothers. They're going to love you."

It didn't take too long to figure out that the blacks hung with the blacks and the whites hung with their own. Being a Mexican hippie from California, I decided I would go over and meet the brothers. The confrontation with those two white guys the other morning had me all mixed.

That incident brought back memories of when I was in high school dating a white girl. Her father came to our front door one morning and told my dad that he didn't want me seeing his daughter anymore because he knew "how Mexicans treat their women."

My father was flabbergasted. He should have punched him out but my father was above that. As a boy growing up in a small town in Arizona, my father knew racism. The white sheriff who ran that town never gave the Mexican kids a chance to be kids. He would drag them in on a whim and accuse them of mischief for the pettiest of things.

In Globe, Arizona, the temperature often climbed to 110 and the only respite from the heat was the public swimming pool. City ordinances forbade blacks and Mexicans from using the pool until the day before cleaning …

Herman led me past the latrines and mess hall to the far side of the camp, where he offered me up to adoption by my new family. The group was waiting for me.

I already knew Benson, a tall muscular bad-ass from Oakland. He was the most politicized of the bunch. He said that he had joined the Black Panther Party before all the shit went down with Eldridge Cleaver. Benson hated the white man and was always talking about how he was just here to organize the black soldiers into groups of radical pacifists.

Olgovey was a northern black from the DC area. Although he partied, he never seemed to get as fucked up as the rest of us. He was a soft-spoken man and he seemed to look a little older than the rest of the guys. He was light-skinned and took teasing from the other fellows who called him "high yellow."

Doc Lewis had just arrived from Fort Sam Houston where he trained to be a combat medic. He was slender and had a likeable personality. He was our platoon medic.

Herman was right. They did love me.

Outside of our little group, nobody really knew anyone else. Blackhorse became a stopping off place for green recruits to acclimate to both the weather and environment. Here the real training took place. I took my basic training at Fort Ord, California and my advanced infantry training at Fort Knox, Kentucky. Blackhorse was the first place that I actually was put in a real combat situation with live ammunition.

And some ammunition? Not so live. This is where I first learned of the punji sticks. These sharp, pointed sticks were tipped with human shit. It caused infections in the wounds. These and the most horrid kinds of booby traps were placed in holes covered with leaves and brush. The Vietcong took pride in placing traps in the most mind blowing manner of concealment.

Every morning our engineers left the gates of the compound to sweep the area for mines. Every evening the Vietcong laid more. Every other day one of our guys would be killed by the one we didn't find.

The Vietcong wanted us out of there, and they were patient and single-minded.

It was easy to get into a groove in our first week in country. Blackhorse was an Army camp, basically the same as others we had trained at. Our barracks were decent enough, just a place to lay your head down at night. There were communal showers and outdoor toilets. The camp smelled like shit because every morning we had to drag the 50-gallon half drums out from under the latrine and pour diesel fuel on them and let it burn. It was really the shit detail.

The base camp also had a PX, a snack bar, and a movie house. Like every other military installation in the world, they had a bar. Herman and I decided to grab a cold one and walked into this little club that boasted a pool table. What we discovered there surprised the hell out of us. They had a TV!

It was funky and old but we watched the Smothers Brothers with the Beatles and got so high that later that night during an artillery exchange we just sat there, watching TV.

"Is that incoming or outgoing?" Benson asked.

"Not to worry, my man; if it's your time it's your time."

Doc was getting philosophical. One week in country and we were becoming believers in predetermination. I swear it was to be a credo we would live by. If it's your time, it's your time. There it is.

Two weeks ago this thought had never entered my mind, but now, out of experience, it had become a kind of religion.

Around 3 a.m. an airplane flew over us and started spouting propaganda in Vietnamese. With its loudspeaker blaring, it circled for about twenty minutes and we couldn't figure out what its intention was. It turned out that there were two regiments of Vietcong around our perimeter and the US Psych-Ops were telling them to give up. I thought that was pretty hilarious because they had us surrounded and outnumbered and we were instructing them to give up. That combination of arrogance and naïveté set the tone for what was to come.

After a week of in country training, we sat ready to go out into the jungle and start the countdown of days until we got to go home. M-16's and ammunition, flak jackets and helmet liners, ponchos and canteens were issued. Some uncaring supply clerk handed me three pairs of socks and four pair of olive-drab underwear. I prepared to go to war.

Thursday May 15th, 1969

Dear Mom and Dad and Sister,

Sorry I haven't written but things have been a little hectic. I flew out in a helicopter last week to the troop's position in the jungle. The first thing that I see when I get off the chopper is a guy with no shirt wearing a necklace of human ears. He has a jar of them. I don't know if he was born this way or if the war made him dinky dao. His angry attitude turns off most of the veterans, but all us FNG's stay away from him because of the necklace of rotting flesh he wears around his neck. It is gritty and the stench of death follows him. His name is Ted Clementi and he is from Ventura. He has been out here for about six months and everybody calls him Sgt. Rock after some comic book hero. He knows what he's doing. Our biggest worries are RPGs (Rocket Propelled Grenades) and land mines. Sgt. Clementi likes to blow things up. On the second day that I am out here, he spots a mine on a trail. He jumps off our vehicle and straps some C-4 plastic explosive to a hand grenade and runs like hell. Everyone's laughing. Lieutenant Cutter is not pleased, but Clementi gets the job done. We have Kit Carson scouts with us. They are former Vietcong who surrendered and came over to our side and their sole job is to be on the lookout for mines on the trails. Clementi always makes sure he has one of them by his side so that he can show his heroics. A grenade without C-4 would do the trick but Ted loves a big explosion so he straps C-4 to the grenade. I am assigned to a vehicle which will more or less be my home for the next year. He is my track commander (TC) and he has decided to take me under his wing. I'm the driver on his track. A track is an Armored Personal Carrier. A crew consists of a driver, two M-60 machine-gunners, and a TC that mans the 50 Caliber Machine-gun. I'm in Charlie Company, Third Platoon, vehicle four, so my call sign is Charlie

3-4 Delta. Delta means driver. There are four of us on it and we live on the track. All of our activities take place on this piece of metal that I call home. My friend Herman is also assigned to my track. He is the left side machine-gunner. The left side guy fires his M-60 directly over my head. I'm glad that I wound up with him. I don't know where Benson and Doc are, but Olgovey is in the same platoon with us. Anyway, this troop I'm in has been in the jungle since March so the brass has decided to give us a rest. They are a little squirrelly. I have only been out here for a month and luckily I've seen no action other than that mine incident. Today we drove into Lai Khe. Lai Khe is the 1st Infantry Division's Base camp. We will be here for 7 days. It was spooky coming here. We drove all day, passing through the jungle, rubber plantations, and grasslands. When we thundered through a village, I really felt weird. We come rambling down the main road with our tanks and tracks and I don't know what to expect. Millions of little kids came running out of nowhere and I'm afraid that we are going to run them over. Everybody starts throwing C-rations and chewing gum and candy to them; and as we move along, the kids always start fighting for the food and yelling. I could see the ones that were scarred from the war. There are little five year old kids with burns, crippled children. Then we pass an orphanage and they just stare at us through the fence. I feel like crying. No one will ever know what it is like to see this war. Every building we pass is riddled with bullet holes. There are B-52 bomb craters everywhere. You should see those craters. You could put our house and garage in them. We stopped in the village long enough to buy Cokes and beer from some little girls. They charged 50 cents a can. Then we take off and come to Lai Khe and never look back.

This week we will be pulling maintenance on our vehicles. Out of necessity, I'm becoming a pretty good mechanic. I don't want to get stuck out in the jungle sometime when my track

breaks down. You know, this is the only war ever to be fought
where the GI can watch TV and listen to the radio. My platoon
Sgt. has a battery operated TV and when we're out in the field,
we watched television at night. On our Way to Lai Khe, Ted
keeps his radio going on top of the track. Yes, I'm in the Iron
Triangle. I don't know where we'll be going next week but I will
stay in touch. I miss you all.

    Love,

    Fred

"What's with the fuckin' ears, man?" I asked Herman. We had
been filling sandbags on the edge of the perimeter as was our custom
late in the afternoon. After four days in Lai Khe, preparation to go
back to the bush was our top priority. Herman grabbed the bags and
stacked them on the side of our track.

"He says it keeps the gooks from going to heaven or some shit.
They believe that if they have any part of their body missing they can't
have eternal peace."

"Eternal peace?"

"That's what I'm talking about. Can't be with their ancestors,
you know, it's that Buddhist thing."

"Buddhist thing? It ain't a human thing. Ted Clementi is one
sick son of a bitch," I said.

"Real hard-ass. Jump up your bones if you don't watch yourself,"
Olgovey chimed in.

"Heard he got sixty ears in them jars over there. Cross him good
and he about to have sixty-two ears and one less nigger going to heaven."

"You calling me a nigger, 'Vey?" Olgovey didn't realize it but
he had just paid me a high compliment. By him calling me a nigger I
finally felt fully accepted into the group. I had a home.

"It's just bad karma, that's all I'm saying. He doesn't have to be
cutting ears off just to fuck with them. Christ, they're dead already.
Let them be."

I stopped short. "Why you all looking at me like that?"

"You got a lot to learn, Freddy Boy." Herman stood up now. "That man Clementi, he crazy, yeah, but that motherfucker will save your life if you keep close to him and learn a thing or two. They don't teach you the things he knows in training. You think that the next gook that comes up that trail and sees his buddy's ears cut off and the Blackhorse Patch sticking out his ass, you think he isn't going to think twice about fucking with us? Pure intimidation, my man."

Olgovey rose and pointed a finger out into the darkness.

"Charlie out there right now looking at you. You don't see him but he sees you. You need a man like Clementi to even out the score. He's a killer and he enjoys it. Cut the motherfucker some slack, Jack. He will take care of you. Let's get some sleep," he said, walking away.

Herman and I stayed up another hour or so after Olgovey left. We sat for a while, not able to talk. It was apparent that still being inexperienced in the ways of war, our nerves and courage would be tested upon going back into the jungle.

"What are you thinking about, Herman?" I finally asked. It was quiet, and it was dark, and the false sense of bravado that preserved Herman during the daylight hours gave way to the deeper Herman I had come to love.

"About if I can kill as easily as Clementi. If I can actually take a life and enjoy it."

"I don't think that anyone enjoys it," I said. "He's just been here a while and seen some shit. When we go out tomorrow you better be shooting over my head, motherfucker." We all knew of many accidents occurring in the past. Drivers always had to have trust in their gunner. It was too easy for him to squeeze off a burst right into the driver's head. "I'm glad you're my gunner. I trust you. When the time comes you will know what to do."

I said this without knowing that I would be the first to be tested.

"Don't worry 'bout a thing, my man. Herman got your six."

The military had a great way of laying out the battle field like a clock. Directly in front of me was 12:00; 90 degrees to my right was 3:00 and if I turned completely at a 180 degree angle to my rear it was 6:00. Funny, the word six also had another connotation. It was the lieutenant's "LT" call sign. In military jargon, an ass and a lieutenant meant the same thing. To my eyes, Cutter never did a damn thing to change that connection in my head. Herman and I decided to smoke some dope while we waited to hit the rack. I must have been in a mood of loving everyone, because I wrote a strange letter to my friend Bob. He was a musician I had played with before I got drafted.

May 15, 1969

Bob,

"Christ you know it ain't easy ...," Living like an animal is quite different then living with them. You'll just never know how fucked up this living in the jungle is. If Charlie don't get you, the bugs will. I'm with the 11th Armored Calvary Regiment. Our motto is "Find the Bastards and then pile on." Remember those things parked on Greenwood Ave.? I'm probably riding around in one of those armored personal carriers that we saw every day. Well it's my home. I could never explain to you what it's like to be in a war. Lee Michaels always sings "How would you feel if you saw a baby burn?" Well, we drove through a village yesterday. Millions of little kids came running out holding their hands up. I waved. They weren't waving man. They were begging. They were starved. So everybody started throwing C-/ rations and candy down to them and I was afraid we were going to run over some of them the way they were fighting for the food. Man what a fucked up thing. I'm getting bitter, real bitter. I hate the rich bastards that are sitting back getting fat off this war. I was crying when I saw these people and how they live. Then we passed the orphanage. They just stared at us and the burnt ones and the crippled, they weren't begging. I could

see that they already got something from the Americans. A little kid gave me the finger and I threw up.

This troop I am with is battle tested and there are some real hard chargers with us. The majority are guys like me and Herman who are still jumpy and waiting for some action. Somebody walked up behind some cat and he turned around and blew the guys head off. Just like that. Guys die, life is cheap here. My crew-I love them-nice guys. Hillbillies and blacks at that; there is tension but still, they might mean the difference between me living or dying. There is such comradeship. Hey what a fucking trip. I mean it!

I really find it hard to tell you what it's like. I'm in another world. Jungles, monsoon, orient, weed, rockets and death. I want to live. The other night we got righteously ripped and we were sitting around when all of a sudden "BOOM!" My friend Herman said "Man, I hope we're not getting hit because I'm too fucked up to walk," He was right. Total oblivion on three hits. No way to fight a war. Maybe the only way. We will see. Well, take care. Write if you can.

Peace,

Fred

II
The Mass

Morning found me sitting by the side of the track. The troop had left Lai Khe six days earlier and I had no idea where we were. Somewhere in the jungle. That's all I knew. I had just finished my morning practice of writing letters home. We had picked up some beer in Lai Khe and now I was having cold spaghetti and meat balls and washing it down with warm beer. It wasn't the worst breakfast that I had ever had. Herman startled me as he approached.

"Man, why you write so many letters? You got a girlfriend going crazy without you? Think anybody care about what you doing over here?"

"It's my family, they worry about me."

"They shouldn't, tell them you're in good hands with old Herman Johnson." He had a beer in his hand, as he spoke.

"My dad built a shrine to St. Jude in our backyard and they go to Mass every Wednesday night in Pasadena to say a Novena. I don't think that they believe I'll make it home alive." I said this trying not to believe it, too.

"So they're good Catholics?" Herman was leaning forward now. An evil grin crossed his face. I could see that this somehow made him resentful. I prepared to get teased. The idea that my family could love me so much, that they would be so concerned for my safety as to sacrifice a trip to Pasadena every week to pray for me fascinated him.

"I wouldn't say they were good Catholics; let's just say they are scared Catholics." I returned the grin.

"What about you, Herman? Who's praying for you?"

"I got a little sister and my mom at home. Pop died when I was six. Moms don't take much to religion. I don't ever remember us going to church much when I was growing up." He started getting mad and upset just talking about this.

"Do you believe in God?" I asked.

"Do you believe in God after seeing what went down here yesterday, Freddie Boy?" he said angrily.

"I don't know what to believe yet," I said. "Yesterday was a mind-blower."

"You better believe it," he said. "This shit for real and this God of yours ain't shit."

This was Monday morning. Just twenty-four hours earlier, the Army had sent a Catholic priest out in a chopper to say Mass. He was one of those real Army lifer types. Probably kicked out of some parish and sent to Vietnam to save his own soul. The first thing we noticed when he stepped out of the Huey were his boots.

"Sho' is shiny," Herman said.

I laughed. Then I noticed something that I had never seen before. He was wearing camouflaged robes.

I stopped laughing.

This man of God, servant of the Almighty and Faithful Shepherd of the Flock was wearing fucking camouflaged robes.

"Check it out, brother. He afraid."

Herman also stopped laughing. "Let's go peep his keyhole."

"What?"

"Check his shit out, man. Drop a dime on the motherfucker. Let's go to church."

When I was growing up in South Montebello, there was an old Mexican Catholic priest, Father Paplito. He used to pick us up every Sunday morning in his rickety old school bus and take us to Saint Benedict's for church and catechism.

"Oh, my God, I am heartily sorry for having offended thee and I detest all my sins because of Thy just punishment. But most of all, because they offend Thee, my Lord, who art all good and deserving of all my love. I firmly resolve, with the help of Thy grace, to sin no more and to avoid the near occasion of sin."

I learned this prayer when I was a kid. It became the crux of my whole belief system. Like many thirteen-year-old boys, the fear of offending God drove hard on me. I memorized the prayer because, as a matter of fact, He scared the shit out of me. I never understood a word in church. The priest celebrated the Mass in Latin and even when Father Paplito gave his sermon it was unintelligible. His thick accent and slow mumbling put me to sleep. Now, here I sat with Herman and he wanted to go fuck with God.

Some twenty or so enlisted men and officers attended the church service that morning. It had rained all night, and as the sun broke through the clouds, a dramatic Sunday morning calmness settled over the men of C Troop. We sat in the mud and tried to make ourselves as comfortable as possible. Many spread their poncho liners on the ground. Some just sat in the mud, unmindful of the horrid conditions. They just wanted to find some peace, find some quiet, some respite from the war. Herman and I stood at a distance.

I noticed Clementi and Jim Gaines sitting close to the makeshift altar. Jim had been in the bush for nine months and thirteen days. We called him short, which meant he had less than ninety days left on his tour. He had been granted the semi-safe position of being the lieutenant's chief bodyguard. For as long as I knew him, Jim Gaines had always been the track commander on Lt. Cutter's vehicle. Lt. Cutter, 3rd Platoon leader, was not considered by many to be a competent leader. He was lucky to have Jim around.

I met Jim the first day that I arrived in the field. It surprised me to see him with Clementi. They discharged their duties with such opposite personalities. Where Clementi had such a loud and obnoxious demeanor, Jim had a peaceful air about him. He disliked Clementi for his cruelty. When we had been in Lai Khe, Jim went into the village and bought me a cheap Vietnamese guitar. Not much of a guitar, but his thoughtfulness touched me. I would carry that guitar with me all my days in the bush.

"Jim, man. You didn't have to do that for me," I managed to stutter.

"I've got my own selfish reasons for it, buddy. I've heard tell that you're a rock and roll star back in the world."

"I was in a band signed with Mercury Records when I was drafted. As a matter of fact, the album was released on the day I was inducted." I said this without bitterness or self-pity. I had already learned Doc's lesson on predetermination. Jim held up the guitar and it was the sweetest thing I had ever seen: painted green, yellow, with an attempted painting of a palm tree. Jim placed it in my hands.

"Play it," he said. "Play me some Hank Williams or some Johnny Cash."

Jim grew up in Farmington, New Mexico and he turned out to be a genuinely kind man. We spent many nights in his track, me playing guitar and he singing country western songs. He never smoked dope. He had won the Silver Star and Purple Heart months before I came into the jungle. Soft spoken and compassionate, Jim did his job quietly and competently, the kind of soldier who did just what was expected of him. Everyone loved Jim.

Father Major John Crow of the Holy Church of the United States of America stood on a tree trunk in a clearing and spoke to us of God's will.

"Men, God intends for us all to be good, effective Christian soldiers," he began. "Your family is proud of you, the nation is proud of you, and God is proud of you. The sacrifices that you are making, the inconveniences that you are tolerating and the suffering that you endure go not unnoticed by Him. He is here with you all in your time of need."

Oh, how we were blessed. God was truly on our side.

Suddenly an explosion ripped through the clearing and I saw Jim blown forward on to the altar.

"Incoming!" somebody yelled.

"Son of a bitch!" Herman grabbed me and threw me to the ground. In the swift confusion and ensuing turmoil I saw Jim Gaines slumped over, trying to grab Father Crow. Rockets, mortars, and RPGs opened a visible crack in our little perch of paradise. It showed the world of horror and terror that was waiting for us just on the other side.

"Medic! Medic!" Clementi frantically tried to hold a bandage to Jim Gaines's stomach. There were screaming men and pandemonium all around us. Herman jumped to his feet.

"Come on!" he said.

I jumped up and we started running for our track. Clementi stayed busy with the wounded Gaines while Herman and I flew behind the two .60-caliber machine-guns on old Charlie Three-Four. We opened fire simultaneously. We were firing blind into the jungle thicket. I had yet to see an enemy soldier. It was pure chaos. Suddenly I heard the whirl of the chopper blade as it readied its engines for takeoff.

"Check it out!" Herman screamed above the noise, "Check it out!"

Goddamn Father Crow was running for the chopper, his shiny new boots filling with the red dust of Vietnam and his starched new camouflaged robes splattered with the blood of Jim Gaines. They whisked him away as if he were fuckin' Tricky Dick Nixon.

Jim Gaines died twenty minutes later.

Herman and I stopped firing and stared down at our fallen friend. Clementi looked up at us and yelped, "He's dead! Saddle up and start the engines."

I did. I dove into the driver's hatch and started the engine.

I was shaking uncontrollably behind the steering sticks. Streams of tears ran down Herman's face. I could barely see because of my own tears. The troop moved out onto the trail and set up in a herringbone formation. It started raining heavily and Clementi and Teddy Jones threw Jim's body on our track behind me. I could smell the blood and red mud that covered him. I looked back over my left shoulder. My God, he looks like a wax figure.

Pale and lifeless, Jim Gaines became the second American and first real friend that I saw killed. I realized then that there would be so many more. Just seven weeks in this lousy country. Where was God? I was no longer afraid of Him. I had found a more clever and elusive enemy. God paled in comparison.

Friday May 23, 1969

Dear Mom and Dad,

Sorry I haven't written for a few days. It's been impossible until now. We left Lai Khe over a month ago and went into the jungle. The first day out we ran into enemy bunkers. We searched them and found ammunition and mines. We killed one VC. I didn't see him, but it came over the radio that they pulled one out. I wasn't scared until I heard that. Then I figured that there must be more. We set up a night defensive position (NDP) in a clearing but it was mined. Two tanks hit them but no one was hurt. Today we went deeper into the jungle and found ten thousand rounds of ammunition. The cache was hidden in underground storage bunkers. We found it because a tank ran over it and fell through. That was a big find so it will probably be on the evening news. We were supposed to go back to Lai Khe tomorrow, but after all of this, we won't. We are setting up a new position now. They brought in some ARVN's (South Vietnamese Soldiers). They are weird. I'm in no danger so don't worry. There isn't any sign of recent enemy activity here. The bunkers are a few weeks old. They think that the VC have moved and left caches of food and ammo for later use. All we are going to do is find them and destroy them. The whole squadron is with us. That's a lot of firepower. Right now, the B52s are bombing the places we were at earlier. Well, I must say that this is exciting. I hope that you're not too worried about me. When I'm in the bush, I can't write every day. We stay pretty busy. During the day we go out on patrols and search for the enemy.

I went to mass last Sunday. They flew a priest out to our position with some hot food and cigarettes. I'm trying to stay dry. The rain and the mud don't bother me too much. I just want you to know that I'm ok and doing fine. I miss you all.

Love,

Fred

PS: I noticed that you are sending air mail. You don't have to. It has to come by air anyway. So buy 6 cent stamps and it will be the same, only you will save 4 cents on each letter. Also, have you received the $250 that I sent? You didn't mention it in your letter. I would like a package. Please send lots of pre-sweetened Kool-Aid and socks. Someone stole my socks!

"Someone stole your socks?" Herman loved to read over my shoulder. He hardly ever got any mail from home. We had stuffed ourselves inside the track trying to stay dry. It seemed to be almost 9:30 p.m. and the first guard shift would be about to start. Clementi always took first watch. One of us had to stay awake all night behind the .50-caliber machine-gun. Two hour shifts each. Mine would be the two a.m. to four a.m. shift. This was the worst shift. That shift usually only let me grab three hours of sleep.

Every evening after the supply drop and the hot chow was served in the middle of the camp; the mechanics would set up huge bladders full of diesel fuel. One by one, each track driver would bring his vehicle over to this bizarre gas station to top off his tanks with diesel.

"I got to tell them something bad," I said. "I mean, they're not stupid. They know it's not a bunch of fun and games. Let's go top off."

We walked toward Olgovey's track on the south side of the perimeter. We passed the lit joint between us. It didn't take much to get us high. The one good thing about the Nam was the great weed. Olgovey stepped out in front of his track to meet us.

"Heard about Gaines," he said solemnly.

"Yeah? Well, don't mean nothing," Herman said.

"Where you been?" I asked.

"I've been back at Blackhorse. Just came out with the re-supply chopper."

"Well, you missed a good time," I said.

We all just stood there not knowing what to say next.

"Hey, Doc came out with me. He's on Three-Eight with Sgt. Mays." Olgovey looked at us up and down trying his best to cheer us up. "He waitin' on you all. I was coming to get you."

"Doc Lewis?" Herman's eyes lit up.

We half ran to Track Three-Eight. Mays looked at us with surprise as we climbed into the back of his track. Mays never seemed to like us much. I know now that it wasn't anything personal. He just didn't like new guys. The nature of the system dictated that troopers would put in their year and leave. C Troop was getting an influx of FNGs as the old-timers were rotating out. He didn't want to know us. I would feel the same way after I had been there for a while. Knowing and having friends like Jim Gaines and then watching them die seemed too brutal. It seemed better to keep everyone at a distance. Too late. I already had too many close friends.

"My man!" Doc looked at us as if he had just found two long-lost brothers. "My man, Fred. My man, Herman. What is hap-pen-ing?"

"Same o' same o'." Herman started laughing now. "Lose one nigger, get another. Uncle Sam just keep 'em coming."

I resented that remark but kept it to myself. Herman hadn't been as close to Jim as I had been. Olgovey had brought back a few bottles of cheap Vietnamese whiskey and we started passing them around. Mays warmed up to us with the booze and by midnight we slumped over each other, completely wasted. We found ourselves feeling confident and warm when all of a sudden Herman realized that time was approaching for his watch.

"Shit! We got to go."

We said our goodbyes to Doc and Olgovey and staggered back to our track. Clementi looked pissed until we slipped him a bottle of whiskey. We climbed aboard and Herman slid behind the fifty. I passed out on the .60-caliber ammunition cases and made it my bed for the night. We used our flak jackets for pillows. Since our sleeping quarters changed constantly, they were usually dictated by the weather. When it rained, which seemed to be all the time, we slept inside the vehicle.

Because Standard Operational Procedure dictated that one crew member be required to stay awake all night behind the fifty, there remained plenty of room for three people inside. On the inside of each track we stacked two rows of ammunition cans. We put our poncho liners and any extra clothes that we had on top of them to make our mattresses. As a crew, we had about five or six blankets. We shared them as we shared the clothes. I don't ever remember seeing anybody in his own uniform. The name tags never matched the person wearing them. I wore the same shirt for twenty-two days once. It said "Kellman." The guys started calling me Kell, and eventually Cal for California. This happened as everything else happened, without me even noticing it.

In the morning, hungover and groggy, Herman and I stood in the chow line near the mess tent. Three hots and a cot. That's what the Army had promised us and that is what it delivered. Doc was adjusting to his first day in the field and Olgovey was taking him around to meet the guys. I never knew what name Mr. and Mrs. Lewis had christened their son. We called him Doc because he was our medic. They called me Cal as it evolved from shortening Kellman to an indication that I came from California. Montana was, well, he grew up in Colorado but for the most part, everything was reduced to its simplest form.

When we saw him that morning, Clementi had a big distorted smile on his face. Clementi never smiled. It looked unnatural on him.

"Going to be a few changes around here, boys."

"What's going on?" I asked. Herman looked worried.

"You're looking at the new Charlie Three-Six."

Charlie Three-Six had been Jim Gaines' assignment. Impossible. There's no way Clementi could be track commander.

"That's not all," he continued. "Sgt. Haynes will be taking over Three-Four and he has his own driver. You and Herman will stay on and be their gunners."

"What?" I looked at Herman. I had never seen him so dejected, and I had been happy being the driver. As a driver, I figured that I probably would never have to kill anyone, unless I ran over him. But now, now I was going to be a gunner. Shit!

"Sgt. Clementi," Herman asked quietly, "Who the new driver?"

"Spec four Billy Henderson."

Doc and Benson had joined us. Herman started getting agitated.

"Billy? Dat silly wabbit!" Herman got mad. "Silly fuckin' wabbit."

"It's OK. Settle down, man," Benson said in that deep bass voice of his.

"What are you talking about, Herman?" I asked. "What are you saying? 'Silly fuckin' wabbit.' What does it mean?"

"You never heard of the rabbit, Cal? The silly fuckin' White Rabbit? That's him. Dumbest white boy I ever come across."

I had never imagined seeing Herman this disturbed. Clementi's smile widened as Doc and Benson tried unsuccessfully to calm Herman down.

Henderson certainly came across as a dopey guy. I mean I just barely knew him, but he didn't seem that bright. I came across him from time to time but had little personal contact with him.

"What's wrong with Billy?" I asked. "Herman?"

This was not a hippie love-in or Woodstock. It was war. The American government by virtue of having a draft system ensured that men of different values and backgrounds would be placed in a life-or-death situation together.

"He called me a nigger."

"Well, you are," Benson said with a smile.

Benson tussled Herman out of earshot and lowered his voice. Knowing Benson's history with the violent Black Panther Party, I figured Benson had just told Herman that he would take care of the problem. I saw Herman relax, smile, and he stepped back into our circle with his usual saunter.

Staff Sgt. Bobby Gene Haynes became my track commander that day. He brought along his driver, Billy Henderson. Billy carried three generations of racism all the way over from Yazoo City, Mississippi. A good ol' Southern boy born in the Delta, he was a lot like the Southerners that I met in Vietnam. He disliked colored people and California hippies. Now he had to live with us and he made it known that he would never be happy about it.

"I stay left gunner," Herman told Haynes.

I was thinking that maybe Herman planned on shooting Billy in the head first chance he got if Benson didn't take care of the problem. The thing about Nam is that things changed on a dime. Adapt or die. It appeared that Herman had adapted, but I couldn't read his mind.

I found myself trapped between two worlds. I was not white; I was not black. The troop was becoming more and more racially polarized. The nation itself was split in half and we were but a microcosm of American society. Muhammad Ali had been convicted of refusing induction in the U.S. Army just that day. Some brothers started passing a flyer around the troop from the Black Panther Party, saying, "No Vietnamese ever called me Nigger." The brothers started feeling that this was a white man's war. The tension mounted.

It was time to decide where I stood. I reflected on my childhood growing up in the *barrio*. All of my childhood friends had been kids of color. My best friends were the Reyes brothers, Bobby and Steve. My neighborhood was integrated and I played with Lyle Groves, the black kid next door. I had dinner many times with his family. When I hit high school I found myself with white boys. They never made me feel comfortable around them. With their pale skin and blond hair covering their ears, they sneered at me and Bobby Reyes. Right now it was not hard to make my choice.

I stood with Herman.

"He stays left gunner," I said to my new commander. "He has more experience. I'll take the right side."

"Fine. We roll at 0600. I expect your weapons to be cleaned tonight and the ammo dry and secure." Bobby put out his right hand. "Welcome aboard," he told us.

"Welcome aboard? This is our fucking track!" Herman flared again, ignoring the outstretched hand. Haynes was speechless and walked off shaking his head.

"Let's go top off," I said.

This had been another hell of a day. Neither of us got much sleep the night before. As we walked off, I had almost forgotten how the day had started, with Herman waking me up for my guard duty.

"Watch time," he whispered in my ear. "Get your ass up, you lazy Mexican. Cal? You hear me?"

I reached up and punched him in the face.

"God damn, Fred!" Herman fell back laughing.

III
The Kill

Thursday, July 23, 1969

0600 came and, true to his word, Bobby Haynes had us up and ready to move out.

"Saddle up!" Bobby began yelling at us to get our shit together.

The radio crackled with more chatter than I had ever heard before. I looked up and saw two gunships moving out over the horizon, heading north. I swung myself behind the right-side M-60 machine-gun and looked over at Herman. He smiled. Lt. Cutter pulled alongside of us and Clementi waved at Herman and me. Clementi looked genuinely concerned for our safety. He clearly knew something that we did not.

"Keep your heads together, boys, keep them clear and keep them down."

He knew about our extensive drug use and during his stint as our track commander he always looked the other way. Today however, his voice had urgency to it. His eyes were wide open with anticipation and he looked as if he wanted to tell us something privately.

He was with Cutter now, and so was privy to more information than any of us had. What did Clementi want to tell us? Why would he care about us? The LT nudged him on the shoulder and they pulled ahead of us. The smell of burning diesel filled the air. Thick black smoke billowed above the tracks as we formed a single line. With our antennas waving high, brushing against the tall banana trees, we moved out slowly and felt ourselves soon showered with falling branches and big thick leaves.

Bobby looked over at me and said, "We're picking up a squad of South Vietnamese soldiers. ARVNs about 5 clicks from here."

A low growl spread through the men of C Troop. We hated those bastards. "We're running single file through a string of VC base camps. Radio silence from here on out. Protect the flanks. Fred, you have the right rear. Herman, left rear." Maybe that's why Clementi seemed so concerned: he wanted us to protect his ass.

We hooked up with First and Second Platoon and moved slowly into the first base camp. It still appeared to be deserted. With all of our firepower, it seemed unlikely that anybody would return. We moved on slowly. The abandoned base camp, littered with bloodstained rags and torn shirts, gave the impression that the VC had used this place for treating their wounded. A group of bunkers covered with sandbags ran in a semicircle around the trail. On the right side of the complex I saw a spider hole. It once had been covered with such ingenious camouflage that it would have been unnoticeable to our still untrained eyes. Now, it stood there wide-mouthed as if asking us to come down and inspect it. We moved on slowly to the ARVN pick-up point.

"There they are." Herman was the first to see them. What a sorry bunch. A seemingly small, dirty, ragtag army. That was my first impression. It got worse. They just kept coming. They were legs— infantry men—and they were notorious cowards. They also smelled horrible. We were not the perfect examples of proper field hygiene. These guys, however, didn't look like they had bathed in months.

"You gemme go? You gemme go?" They kept asking this over and over again. Finally, I understood what they wanted. They were dog tired. They wanted a lift.

"Okie dokie. You number one? Yes? You kill VC?" I wanted to know. We helped as many onto our track as we could fit. Still they kept coming. We started to push the extras over the top. As they scrambled to fill all of the other tracks in Third Platoon there were still about fifteen left with nowhere to sit. It became a brutal kind of musical chairs. When the music stopped and there remained no more empty seats, you stayed behind and died. They panicked and started climbing back onto the vehicles, desperately searching for an empty spot. Bobby drew his .45 and fired a round into the air. They stopped scrambling. Lt. Cutter ran back to see what all the commotion was about.

"Look, sir, there just isn't any more room back here. They'll restrict our field of fire." God, I was learning how to speak Army. A lot of good that did me.

"Pile 'em on and when we hit the base camp you may dismount them."

"Throw them off, sir?"

The LT walked away. We piled them on and moved out. Bobby slipped the .45 back into his holster. I was thinking, *man I should grab that .45 someday and take it home.* No one will ever miss it. What a great souvenir.

I looked up and noticed a sixteen-year-old boy looking at me. He had the Army of the Republic uniform on and filthy green socks and sandals. His helmet liner was stuffed with tree branches and leaves for a very impressive camouflage. Draped across his shoulders were two bandoleers of ammunition. This pip-squeak was carrying a heavy load. He took off his sandals and socks and I spotted the jungle rot on his feet. Three toenails on his left foot were missing. The skin on his feet was a mixture of green, dark red and black. As he massaged his feet, he had a toothless smile of genuine relief. He gave it to me. I refused it.

"GI numba one," he said. "Numba one USA." He waved his free hand around in a broad wave over the troop. Yes, we were number one. No doubt about it. We had so much firepower sitting on that trail and so much more in the air with the helicopter gunships, we felt invincible. I looked down at his feet. He was rubbing his left foot again, trying to get some circulation back and clean off the rot. He still had the smile.

We stopped suddenly. The lead elements had entered Base Camp No. 2. Herman lit a pipe and we took a few hits. The Vietnamese just looked at us. We were used to this stop-and-go routine. A few people would dismount, clear the bunkers, and we would be on our merry way. Suddenly the radio popped.

"All units, be advised, enemy activity in the area."

Shit, I hated those words.

The radios started chattering again. So much for radio silence. Now the word was coming down the line to dismount the ARVNs. We did.

"*Di di*," Haynes started yelling. "*Di di mao!*" They didn't move. "Get the fuck off of my vehicle, now!" They didn't respond to English any better than they did to the Vietnamese. Bobby yelled some more. Herman flew into a rage. He started cussing loudly and throwing them off the track onto the ground. Herman looked skinny but he was tall and strong. He picked them up by their shirts and flung them over the side. The kid with the bad feet still sat there smiling. Bobby pulled the .45 from his holster and pointed it at his head. He jumped overboard. We sent them out to check the bunkers. We were deep into Vietcong-held territory. At the front of the column somebody reported a cooking fire burning.

Bobby pointed to the very last bunker on the right side. The boy walked over like he was strolling in the park and without even taking his rifle off his shoulder, peered into the bunker.

I stood alone on the back of the track watching the little boy with sore feet. He stuck his face into the bunker opening and in a flash of light his head exploded. I smelled the white smoke and burned flesh. The sound of an AK-47 assault rifle rang out in my ears. My boy fell backward, and to my surprise, the Vietcong that shot him jumped up and started running across my field of fire. Time ceased to exist. All I could do was fixate on him. All movement was reduced to single-frame imagery. I stood there behind my M-60 machine-gun. I didn't move. I watched. I saw in detail all of the events unfolding before me.

The Vietcong darted out of the bunker wearing black pajamas and sandals made from truck tires. His pajamas had become caked with dry mud and fresh blood along the side of his leg. His black shirt was torn around the sleeve, as if someone had grabbed him there and he had broken free. I randomly wondered how it happened. He wore a straw peasant hat, wide at the brow with a red bandanna tied around his forehead. He was really digging in, running with everything he had and churning up mounds of mud in his wake. He glanced up and noticed me sitting there very still and quiet. One eye was almost swollen shut from a gash across his eyebrow. He wasn't zigzagging or trying to be elusive. He was running in a straight line to the edge of the clearing. He carried something in his right hand. All this was happening in slow motion.

At that moment, there was not a sound in my world.

I glanced to my left and saw the white cloud of gunsmoke still lingering in the air. I looked again and realized what the VC held in his right hand. It was the same AK-47 that he had just used on the boy. My heart was pounding, blood pumping through my veins rushing to my trigger finger. The world remained in slow motion. My head spun out of control.

I'm going to kill him.

I can't kill another human being. This is a father or brother or son. How could I ever live with myself? I can't kill. I can't kill. I began to cry.

He stopped running and pointed the rifle at me.

My first burst of fire cut him in half.

The sound of my gun discharging woke me out of my trance. I became conscious of Herman and Bobby hitting me over the head. They were yelling.

"You killed him!" Bobby screamed.

"Shot the motherfucker up his ass!" Herman's eyes opened wide and danced around the scene.

I looked at them. A huge smile crossed Bobby's face. A genuine happiness spread through the track crew. Even Billy Henderson stuck his upper body up over the driver's hatch and gave Herman a high-five. I felt like a baby that took a crap in the toilet for the very first time. Everyone became so proud of me.

"You're a big boy, now, yes," pinching my cheek, making those eyes at me. "You're a big boy, now, *mijito.*"

Thoughts of any right or wrong ceased to exist for me. No lingering doubts about my circumstances remained. I had arrived at war and it all just boiled down to survival. No thoughts of love and peace crossed my mind when Charlie aimed his rifle at me. Since the beginning of mankind, it had been kill or be killed. There it is.

Lt. Cutter looked at the dead kid and the VC. He reported the body count to headquarters, "Two confirmed enemy KIAs. No friendly casualties."

I started breathing again, astonished at his statement. How convenient for the Americans that they all looked the same. Well, they could have been related for all I knew. This was a civil war and we were right in the middle of it. Vietnam was a war of attrition and the only thing that matters was that at the end of the day we report a high body count.

We moved on. First Platoon had the lead and we found Base Camp No. 3. It was *not* unoccupied. I was still thinking about the events that just went down when a cacophony of AK-47s and RPGs startled me back into the present.

"Ambush!" somebody cried.

Herman and I opened fire at an unseen enemy. I shot an empty hammock. Herman killed a bowl of rice. First Platoon started coming back alongside of us so I stopped firing. It only took ten minutes. I saw the guys in First Platoon stacking twelve dead Vietnamese. Four more were captured and blindfolded. Lt. Cutter called in another body count. I couldn't help wondering how many of the dead were really on our side. It had been quite a day. Exhausted, I watched as Clementi unsheathed his knife and walked toward the bodies. Closing my eyes, I collapsed on the floor of the track.

IV
Jimi in the Jungle

Monday July, 28, 1969

The sun started dipping low behind the hills. Most of the track crews already had their guys out and back from setting up the night traps. Herman glanced at me with mischief on his face. "Ever heard of orange sunshine?"

"Yea, what about it?" I had dropped acid every Sunday at Fort Ord. Everyone had. It was the summer of 1969 and we were young men far away from home. My buddies back in the World would write to me about their fantastic acid trips. Back in sunny California my friends were enjoying life. They were taking pleasure in their youth with all that it encompassed. Fast cars, hippie chicks, free love and music. I was envious. "What you got?" I asked.

"Cal, we going tripping tonight." Herman brought two tabs of acid out of the cellophane wrapper of his Kools. He put one under his tongue and handed the other one to me.

Without a thought I took it and said, "It's Howdy Doody time." We walked out into the night together.

I looked into Herman's eyes and they were fearless. Bright, shiny, and bold as love. We walked in the warm night air and talked.

We talked about his father, how he was murdered when Herman was a kid. He told me about how he grew up on the streets of Detroit. Poor, lonely, and sometimes bitter, he managed to survive on his own.

He told me that he learned to drive by stealing cars, learned to read by reading the Detroit Free Press in juvenile hall. I was amazed at the story of his youth. I had had a wonderful childhood. My mom was the den mother of my Cub Scout troop. My father coached Little League. I was loved by my family. He had none.

"Cal," he slowed down. "You a brother to me. I mean, you know, we all brothers out here, but you my main man."

"Main man?" I mean, I had been *man*, even *my* man, but never *main* man. I thought about this for a moment.

"Main man it is."

We continued to walk. Dusk was falling as fast as we were coming on to the acid. I could feel the blood running through my veins and the ungodly weight of my jungle boots. I looked down to the end of my legs and saw two of the ugliest monsters I had ever seen. The green and black boots against the red clay were so vivid. They were alive. I stopped in my tracks.

"What?" Herman pulled up alongside of me. He looked like a shadow. His black face stared at me with the sparkle missing from his eyes. He bent over and leaned on his right knee and in a quiet voice asked, "What's wrong Cal?"

"Herman, I can't walk." The boots seemed like lead weights. I was getting scared. I had heard of people having bad trips and flipping out. Had people become paralyzed because of bad acid? What was going on? A small monkey ran across our path. I became a monkey. I stared down at my feet again. I had monkey feet! "I can't move, man." I felt petrified.

"OK, OK, sit down. What's wrong? You sprain an ankle? Let's rest." Herman sat down.

I sat next to him and looked at my boots again. They were crying now. Howling, as a matter of fact. They were screaming at me. Herman lit a Kool and gave it to me. He lit one for himself. I reached over and unlaced my boots. First my left and then my right, and then I tugged and pulled those monsters off my feet. I smiled at Herman much like the young Vietnamese boy had smiled at me. While I had rejected that young man's gaze, Herman returned my smile. I felt a warmth spread all over me. I lay on my back and wiggled my feet in the air. I could move my feet again.

"Man, what the fuck wrong with you? You tripping, Fred?" Herman started laughing and lay beside me. We had no idea of how far we had wandered away from the troop. At that moment we didn't care. Summer nights in Vietnam are beautiful, and the hot humid air sent our minds spinning until we were lost in another world. We let our heads be comforted on the soft mounds of dirt. We wrapped leaves over our bodies and entered into a world of peace and splendor. The lush dark green growth of the jungle's flora seemed to offer safety from the night.

The next thing we knew, we're covered by the crawling jungle. Scorpions, bugs of all shapes and sizes, and varied species of worms crept over us in silence. First I heard a faint gasp, then an utter of profanity, and then the full blown screams of the two man-children, Herman and Fred. The soft mounds of dirt that we used for our pillows were actually ant hills. Red ants, to be exact. We called them fire ants because their bite burned with such an awful intensity.

"Son of a bitch!" Herman jumped up and started flinging his arms in the air. He ripped his shirt off over his head and started slapping his face and chest. "Son of a bitch!" The ants crawled all over his face and neck. Huge welts started popping up on his forehead. I jumped on him as I would a man on fire. He was burning to death in front of me.

"Herman! Herman!"

My right hand ignited into a ball of fire. His face melted and my chest exploded. The earth opened up and shook with a mighty force that dropped us to our knees. I grabbed his face and rubbed it in the dirt. He stuck my burning hand into the ground and we looked up to see every particle of air, every molecule floating in a sea of red. We were tripping.

We fell back to the ground laughing.

"You OK?" I asked.

"Fine as dirt." Herman stood up and put his shirt back on after we somehow had managed to knock off all the ants and bugs. He looked at me with utter amazement. Then he looked down at my feet. "You know," he said, "your feet are invisible."

"What?"

"Your feet. I can't see them. You invisible." Herman slipped his shirt back off. We were so high that we thought if we could take our uniforms off, we would become invisible and be able to find the troop and sneak back in without getting caught by either side. We stripped naked and stood there under the quarter moon.

"Hey, Freddie Boy, where are you?" Herman was giggling. He extended his arms out and stumbled about like a blind man looking for me. I brushed alongside of him and fell to the jungle floor, laughing hysterically. We were having a great time. It was just the two of us playing blind man's bluff in the middle of the night. We had been making quite a ruckus with all the screaming and yelling. Now our laughter seemed to carry out into the night like a rocket launched deep into enemy territory. I stopped laughing and moving about.

The enemy!

"Herman!" I said in a lucid moment. "Where the fuck you think we're at? We've been out here for more than three hours. Where's the troop? They must be looking for us."

We got dressed in a hurry. Herman looked up into the night sky for any sign of C Troop. Maybe we would see a green flare, maybe a smoke grenade. There was nothing but millions of tiny stars dotting the blackness. It turned cold at once. I was losing my high fast and butterflies were fluttering in my stomach. Fear was growing steadily in my body.

We still had our Claymores and trip-flares. We each had our M-16s draped around our shoulders. We were not carrying any extra ammunition or water canteens. We were only supposed to go a few hundred meters beyond the perimeter and get our asses back as soon as possible. The drugs had distorted our perception of time and space. We simultaneously realized that we were lost. Horror and dread set in immediately.

"Shhh!" I said.

Herman sat upright and started laughing and yelling, "Hello, hello! Is anybody out there?"

Fuck! "Shut the fuck up, man!" Half whisper, half shout.

He looked at me with the face of a child and scrunched down holding his private parts, his face withering in pain. He looked like he was about to cry.

"I need to go, I need to go! I can't hold it anymore! I got to go now!" he yelled.

I jumped on him again, not to save him from a burning ant death, but to kill him. I slapped my left hand over his mouth and used my right hand to hold his face down.

"God damn it, Herman, shut the fuck up!" I looked down to see that he had wet his pants. He was glaring at me with anger in his face. "You don't have to be so pissed off," I said.

We started laughing uncontrollably again. It's the funny thing about acid. One moment can be so serious and the next moment completely insane. There still was the matter of us being lost in enemy territory and the fact that no one in C Troop appeared to be looking for us. This brought us both back to the dismal reality that we could be stuck here all night.

Herman finally stopped laughing long enough to put together one thought. "OK, let's think about this."

"Let's head back the way we came in," I said.

"We don't know where we come in, Cal."

"The sun was over our left shoulder. It set over that hill right there."

"We are in a fucking valley. There are hills everywhere.

How can you be sure which hill the sun set over?"

"Our left shoulder, man, it was our left shoulder. Didn't you notice?" I was getting exasperated.

"Your left shoulder is dependent on the direction you are walking. My left shoulder is facing that hill. Yours is facing another." We stood facing each other. He pointed in both directions, crossing his arms, like the scarecrow in *The Wizard of Oz*.

"But the sun was over our left shoulders, so that means we were walking north. Let's head back south." This was making sense to me now. I was getting my bearings.

"You a fucking compass? How do you know which way is south? You a Boy Scout?" Herman wasn't laughing anymore. He had a serious frown going. "Let's head back toward that hill. I think that's the way we came in. We can get our point of reference at the crest. Let's go."

I slipped my boots back on and we went. It was a fast crash. A high-killer. Reality was bringing us down fast and my boots became just footwear again. Necessary objects needed to carry me out of this nightmare. Herman had a look of seriousness about him that I had never seen before. The look on his face unnerved me as he moved with newfound purpose. Every tree and bush looked the same to me. Every animal trail, every tree stump and every inch of that red clay floor looked as virgin and untouched as the surface of the moon above us. Man had landed on the moon just the month before, and here we were walking on alien territory trying to find our way home.

"Shit!" Herman slowed and turned to me. I think it was mostly the acid but I experienced all of Herman's complexity that night. I saw his strength and leadership capability. I laughed at his twisted sense of humor. I saw the street smart problem solver in him. Now I witnessed a dejected young man. I sat next to him.

"Let's try to get some sleep." I was getting tired and my feet were sore. God knows how far we had walked. The temperature had dropped a good ten degrees and the moon hid behind some clouds. Not rain, please not rain.

Of course it started to rain. Misery begot misery. It was our own fault that we were in this predicament and we knew it. Shit. At that moment I was prepared for the worst. I knew that Charlie would find us before C Troop did. We had been so loud and careless and now we were ready to accept the consequences of our actions. I reached into my rucksack and pulled Bobby Haynes' .45 out and waved it in the air.

"Whatcha doing with that, Cal?" Herman asked calmly.

"I lifted it off Bobby as he slept. You know I always had a thing for that gun." Weapons in the field were easy enough to get but I wanted Bobby's. I lowered it to my side and fumbled with it. I turned it over in my hand and ejected the clip. It held six bullets. I slid the clip back in and chambered a round.

Herman looked at me. "You got a crazy look in your eyes, nigger," he muttered.

"You know, just in case," I said. "Yeah, just in case."

Herman looked sad, his eyes slowly turning red and his face, already black as coal, seemed to take on an even darker tone.

"Give me the fuckin' gun. You don't have it in you, Cal."

I don't know what I had in me right then. I was empty inside. Jim Gaines' face appeared to me and I fought back a scream. What the fuck had we done? Of course I didn't have it in me to kill ourselves. We had all heard stories of the NVA torturing their prisoners. We had been drilled never to be taken captive. I have never felt the deep emptiness and desperation as I did right then. I thought of my mother.

Do all dying men think of their mother? Clementi had struggled to keep Jim alive. Everyone that I knew had that survival instinct in him. Even the guy I killed had it. I saw it in his eyes. It wasn't fear that I saw; I now realized this. It was the survival instinct. That's why he ran so hard. That's why he turned and raised his gun before I shot him. No, we were not going to give up hope just because we were tripping and lost. We would find our way out of this mess and have a good laugh over it back with the troop.

" ... Purple Haze, all in my eyes ... " That musical refrain hit my heart. It meant that we were no longer lost in the jungle with NVA and Vietcong surrounding us at every step. We walked from behind a hedge into a clearing to the scene of three Blackhorse troopers kicking it back in worn lawn chairs listening to Jimi Hendrix on a cassette tape player. They were wasted on good smoke and were passing around cans of Budweiser. We introduced ourselves; the self-appointed leader of that little band of merry men was Darwin Anderson.

"My friends call me Dizzy," he boasted. His eyes were glassy and he had one lazy eye that jetted out to the left at a slight degree, giving him the appearance of being faintly cross eyed. As if reading my mind he said, "Don't let the lazy eye fool you. I'm a hell of a shot. I qualified as expert on the shooting range in AIT. This here is Jenkins and the guy with his head in the bucket is Terrance Love. Everyone calls him Terry. Where did you guys come from? I thought we had this spot all to ourselves."

"I'm Fred and this is Herman," I spoke up. "We had some acid and we dropped it last night."

"Wow! That's pretty heavy. How was it, or should I say, how is it?"

"We're crashing pretty hard. Lucky for us we ran into you dudes. What troop you in?"

"I know you, Fred. They call you Cal. We are from C Troop, Third Platoon."

"Can you take us in?" I asked.

Dizzy looked us up and down and said, "Had enough on the outside? Sure, we can take you in."

We followed our new friends through a maze of overgrown hedges and little animal trails. We came into the perimeter right in front of Olgovey's track. No one was around and we just sort of slipped back behind our lines. Surprisingly, no one was looking for us and Herman and I made a beeline to Charlie Three-Four. Also a surprise, Bobby Haynes never made a big deal out of us disappearing for a night. It was our secret and we never had a hard time looking each other in the eye and talking about everything under the sun. Everything that is, except the night that Fred and Herman went missing.

V
Dizzy

Bob,

Darwin Anderson is another good friend. We call him Dizzy. The name speaks volumes. Like Herman, he is also from Detroit. He and I hit it off from the very start. He's been here longer than me and Herman he is also a driver. When we are in the rear we work on our vehicles together. We are in the rear now. The Squadron lets us come into other unit's base-camp every four to six weeks in order for us to have a stand down. We use the time to work on our vehicles, clean our weapons and have a few days rest. Usually the unit that we visit will throw us a party with steak and beer and some of them throw in a movie. We watch these movies on what I can only describe as the strangest drive in theater that I've ever seen. We line our tracks up like we are at a drive in theater and watch the films from the top of our vehicles.

Peace,
Fred

Tuesday, September 2, 1969

Dear Mom and Dad,

Man this army is messing me up. I can't even spell anymore. This is the third try for this letter. I had a nice rest in Bien Hoa. It is right next to Long Bien. It has a four lane highway and modern buildings. They even have steaks and cheese burgers. It made me mad to see these guys stationed there. They don't know the same Vietnam I know. I just hope they let me go into Special Services in December like they said.

We are still around Loc Ninh. We lost our platoon Sgt. And his loader a few days ago. We were going through a jungle area and a tree knocked the handle back on a machine-gun – then another one fell on the trigger and it went off. They were in front of it. It was a freak accident that really makes you think that if it's your time to go – you're going to go. Just like one night when we got mortared. Two of my friends, Tommy Cruz and Teddy Jones were sleeping outside of an abandoned French villa about three feet apart. Around two AM a mortar shell came screaming through the night breaking the dark silence. The shell landed with a loud thud waking them both up. The close miss sent them scrambling to their feet. Other live rounds hit their mark and caused havoc in the NDP. If God wants you he will take you. If he doesn't, you will live. My two friends are still alive. I hope you don't worry too much. Just keep praying like you have.

I haven't gotten your goodie box yet. Get some tortillas and wrap them in tin foil and send them. I bought a tape recorder when I was in Quon Loi. It's a cassette and uses cartridges. Tom Kendall is going to send me some tapes. I got a letter from John Westfall. I have to write back.

Sorry I missed Barbie's birthday. I should have written. Yes, send me the camera. I'm driving now. It's not too bad. Just a lot of work to keep the vehicles going. I enjoy driving though; it's kind of cool because you can drive those A-Cavs anywhere. It has rained every day since I've been here. Sometimes I feel like I'm driving in a lake. You should see the mud.

I was just interrupted to go get fuel. I'm back now. We are set up in a clearing sort of like a pasture. The scenery is so beautiful. I can see the Black Virgin Mountain. It is a huge steep black looming mountain with a Special Forces camp on top and one on the bottom. It is the worst place in the world to be. On your map it will say Tay Ninh. Could you find Lai Khe? Ben Cat is the village by it. You should have seen these cute little Montagnard girls about four years old. When we were at LZ Kelly they followed me everywhere I went. It made me homesick because I miss playing with Wendy and Barbie.

My platoon is going on a dismounted ambush patrol tonight. I'm the driver so I won't go. I'll stay at the NDP (night defensive position) with my vehicle.

I can hardly wait to be in the peace and quiet of Montebello again. I'm missing everybody and everything. I love you very much. Just remember that I'm fine and doing the best I can. My tape takes the same cartridges as the portable Lance has. Try to send me some pre-recorded albums. He knows the size.

Love,

Fred

Friday, September 5, 1969

It has been two weeks of constant skirmishes here in the Michelin rubber plantation outside of An Loc. The rubber trees are planted in row upon row of straight lines just wide enough to drive our tracks through. The NVA is very active on these plantations and we see signs of them everywhere. Lt. Cutter and Capt. Riddle have decided to have us move through here in a straight line abreast of each other.

Sgt. Mays' track is on our right and Clementi is on our left. We move out cautiously at first and find no resistance and soon we are rumbling full throttle through the trees looking for anything that moves.

This is a fucked-up way to do things. We are called scouts but the way we do our recon is to just let it all hang out and wait until we are ambushed. The bad guys can hear us coming for miles around and I am starting to feel boxed in inside these trees. There is not much room to maneuver about in here. As Dizzy pulls up next to me we come to a halt and he yells at me over the engine noise.

"Slow the fuck down, man!"

I let the motor idle down so I can hear him better.

"This ain't no race, you're going to drop a man!"

Now that pissed me off. In all my months of driving out here I have never dropped a man over the side. Not even those stinking ARVN's when they pile ten or fifteen of them on my track.

"Fuck you, Diz!" I yell back.

He's just messing with me to break the tension. We are stressed because the dog-days of August came roaring through our platoon like a hurricane and September is not starting out any better. We are once again just waiting to be ambushed. Hell, yes, I'm going to race through this plantation. The sooner we clear it the better. And what is with these constant stops? We just make for better targets when we do this. Cutter can't read the goddamn map. Gaines would never let this happen. He always took care of the LT.

"LT lost again?" I ask Dizzy.

"The old man wants us to meet him at some old plantation house," Dizzy replies.

It looks like Capt. Riddle is actually going to be coming out to the bush tonight. Good! That means hot chow for supper and maybe some beer.

The headset in my helmet starts to crackle and I hear Bobby telling me to turn left and fall behind Sgt. Mays.

"Fall in single file."

I put it in gear and head out behind Mays. Can't Cutter make up his mind on our formation? It must be Riddle trying to throw his weight around. Somebody's fucking up. Before long, our column picks up speed and we head out for that plantation house some thirty clicks away. After a little over an hour or so we reach the ruins of a formerly impressive compound. During the French occupation this must have been one hell of a set-up.

As we draw closer I see the bombed-out portions of roof that have collapsed inside and the bullet holes that nearly tore down what little is left of the walls. Vegetation creeps up the burned-out columns of a once magnificent house. We dismount and explore it more thoroughly. I see Herman on the far side of the ruins and look at Dizzy. He smirks and we walk up to Herman and slap hands.

"Look like we got our hotel for the night," Herman says.

"That so?" Dizzy asks.

"The old man is coming out to meet us here," I say, and just then we all look up to the noise of a helicopter flying in low.

"Here come the muthafucka now," Herman sighs. The chopper lands and out steps Capt. Perry James Riddle. With his crisp clean fatigues and big black cavalry hat, this son of a bitch is making a very big target. Everyone knows you don't salute in the field but Riddle is walking around saluting everyone he encounters. The three of us make it a point not to get anywhere near Riddle, but as long as he is going to be with us tonight we'll see if we can have some fun.

Bobby has been looking for me and he finally catches us near an old campfire site left by the former occupants of the house. Probably a company-size unit of NVA camped here a few nights ago. Well, it's ours now.

Bobby wants us to set up house. "Come on, you guys, mount up. Fred, move the track into the NDP next to number Three-Three."

Herman and I jumped aboard and I hit the engine and moved into position. As I did this, Herman started getting the trip-flares and Claymores ready. We had our routine down so well now that we moved without speaking to each other and set the shit up real pro-like. Gone was the guessing and fear that used to grip us when we did this little task.

Tonight, though, things would be different. As I brought the wires for the Claymores to the track, Bobby nudged me and whispered in my ear, "Run a wire back from the trip-flares. Let's have some fun with the captain tonight. Don't say a word to anyone else. Just do it."

So tonight, Bobby and I have a little secret. I run the wire back and rig it to the cupola right next to the .50-caliber. I don't even tell Herman what I have done. I don't give it a second thought. I'm just following orders.

As expected, we get hot food flown out to us from base camp. Dizzy, Herman, Doc and I sit in the ruins and build a fire. Too bad we don't have marshmallows, but we do have cold beer, one of the benefits of having the old man with us. You know, you have to take this war a day at a time and when you have days and nights of quiet peace it makes it all the more bearable for when things get hard. I take my shift behind the .50 and the night goes by swiftly. I look at the thousands, millions of stars out tonight and think of home. I wonder what my friends are doing right now. It's OK.

I think that I just might make it out of this place alive.

VI
The Probe

My shift ends and I go to bed. It's a hot night as usual and I go to my newly found sleeping spot under the .50. Last week I found this bed quite by chance and have been sleeping here ever since. I take my shirt off and use it as a pillow and stretch out beneath the barrel of the .50-cal and close my eyes. I'm so tired that I forget about the wire I brought back for Bobby. He takes his turn behind the machine-gun and starts his two-hour watch. I dream of the Roxy and the Whisky a Go-Go. Somewhere between those two clubs on Sunset Boulevard, a five-car pileup slams into me.

An earsplitting hammer of metal-to-metal wakes me up and fire is burning my chest. The ejected shells from the .50-cal are falling on my bare chest and the deafening noise of the killing machine is shattering my eardrums. Bobby has pulled the wire and set off the trip-flare right in front of our track. Now the perimeter opens up and every track in C Troop is firing their .50- and .60-calibers in a tremendously hideous cacophony of brutal ambush. The night is battered alive by the full sound of screaming men and loud explosions.

Man, let me tell you that the look on Capt. Riddle's face is well worth me getting my chest burned. Riddle comes charging into the center of the NDP looking for a bunker! His pale white face ready to crumble in fear. His teeth chattering and feet dancing, Riddle is a man on the Panic Express heading out of the station at light speed! Bobby and I start laughing hysterically, like two hyenas in the bush.

Bobby soon realizes that he has set off a shit storm and quickly needs to restore some order.

"Cease fire, cease fire!" he screams.

"Cease fire! Stop shooting! Cease fire!"

Gradually the troop realizes that there is nobody firing back at us and order is restored to this once-peaceful night. Nobody sleeps the rest of the evening and we pop flare after flare into the night sky and even though I know it has all been a hoax on the old man, I am hyper-vigilant myself, telling Herman to keep his eyes open.

In the morning, Herman and I walk out in front of our track like we do every morning, to bring the trip-flares and Claymores back in and pack them up till the next evening. Groggy and tired from another sleepless night, Herman and I don't notice it at first. I smile inwardly still thinking about Bobby's little practical joke on Capt. Riddle, when I see something glittering in the morning sun. It stands about fifty feet away.

"Herman!" I say softly. "Check it out." I nod toward the object when it suddenly comes into focus and my heart freezes. An RPG sits at the ready to blow Charlie Three-Four to Kingdom Come. A blood trail runs off into the bushes.

VII
The Mighty 590

Saturday, September 6, 1969

The morning is a blur. Last night and today are meshing into one horrific nightmare as the series of events becomes crystallized in my brain. Bobby laid the trap, I baited it, Charlie took a big bite and here we are. Dizzy has a fire going and we make some coffee.

"Christ, you guys are lucky," Dizzy frowns.

"Maybe," I reply. I am quivering inside. I thought that I had experienced fear before but what grips me at the moment is not a fear of the unknown but of the known. I knew that RPG was taking dead aim at me and sure as shit I would have been a goner. Maybe I was lucky last night, just to get killed today. It is first light and Dizzy and I try laughing it off, but man, I was scared.

To deal with the stress, my brain detaches and up I soar over the open fire. I look down and watch the men of Third Platoon Charlie Troop drink coffee and smoke cigarettes. I watch as Capt. Riddle walks up to us and says, "We need to send a dismounted patrol out in the jungle and follow the blood trail. Let's see where it goes."

My body falls back to earth. I feel like shit. I am nauseous as we pull on our packs and tread lightly down the blood trail. It's like some crazy graffiti artist took a can of red paint and sprayed a gang name across the bushes. We lose it at the edge of the jungle and pick it up again some twenty meters up a small hill. We separate. Montana is a big guy so he carries the M-60. His blond hair is a pale yellow in the overcast sky. His muscles are well defined and he walks with a gutsy gait that most of us find hard to keep pace with. Dizzy and I make up the rear of the detachment with Herman and Doc just in front. Clementi takes the point.

We disperse into the double-canopy bush. It's too small an area for our tracks so it's hump time again. At least I'm not on point. After several hundred meters Clementi raises his hand and we freeze. He sends a quiet order down the line: "Rivera, up front!"

No, God! What does he want me for? I move on up the line and find Montana and Clementi waiting for me.

"You guys set up a firing position here."

That's all? Whew! "OK," I mutter and look into Montana's eyes and they're cold and dead. We set up and I bring out my ammo and lay it ready for reloading his machine-gun. Montana dips into his pocket and pulls out his cigarettes. He offers me one and lights his own with a Zippo.

"So, how you be, Cal?" he asks. "You had a pretty close call last night."

"Yeah." I move back and stretch my legs. "We aren't going to find the sons-of-bitches."

"Clementi will find something," he drawls. We settle in and watch the last of our detachment disappear into the foliage. We wait for some twenty minutes before we hear a noise coming back on us. Montana tenses up and sits upright. I do the same. It's Clementi leading the patrol back. Montana relaxes and picks up his gun as I stand up and gather the ammunition at my feet.

"All clear?" I shout to Clementi.

"We lost the trail back on that slope," he says. "Fall in and let's get moving back to the troop. We have a lot of ground to cover today and we just wasted our morning."

Montana stands up next to me and yanks out another cigarette. Suddenly a burst of machine-gun fire cuts Montana's left leg apart at the knee.

"Holy shit!" I scream and fall back to the ground. Clementi

opens fire and I see two figures out of the corner of my eye go flying by on the right.

"Doc! Medic!" we cry as the gunfire escalates into a full crescendo of chaos. I cradle Montana's face in my arms as he shrieks out in pain.

"Doc!" I yank out one of my ampoules and shoot the morphine through his pants into his upper thigh. Lewis runs over at full throttle and cuts away Montana's pant leg and wraps a tourniquet around the injured leg. Montana continues to scream as the bullets bounce from the trees. I pick up the .60-cal and open fire in the direction that I saw the movement and Clementi yells a cease fire.

"Stop firing!" he repeats. He points at me and motions that I should go check on the damage.

I crawl to the spot where two bodies are sprawled on the hill. One has an open chest wound that killed him outright. The other is vertically shot up and down the left side of his body. His brains are splattered across his uniform and I wonder, "Are these the guys?" I strip them of all documents and place the contents into a plastic bag. I will later turn them over to the CIA when they come to verify the body count.

What a way to start your day. We evacuate Montana on a chopper and regroup on the road.

My crew this day is Bobbie Haynes as track commander and Herman and Boober as my gunners. I grab an M-79 grenade launcher out of the armorer's vehicle and don the CVC helmet and plug into the radio network of the platoon. We swing wide around and form a single-file line that winds through the rubber plantation like a giant snake. We fall in behind Second Platoon and move out.

The snake is hungry, having tasted the blood of two North Vietnamese Regulars. The sun peeps out of a dark cloud formation, like a sniper overlooking his prey. A few raindrops fall and the smoke from the engines stagnates in the sticky hot air. Herman leans forward and hits the back of my head, "You got smokes, Cal?"

We move out. I am feeling good after having a hectic morning with the dismounted patrol but things are OK now. Things are back in order, the way they are supposed to be. I am the tenth vehicle in the line. I am not thinking much except about the way Montana's leg looked in those bloody trousers. I had seen plenty of disfigured bodies by that time and was always amazed that we were as ruthless and inhuman as our enemies. As if to prove my point, suddenly the lead vehicle in our column hits a mine and everyone starts yelling.

"RPG! RPG!"

The radio in my ears starts shouting and squawking.

"Herringbone!"

This means that we deploy with every track facing the opposite direction on a forty-five degree bias, just like the name suggests. We open fire and I spot a rubber worker cut in half by a .50-caliber machine of death and destruction. His only crime was working in the rubber at 11:30 on a drizzly Saturday morning.

We add another body to the count. Three before noon is not a bad beginning for the killing machine. There is a lull in the action, and we roll on.

Around noon word comes down via the CVC earpiece that Alpha Troop is in heavy contact a few clicks to the northeast. We are sent to the firefight.

By the time we arrive, Alpha Troop has already broken contact and as I drive up that little rise I see the guys standing at the crest of the hill. They are smoking cigarettes and just sort of hanging around their tracks. They have a few blindfolded prisoners with their hands tied behind their backs. I look back at Herman and in turning I see North Vietnamese Regulars in brand new fucking uniforms crawling on their stomachs toward Alpha Troop. This time it is me who screams into the radio.

"Left side! Left side!" My heart is pounding and the blood leaves my face as I see more NVA in that single glance than I have seen in my whole life. They are like soldier ants in their coming. Steady moving forward for a sweet ambush. The men of Alpha are completely unaware of the danger that awaits them. Others soon pick up my cry and the troop turns left in a grand motion and opens fire on that nest of enemy agents. I spray the bush, as we come out of the rubber into the same sort of terrain where we had followed the blood trail.

Alpha Troop soon mounts their vehicles and joins in formation leaving behind a track and five crew members to mind the prisoners until they can get some aircraft to evacuate them.

I hear on the radio that Delta Company and Bravo Troop are also in the area and we race to form a full squadron fire-force that will be able to smash the thousands of NVA that now hold the jungle. What a mighty force we are. We do not know it yet, but we have stumbled into the 590th NVA regiment straight off the Ho Chi Minh Trail by way of Cambodia.

An NVA Regiment is made up of some 2,500 troops and we have disturbed the hornet's nest. They sting us with heavy AK-47 fire and .30-caliber machine-guns, but the most dreaded weapons they have are RPGs. They have rockets and mortars and the sky around me feels like the Fourth of July.

We inch forward, always firing. Herman's barrel becomes too hot to touch and we steadily fight them for a good two hours before I notice that it is raining. My job as driver is to give my crew the maximum effective field of fire while keeping us abreast of the rest of the squadron. This is difficult, given the false starts and stops of the vehicles next to me. Don't move out in front of everyone else or you will be shot. Don't fall too far behind or you might fire on friendlies. It is all I can do to keep us straight and shoulder-to-shoulder as we inch up taking hard-fought ground as we drive.

Deeper into the jungle we go.

Blam! Dizzy's track takes a glancing blow from a rocket propelled grenade. I see the two NVA troops who shot it and bring my own grenade launcher to my shoulders and blast them out of existence. Bobby lays down heavy fire from the fifty and we move forward.

I look over at Diz and he glances back at me and mouths "Thank you" and grins. Still the bullets keep flying. I can hear them ricocheting off of Herman's gun shield as I duck my head in and out of the driver's hatch, finally coming back out to gather my bearings. The fourth hour makes this the longest firefight anyone of us has ever taken part in.

As we crawl forward I pass dead bodies lying in the heavy downpour. Their bodies are swelling in the pools of mud, water and blood. Lifeless they lie, as if they are waxen images emerging from the soaking red earth.

On we trudge.

Relentless is the rain of bullets and another track takes a direct hit, this time from an RPG. I see Doc Lewis rush to their assistance and administer aid to staff Sgt. Saunders, who has shrapnel all down his back and legs. There is not much Doc can do and Sgt. Saunders becomes our first fatality of the day.

I turn up front and lurch forward another couple of meters when I see Capt. Riddle armed with just his .45 pistol dismount and start walking out in view of our line of fire. He is like some crazed madman yelling and screaming obscenities to the half-seen enemy. We probably should shoot him ourselves; his ranting causes a tragic thing to happen.

Because he is out front of us, our gunners have to stop firing, and that is just enough to let an RPG crew move out in front of us and fire a round that takes out Boober and Bobby directly, and blasts me out of the driver's hatch some ten to fifteen feet. The noise is deafening and the blast blinding and I lose consciousness.

I come to with Herman on my lap.

All I know is here I am with Herman and he has taken a BB-size piece of shrapnel to his carotid artery and he is bleeding profusely. I cup my hands over his neck and fail to stanch the bleeding and cry, "Herman! Oh shit, Herman!" Tears flow down my cheeks and mix with the rain and I cry harder as the life flows out of him a crimson stream. Blood gurgles out of his neck and no matter how hard I try

I am powerless to stem the flow. He lies in my arms wide-eyed and lips quivering and struggling to form a word. The Herman I love. The Herman I share my cigarettes and food with. The Herman I trip with in the jungle lies here dying.

I lower my ear to his mouth and I hear him trying to speak. Against all of the racket on the field of battle — machine-gun fire, shells exploding, people screaming — I think I can make out one syllable in Herman's breath.

"Ma ..."

Do all dying men call out to their mother as they die? My best friend in the world sighs and stops breathing. Dead, in my arms. I am devastated and I cry inconsolably. This is truly the low point of my twenty years on this planet. Where is God now? We were right to have made fun of Him.

Gradually sound returns to my ears and the battle scene comes into focus. I reach down and close Herman's eyes and Benson comes over and removes Herman's boot laces and pockets them. I have no idea why. Benson and I cry together as we lift and carry Herman to the rear of the line.

I stumble aimlessly for a few minutes alone on the battlefield. I notice a whole other war going on in the rear as I see our docs working on the wounded. I see Bobby and Boober's bodies lying there while people I've never seen before are coming in on choppers and bagging them and resupplying us with ammo and extra barrels for the machine-guns. It's like being backstage at a concert.

The explosion hurt my back and I go up to Doc Lewis and get something for the pain. As I gather myself and consider the last five hours, I see Dizzy wildly waving at me to come over to his track. They lost a gunner when they were hit and I climb aboard his vehicle. I take my place behind the left .60 and start firing as if nothing had happened. How long can a man operate on pure adrenaline?

Herman's blood is washing away in the rain, running like a river down my pants and filling my boots. He is lost to me again. I cock the sixty and angrily fire into the dense bush. We move forward. Thus begins the sixth hour of what is to be an eight-hour firefight.

Outnumbered seven to one, we continue our advance on the heavily fortified jungle strip outside the Michelin rubber plantation. There is now an unlimited supply of ammunition and I fire, and as Dizzy drives us to the left, then to the right, we continue to fire in the pouring rain. Steam rises from the barrel of my machine-gun and by now the noise is deafening. Somewhere or other I lose my CVC helmet and the rain pours on my head and down my face to my chest. I am wearing only a flak jacket above my waist and my bloody trousers continue to cascade blood onto the floor of the track.

At the beginning of the seventh hour my gun jams and I yell at Dizzy that I need to change barrels. My barrel has melted in the center from the heat from the *thousands* of rounds I have fired. I jump overboard and run back to the road and the behind-the-battle chaos.

I see Doc Johnson working on Doc Lewis. Lewis took some shrapnel in the neck and face and is lying there writhing in pain. I gave him one of my remaining ampoules. There is a triage area where the seriously wounded are staged for quick evacuation. I look through some wooden crates for a sixty barrel and find them sitting under boxes of ammunition. I grab a box of ammo and two barrels and some grease and start making my way back to the front line. As I move forward I hear a voice.

"Fred!" Teddy Jones screams, "I thought you was dead."

"Not yet."

"Where's your crew?"

"All dead."

"We got hit."

"Yeah, I saw that."

Teddy had been with Staff Sgt. Wayne Saunders when he was killed hours ago. Teddy held a bachelor's degree from LSU. A northern black who by fate or circumstance had wound up out in the jungle with us. I always thought that Teddy should have been an officer. He had that air of authority. Maybe in another army at another time he would have been a major. Now he was disheveled and pale in that late afternoon rain. He and I had hung together a lot with Herman and Doc. Now I am looking at my friend Teddy with a sullen detachment, given that my best friend had just died in my arms. We lock eyes and I am just about to speak when his face suddenly contorts into an anguished grimace.

He falls in place not three feet from where I stand. He lies there glassy-eyed and a gurgle comes from deep in his throat as he gasps his last breath. I swallow the lump in my throat. If he had not been standing there the bullet would have burst through my chest and I would have been dead.

Oh, Teddy, bless you, I think, as I pick up my feet and beat back to Dizzy's track. Like a maniac I run past the inferno that used to be Charlie Three-Four. Its black smoke billows up into a noxious cloud.

I think about the eye contact Teddy and I had made just before he was killed. I was the last thing he saw before he died. I was the last thing that Herman had seen before he died.

"Holy shit!" An explosion to my right pierces my ears and knocks me sideways. Stumbling, I pick up my ammunition and reconnoiter my way again to the front. There is a war going on and this is nowhere to sit and think about the day's events. Right now the 590th NVA Regiment has engaged us and it is my job to stay alive.

I have no idea how many of us are wounded.

As hard as I try, I cannot get Teddy's eyes out of my head. What had he seen? Where did he go? Were he and Herman looking down together at us as we continued in this folly?

"Jesus Christ, I want out!" The voice inside me screams as I scramble back onto the track.

"Dizzy," I shout, "Teddy's dead."

Dizzy nods toward me and says, "Hurry up and get that barrel changed out." Diz is keeping his cool and I grab a pair of asbestos gloves and unscrew the barrel. I dab a little grease to the end and put the new one in place in less than two minutes.

The last hour of battle is fought hard, as a war of attrition would have it. Everywhere I look is chaos and devastation. Young men are crying and being transformed into hollow, sad carriers of pain and remorse. Those of us who see death up close like this know that life is callous and cheap.

We cease fire when there are no longer bullets flying out of the bush. Their guns are silenced. This is not another lull in the battle. The battle is over. We just know it.

Now the hard part begins.

The cleaning up and taking inventory of the dead and wounded from both sides commences with Lt. Cutter coming up to me in the sudden quiet. "Dizzy and Fred, go police the bodies."

This was the gruesome task that Herman and I often performed after firefights. Now it's me and Diz. We are sent out with plastic bags to go through the pockets and personal possessions of the dead North Vietnamese soldiers. Some of the bodies are so devastated and destroyed that they are just bloody rags full of raw tissue. Dizzy and I do our job.

"This is fucked up," I tell Dizzy.

"My ears are still ringing," he says, as he props a body up and starts going into the pockets. It is like we're picking cotton; we are harvesting the fields for information.

I roll a stout bloody body to its side and grapple with its hind end as I pull out a wallet. I look inside and see a photograph of a young family of four. Who killed this guy with two children? I remember back to the day that Jim Gaines was killed and how Herman and I had reacted like two scared little boys. Now there was no fear. I am astonished at what I have become in just a matter of four months. The carnage that is splayed open before us is as gruesome as war can get. Dead NVA are lying out in the open. Some are hidden like Easter eggs. I notice that Diz is as adept as Herman in doing the devil's task we are assigned.

I look to the heavens and yell, "Is this all you got, Motherfucker? Is this as ugly as you can get?" I immediately regret flaunting my scorn at the Almighty, as what comes next is His instant answer.

"FUCK IT! FUCK IT! FUCK IT!" I yell, as a hand comes off the arm when I pull on it. I am sick and vomit all over the body next to him.

"Take it easy," Dizzy says.

"God is cruel, Diz." I throw the hand down and, weak in the legs, move on to another body.

"Herman didn't have a chance. Did you see it? Small as a fucking BB and right to his artery. Christ, it's like he was meant to die today. It ain't right, Diz. Life is too mean."

We count more than two hundred dead out in front of Charlie Troop's area of operation. The majority of the enemy has slipped back into Cambodia where we are unable to pursue them. I take some Cambodian money off of one guy and slip it into my pocket.

As I survey the afterglow of that long, hideous firefight, I realize that I am no longer a wild-eyed kid just off the plane from Los Angeles. I am a haggard veteran and I need a joint. There is a giant upheaval shaking the terrible foundations of my being.

Thus began a new war: the battle for my soul.

VIII
Youth in Asia

I lit a cigarette and turned to Dizzy. By then Benson and Billy had joined us just inside the perimeter. We all headed on back toward the road. Three choppers had their blades rotating in an idling position and the noise became louder as we stepped over war's landfill: shell casings and discarded weapons and barrels. We started looking around us for friends, who might still be standing, or stacked up and breathing, ready to be dusted off. Who had made it? Who did we lose?

"They got all your crew," Benson said above the noise. "Herman …"

"I know."

"Haynes, Boober, and what the fuck was his name?"

"The new guy?" I asked.

"Yeah. What the fuck was his name?" Benson asked again.

"Cooper, or something," I said. "He just came out last night." Cooper had just come out to the platoon the previous evening during resupply over at the French ruins. Man, that was a long time ago. Last night we must have brushed up against that NVA regiment and they probed us. That seemed like such a big deal at the time. Bobby told me to run that wire back and I did, and we showed them how powerful we are. That's why they waited till the morning to hit us.

I took a drag off my cigarette and started to consider the scene. There were still thousands of them out there and here we were sitting around smoking and kicking back like Alpha Troop had this morning before this whole thing blew up. I grabbed an M-16 off the nearest track and chambered a round. I didn't live through the firefight now just to get taken out by a sniper.

"David Cooper," I whispered. "Fucking guy killed on his first day out here."

"That sucks," Billy said. I looked at Billy for a hard moment.

What a stupid motherfucker, I thought. "It all sucks, man," I moaned.

One of the helicopters took off right then and the wind rustled up the spot where we were standing. Benson's hat flew off and that reminded me that everything I owned in this world had just gone up in flames with Charlie Three-Four. My letters, writing material, and clothes all gone and my guitar burned up with them all. *Shit.*

I looked at Benson as he chased down his hat. He turned and looked at me and we caught eye contact the way Teddy and I had earlier. Benson started to cry softly and it was contagious. I broke down watching the big man weep.

"Herman ..."

The tears ran down my face and I wiped them with the back of my hand and got blood all over my face. I cried and didn't try hiding it from the other guys.

The afternoon had brought a break from the rain and our clothes and boots were starting to dry in that hot, humid weather of the jungle. A second chopper took off and we walked to the one remaining. It contained the last of the wounded and we saw our friend Doc Lewis lying on a stretcher.

"Million-dollar wound," Dizzy told him, as he leaned in to punch him lightly on the arm. This brought a smile to Doc's face and he grimaced at once as the smile brought back the pain. We would never see Doc Lewis again as the severity of his wounds won him a one-way ticket back to the US and he disappeared into the VA system as many others had done before him.

Lt. Cutter came walking our way as Doc's ride home slowly lifted above our heads and disappeared into the late afternoon sky.

"Get ready to mount up."

We started to gather the weapons and saw the giant stacks of resupply items that the helicopters had dropped off. I grabbed some uniforms, sizing them up the best I could do on short notice. Benson grabbed the smokes. We got a carton of Kools each. All the gunners came over to that pallet and just started grabbing extra munitions for themselves. They dragged what they could back to their respective tracks. Diz and I made two trips back and forth to his vehicle and I moved into my new home. Charlie Three-Three would be my new hang from here on out. I hoped so, at least.

The engines started to crank over and the platoon soon turned toward the road and met with heavy traffic. The whole squadron was here and trying to detach from each other became a horrible mess. It was like trying to leave Dodger Stadium after the 7th game of the World Series. We formed a single file moving back and forth to make a U-turn. Multiply this by fifty and you get the idea of how many tracks and tanks there were grinding up the earth. Like tractors and bulldozers at a swamped construction site we were oppressive on Mother Earth and soon the mud was starting to grow deeper in our tracks. It had rained all day and now we pushed the rain-swollen earth to its limit. We were stirring mud soup with our machines.

When Third Platoon joined the rest of Charlie Troop, the sun was already starting to set. We formed up on the road and let Alpha and Bravo Troops move out in front of us. This took over an hour and now it was really starting to get dark.

I asked Dizzy for some writing paper and started a letter to my folks while we waited for our turn to roll. Delta Company fell in behind us and we all started to move out slowly. I put the paper and pen away and checked my weapon.

No dinner tonight, I thought. We moved on. Slowly rumbling down that muddy dirt road I took my first reckoning of our situation.

Six dead in Charlie Troop, five in Third Platoon, alone. Twenty-some wounded and dusted off. They would bring out their replacements tomorrow but tonight we would have to square up short handed. I looked up and saw the colonel's personal Huey flying over us. It must just be a big chess game for him. He was now moving his pawns into another defensive position to watch out for their knights.

I turned my barrel up to the sky and took aim at him. I sat back and watched as I blew him out of the sky and the game was over, but suddenly Dizzy brought me out of my daydream.

"Top off?" he asked.

"Whatcha got?" I shot back.

He stood up in the driver's hatch and turned and handed me a lit pipe full of weed. I took a hit and it was good. Amazingly enough my little daydream soon sounded like it might work.

"If I could only-"

Shots rang out on our left front and I swung the gun around and opened up just inches from Dizzy's head. We were getting hit again. We were getting hit again.

"WE'RE GETTING HIT AGAIN!" Dizzy screamed.

Swoosh! An RPG shot around our front and exploded in the jungle. Within minutes our war machine was running at full throttle again, spitting out death and destruction at the unseen enemy. This time they had the high ground and we were sitting ducks on that muddy road. Bullets bounced off of the gun shields and the sides of our tracks.

Boom! We heard the retort of the big guns on the M-48 tanks in Delta Company.

It was louder than before. They must have been right on top of us. We turned into the field of fire and everyone started lining up again in that same formation that had been so successful all day. We moved in a line toward the NVA. Never stopping, we moved up but they moved back and this started to open some ground between us. This was good. We were better like this at a distance.

This firefight lasted about three quarters of an hour and soon the NVA disappeared again to live on to fuck us up another day.

The colonel gave the order to the company commanders that he wanted a full squadron NDP. The captains all got together and talked this out. Where could they find a big enough field to house the entre squadron?

It was probably the idiot Capt. Riddle who suggested the original battle site for before we knew it we were turning around and heading back to the big muddy field. The logistics of this move were enormous. There were hundreds of tracks and tanks that needed to be repositioned and this made the mud deeper. By the time Dizzy had moved us into position it was ten p.m. Everyone was drained and too tired to give a shit.

"Claymores and trip-flares!" shouted my new track commander, Sgt. Harold Jenkins. Jenkins was a New York hippie who shared my passion for rock and roll. Harold claimed to be a drummer back in the World and this sealed us tight. I was glad to be working with him and he made me feel welcome on Three-Three but still it was time to put out the shit.

Dizzy came up to me and handed me the trip-flares. He took the Claymores. As we stepped off the vehicle we were immediately swallowed up by the mud. It was knee deep and you could hardly move in it at all. I felt like I was moving in quicksand. Dizzy and I held our arms up over our heads and trenched our way to the perimeter. This was a fucking joke!

It *had* to be the idiot Riddle's idea to camp us here. We set up the mines and moved slowly back to our vehicle. I grabbed one of my new shirts and wiped my arms and chest with it. The inside of the track was now slushed in mud, which piled inches on the floor. I sat down with the mud pooled around me. I looked around at my new home. There was Dizzy and Jenkins and the other gunner named Dale Darnel from Wichita, Kansas.

Dale was a weird guy. He was very hyper and kind of fidgety. We worked out the sleeping quarters and Dale took the first guard duty. The three of us started smoking and playing cards while Dale sat astride the M-50 machine-gun. It had been a very stressful day and we were just trying to relax and forget ourselves when we heard Dale say, "Hey, give me some water."

Nobody paid any attention to him and we kept on playing cards when he said again, "Hey, *give me some water.*"

I forget what game we were playing but I know it was Dizzy's turn when Dale stuck his arm down the hatch holding a live grenade with the pin pulled and again demanded, "*Hey, I said give me some fucking water!*"

We scrambled out of that vehicle and fell down in the mud and I swear I almost died of fright. Now Harold was as full of mud as Dizzy and I were. Darnel wasn't backing down and Diz called out to him to put the pin back in the grenade. Dizzy started talking real nice to old Dale and he tried getting him to put that grenade down but Dale just grew angrier and angrier. I crept back inside the track and grabbed a canteen and raised it up to Dale Darnel's empty hand and he took it. He grinned and gave me the grenade minus the pin.

I had to disarm the damn thing by unscrewing the cap and taking it apart. Everyone returned to the vehicle and Dale took the canteen and went back up to the .50-cal.

The inside of the track was a muddy mess. No one felt much like playing cards anymore and we settled in to quiet chat replaying the day's events. Everyone agreed that Darnel was a crazy asshole and he just sat guard above us as if nothing out of the ordinary happened. Such was the day.

Everybody in the troop kept to themselves that night. We were knee-deep in the mud and that didn't make socializing that much fun. Everyone stayed with their own crew. At midnight Dale finished his shift and it was my turn behind the fifty. I arose and clamored to the top of the vehicle still groggy and unsettled. I was tired, but out in the jungle you got in the habit of running on four hours or so of sleep. I took a sip of water out of the canteen I had given Darnel earlier in the evening. The water tasted good.

It was a still night, humid and hot, and I slipped on the flak jacket I had worn earlier in the day. I gazed out at the darkness and noticed a Special Forces camp a couple of clicks to the east sitting on a low hill.

I did not see the first explosion, but I sure as hell heard it and jerked my body upright and grabbed a helmet that was lying on top of the vehicle.

BOOM!

Another explosion to my right left mud splattering up all over my face. I could hear mortar tubes popping five hundred meters out in front. The thick mud caused the projectiles to bury themselves three or four feet into the ground before exploding. Like in past encounters, instead of spreading shrapnel, the ordinance scattered mud all over the place.

Everyone was awake after the first thud. It's funny but nobody opened fire. What were we to shoot? The NVA were ghosts and after what we had been through this little mortar attack was more of a nuisance rather than anything to get excited over. That NVA regiment was just letting us know they were still around. As it turned out, they decided to probe the Special Forces camp instead of us.

Big mistake!

At once we could see their green tracers firing into the camp on the hill and the red tracers of the friendlies firing back. I was looking right at the camp when they blew their first circle of fu gas. The Special Forces had placed napalm around their perimeter for just this purpose. If they were probed, they would detonate more fu gas and incinerate anyone caught in the wire.

Dizzy came up on top and sat with me and watched in awe as the entire sky lit up in flames. With the red and green tracers flying about we felt like we were at some Fourth of July picnic. Oh, let's not forget the splaying mud. We started laughing.

"Fuck!" Dizzy said as Special Forces blew their First Circle of Hell.

Jenkins and Darnel joined us and we all enjoyed the light show together. By then the mortar attack had stopped. I guess the enemy moved their concentration onto the Special Forces camp.

September 7, 1969

Dear Bob,

Just a short note while I have some time. I don't know what to say. Thank you and your woman for writing to me. It really helps. Keep visiting my mom. It's so hard for me to keep writing lies to her. I'm miserable but you get used to it. I've seen bodies with their heads blown off, no arms, and no legs. It doesn't bother me to see dead NVA or VC. They don't look real. But it really fucked me up to see a dead American. It hits hard when you lose a friend. Such a comradeship. I had to carry his body to a helicopter and cried my head off all the way. I know I'll be fucked up in the head when I get back if I keep thinking about all this fighting. It's a way of life now trying to keep alive. We are by the Cambodian border. It's a bad place to be. I got a letter from Olivia and she asked me what I do in my spare time. WOW! What can you say? Sometimes it's cool though. It's such a beautiful country. When things seem fairly secure we get high and go driving around digging the scenery. What a joke! Man how are things back in the world?

Write to me and fill me in on what's happening. Tell Lance to write. He hasn't written to me since I've been here. Don't think I'm down. I'm going to come home in May.

Keep cool.

Fred

After I finished writing to my friend Bob, I sat down and wrote lies to my parents. I never could bring myself to tell them the truth of what this war was really like. Still, I wrote home as often as I could.

The rain, the mud and the killing did not deter me from giving my family assurance that I was still alive.

September 7, 1969

Mom + Dad + Sis

I'm fine. It's 8:30pm and I'm writing this by flashlight. We are in a Squadron NDP along with some American Infantry. We have a lot of people here. No, I wasn't on that track that hit the mine. No one was hurt. Just the track. Third squadron is supposed to relieve us soon. They just got their Sheridens. We were the first to use them. Now the whole ACR has them. Well, I have to go on guard now so I hope your all fine. I'll try to write tomorrow. I love and miss you very much.
Fred.

With the new day came some peace and quiet. Peace talks were taking place in Paris and they were arguing over the size and shape of the table. What fucks. Bring them down here in the jungle with all its rain and misery. I stole a glance at Dizzy and found him smiling softly at Dale. Dale was very animated as he opened a can of peaches from the C-rations.

"I'm getting out of this fucking place, man." He set the can of peaches down on a box of ammo. "It's getting pretty funky and yesterday and last night we were fucked."

"You crazy bastard, you pulled the pin on a grenade on us," Dizzy said. "You're wrapped too tight right now. Maybe you do need to leave the theater."

"Exit to the left, please," I added.

Dizzy picked up the canned peaches and drank some of the juice. He stared at Darnel and said without smiling, "You could have killed us, you crazy son of a bitch."

Darnel grabbed the peaches and looked at all of us. "I'm sorry.

I'm sorry, OK? You know I wouldn't have dropped the dime on you all. It's just the fucking stress."

"I've got your stress right here, motherfucker," Dizzy said as he grasped the can of peaches and threw them out into the jungle.

We were still covered in mud and it was tough to maneuver through the camp as we were knee-deep in the muck. Diz and I retrieved the Claymores and trip-flares and we both looked across the perimeter to where the coffee was.

"I'll go," Dizzy said, and off he stumbled to get us some hot coffee.

Jenkins ambled over to where we had been standing and stood before Darnel, who just stared back. Finally the sergeant said, "Clean the inside of the track."

He had to say it just once, and Darnel was all over it. He knew he was getting off light and Jenkins was not going to write him up over a lapse in judgment.

A lapse in sanity was more like it. But what, if anything, was sane?

IX
The Way we Mourn

At 10:15 a.m. on Sunday, September 7, we moved out of the killing zone. We drove past An Loc away from the Cambodian border and moved into a base camp in Quan Loi for some much-needed rest and retooling. We limped into the camp still full of mud and blood. Our vehicles needed maintenance and our bodies needed a good cleaning and some rest. It felt good to shower away the mud, and remaining traces of Herman's blood. I stayed in that shower until the bucket went dry.

By nightfall the heads had found our own hooch and cots with clean sheets. In the rear you hung with your friends and I could probably go two to three days without running into people like Billy Henderson. I always hung with the brothers, as Herman and I were attached at the hip for so long.

Now it was time to hold Herman's wake.

The chaplain had arranged for a memorial service for the six dead members of C Troop to be held in the morning; this evening, we would say goodbye to our comrade in our own way.

The brothers came from all four platoons. We even had guys show up from Bravo Troop. The pipes were lit and passed around with a few bottles of beer that Olgovey managed to snag. Much was made of our friendship — Herman's and mine — and the fact that he died in my arms. I did not know until then that Benson and some guys had made an intricate braided wrist band from the laces of Herman's boots.

Benson came out and presented it to me. I stood and held out my arms. Benson moved in closer and I embraced him with the only hug I had ever given another man in Vietnam.

"Thank you, my brother," I said softly. "I will wear this bracelet till the day I die."

Two white guys I didn't know happened to be walking by the tent and as they saw this one of them yelled out, "Nigger lover!"

You have no idea, I thought.

We talked about Doc Lewis not being with us anymore and we smoked a bowl to him. We smoked a bowl to Bobby Haynes and one for Wayne Saunders. By then we started losing guys, as they had smoked so much weed they were passing out left and right. Dizzy and I had a high tolerance and we made it to the end with Benson and Olgovey and a few others. Everyone found a cot or a piece of floor and we all had our first good night's sleep in over a month.

In the morning Dizzy and I awoke still groggy from the previous night's proceedings. After a real breakfast and hot coffee we went to the motor pool to work on Charlie Three-Three. We had abandoned Charlie Three-Four to the jungle and mud. After stripping the vehicle of all the radios and weapons we just left her there with the hundreds of dead NVA.

I really started to mourn Herman. He and I used to work on Three-Four together. Now it was me and Dizzy on Three-Three and the ghost of Herman Johnson.

We drove the vehicle to a wash area and stripped her so we could wash off the entire thing. This was not an easy process. We removed the cans of ammo that were stacked inside, the M-16s on the side, and the heavy machine-guns on top. We worked in that hot morning air for two hours before we were satisfied that she was as clean as we were going to get her.

Around the start of the second hour my back started hurting, where I was sore from being blown out of the track just two days before. I worked through the pain and finally told Diz we had to cool it. Diz took care of putting the track back together—ammo cans, M-16s and all.

It was just our luck to have Gen. George Patton's son as our colonel. He had a lot to live up to, so he wound up giving us a miserly total of two days out of the field. On the third morning we mounted up and thanked our hosts for their hospitality and headed out toward An Loc for security duty.

Where Quan Loi was a village, An Loc was a small hamlet and setting up security around it was a piece of cake. We had done it before with no contact, so everyone was happy in that column of dust heading down Highway 13.

An Loc was close to the Cambodian border and the giant firefight we had was no more than a few clicks away. It was a friendly village and we meant to keep it that way. We arrived mid-afternoon and the first thing we did was break down brush and small trees with our vehicles to set up an LZ and a NDP that we could use every night after patrol. We would sit outside the hamlet by day, or we would patrol around the perimeter and set up in different places every day.

One early evening, as soon as we had set up our night defensive position, we fell into playing cards. Jenkins, Darnel, Dizzy and I liked to play tonk. Tonk is a back-street game played in the black ghetto, a game Herman had taught me and I had in turn taught the crew.

Lately our crew had taken to just hanging together and not walking around visiting our other friends. The grenade incident was history and not brought up in conversation. This night we were talking about baseball. Dizzy and I were arguing about who was better, Al Kaline or Willie Davis.

"Willie Davis has speed with his power," I said.

"Kaline can hit the ball farther. The only speed he needs is in his hands and they are fast enough." As Dizzy said this I felt my left hand start to burn. I looked down and saw a scorpion crawling down my arm.

"Fuck!" I swiped the insect off of my arm. Immediately I felt nauseous, with a cold sweat covering my upper body. This fucking jungle! I saw the scorpion on the ground and stomped it. I stomped it for Herman, I stomped it because of the mud, I stomped that bug over and over again until I got dizzy and had to sit down.

"What the fuck?" Dizzy asked as he placed a steadying arm on my shoulder. I felt weak and a little unsteady and Jenkins came around the makeshift table and looked in my eyes.

"What the fuck?" he echoed Dizzy and he soon enough realized what had happened as I pointed to the dead scorpion.

"Darnel, get a doc," he ordered, and Darnel took off into the night to find a medic. We were still waiting for Doc Lewis' replacement. Darnel had to go all the way to First Platoon to find the troop medic, and he came back with Doc Sykes. We did not know him well.

"What's going on here? Snake bite?" He sounded like a grumpy old man.

"Scorpion," we all said in unison.

"Well, well, well. Hurt much?" he mumbled.

"Burns like hell," I moaned.

He reached in his bag and pulled out a syrette of morphine and plunged it into my right arm. He looked at Sgt. Jenkins because after the initial treatment, it was all about rank and following the proper chain of command.

"Try to keep him out of the sun tomorrow and you better give him first shift on guard duty tonight. Scorpion will make you sicker than shit but it won't kill you. Call me on Alpha Two-Six if you need me but it ain't no snake bite. Your boy will be all right. Just let him heal on his own."

He grabbed his bag and I thanked him and he strode off into the darkness where he had come from and our little crew tried to settle back to some normalcy for the night. There it is.

The biggest problem with the kind of duty we were pulling was that it meant that every few nights our track was expected to team up with other guys and go out on either a listening post or ambush patrol. I don't know which one was more frightening. On LP we went out in the jungle and set up in a hole or found some sort of hiding position and just waited for enemy soldiers to pass by. We were not to engage the enemy but only listen and report on their movements. On reflection, I found that this was the scarier of the two because on ambush patrol you had to engage the enemy, and therefore were better armed. We usually carried a heavy machine-gun out on those missions.

The enemy patrol usually consisted of only four fools, and the fact that we carried a .50 clearly gave us the advantage.

One night Jenkins came up to me and Dizzy and said, "You two have LP tonight. Get with the crew from Three-Two and go."

We walked over to the other vehicle and told Sgt. Mays that we were told to report to him. He jumped over the side of the track and looked us over.

"Thought you was bug-bit?" he said, eyeing me up and down.

"Better now. Been a few days. Who you got?"

He spat out his chewing tobacco and said, "I'll give you Benson and Harvey. Go out and tear them up."

"Thought it was a LP?" I said, "and who in the hell is Harvey?"

"Harvey came out with the chopper tonight," Mays said, as he took another dip of chaw.

"You're giving us a FNG to take out on his first fuckin' night in country? Come on, Sarge, be reasonable," I complained.

Mays stared back at me and glared, "He goes."

I looked at Dizzy and frowned just as Benson came out of the track with his M-16 and helmet. Joe Harvey came into view at the same time. There he stood, all five feet two inches of him in his brand-new bright green fatigues and shiny new boots. As Herman would say, "Sho' is shiny."

"Hello," he said.

I just looked from Benson to Dizzy to Sgt. Mays. Joe stood there with his brand-new duffel bag and a uniform that looked like it was just issued that morning. It probably was.

"How long you been in country?" I asked.

"One week," Joe Harvey replied.

That was enough for Benson to smile and look at us and say, "Gotta break the muthafucka in sometime. Might as well be tonight. Ain't nothing going on that the three of us can't handle. Lighten up, brothers, and let the boy become a man. Let him be all that he can be."

I sighed and looked at Benson and said, "He's your boy tonight."

I grabbed a flak jacket and threw it at Harvey and, finally smiling, I said, "Put this on and keep it on. It will save your life. We're going on an LP and that just means you keep your mouth shut and keep from moving around and stay real still. Think you can do it?"

"Yes, sir," he replied.

I pushed him onto the ground and said, "I ain't your *sir*, shorty, and if you ever salute me in the field again, I will have your ass. Let's go, Benson. Take your boy." Harvey's uniform was dirty as he picked himself off the floor and adjusted his glasses.

Lt. Cutter walked over with a map and gave us our coordinates for the night. We were to set up about 500 meters out front of Second Platoon's position. The four of us walked across the perimeter and checked with the guys in Second Platoon. They showed us where their trip-flares were.

We were to make a path out in front of them and they were instructed to hold their fire that night, as there would be friendlies out in front. Benson had the map and eventually we found our position. We dug in for the night. We turned down our radio and went radio silent for the evening. We spoke sparingly in hushed whispers and divided up the night as to the guard shifts. It was to be Benson, Me, Dizzy, and the new guy would go last.

At midnight I took over guard duty. All was quiet as I lay in the brush, still as can be. The moon was out and gave off a soft glow, illuminating the landscape in a dark blue hue. The world was sleeping, peacefully, it seemed.

The peace was shattered around 1:30.

Joe Harvey sat up in his sleep and yelled, "I got to piss, piss, piss,

piss, piss!" Benson awoke immediately as I jumped on Joe Harvey, covering his mouth. Benson pushed him back flat on the ground. The world woke up immediately, and erupted with animal and insect noises. We were scared. This FNG talked in his sleep and within seconds a machine-gun opened fire on our position. We hit the dirt.

Dizzy got on the radio and screamed, "Papa Charlie, this is Eagle Three, we have contact!" He repeated, "This is Eagle Three, our position has been compromised." Immediately flares flew from the troop NDP and within minutes we heard the engines come to life on the vehicles of Charlie Troop.

We tried to return fire, but without a machine-gun, we were outgunned. Green tracers lit up the night and machine-gun fire burst through our position. I turned around and found Harvey slumped over his firing position. A bullet hole through his head, he stared back at me with unseeing eyes.

Dizzy popped red smoke to mark our position as we heard our tracks start to pull into position behind us. They came up over the left side and we watched with pleasure as one of our gunners took out the enemy machine-gun position.

As our tracks passed by, Dizzy and I jumped aboard Three-Three as Benson found his way to Three-Two. As Three-Three rolled slowly away, I watched as Doc Sykes bagged Joe Harvey and loaded his corpse into a chopper.

Joe Harvey went to war for one day. Doc Lewis's words came back to haunt me ... "If it's your time, it's your time." There it is.

I hardly thought about Joe Harvey after that night. He was a ghost that had appeared in our combined vision within a hellish nightmare. No one made friends with FNGs for that very reason.

We regrouped in a column and searched the area, but did not find the machine-gun nest. We never expected to. The Vietcong had tunnels where they scampered to after small actions like this. The NVA were welcome to them whenever they fought in the South. They knew better than to mess with the whole troop, but a small patrol was a different matter. Their ability to hit and run and completely disappear was frightening. Finally we made our way back to the NDP.

Jenkins and Darnel wanted to immediately know everything that happened. "Did he really take one in the head?" Darnel asked with shiny clear eyes. He was still in an excited mood from the little skirmish, as we were all hyped up on adrenalin. Whether ten minutes or eight hours, these firefights raised our level of consciousness.

We were warriors now, fighting an ever-elusive enemy.

X
The Volunteer and Jack Ruby

September 20^{*th*}

Mom and Dad,

It's been a few days since any mail has gone out or come in. I'll write while I have a chance. Here is some good news. We've been working around these villages since we came out. We're sitting on this hill right now overlooking two villages down in the valley. It is so beautiful. This place is so green. We are helping the people to build churches and stuff. This is a pacification program to get the people to trust the government for when they have elections after the peace talks. During the day we play baseball and volleyball with the villagers and at night we sit outside the village to guard it. The kids are so cute. They swarm around us all the time. I'm happy that I'm being given the chance to live with these people and help them instead of fighting and killing them.

I got your letter where you wonder about me not hearing the rockets. Mom, this is really weird. When someone shoots at you, you don't realize it.

Love,
Fred

It's true that those weeks were sweet duty. It's like we were simply lifted out of the ugliness and lulled into a peaceful, warm feeling. We engaged with the people and that gave us comfort and reminded us of our families back in the world.

One afternoon we sat single file on a road right outside of the southern edge of An Loc. Not much was happening and we were pretty much removed from the war. We still carried loaded weapons with the safety off but we never realized that we were getting lazy and careless. We had plenty of everything that we needed and some guys had C-rations hanging off the back of their vehicles. I was standing on the road with Benson and Dizzy when we saw movement at the end of the column.

No one was supposed to be there. We were all accounted for up front. Again we saw the sudden movement of somebody taking cover behind the last track. We all reacted at once and Benson and I each fired a shot. We ran to the back of the column expecting to find a Vietcong sapper but instead we found a young boy of about thirteen lying in a pool of blood. He was just trying to steal some food and one of us killed him. Benson yelled for a medic and my heart broke as I realized what we had done.

"God damn it!" Benson yelled, "Stupid fucking kid!" Benson was getting worked up into frenzy. I stood there looking down at his body and started crying and pounding my fists into the trees. Benson fell to the ground and started crying too.

Cutter and a bunch of others came over and tried to convince us it was not our fault. He took us both aside and said, "I'm sending you both back to the rear for a few days."

Benson stood up and I came around to his left side. Was he going to reward us for killing a kid? "That won't be necessary, sir," Benson said to the lieutenant. I looked at him, and Benson was standing tall and he became animated, "We can carry on, lieutenant. I don't know how Cal feels about this, but I'm good to go and want to stay here in the field."

What was I to say? That I was a coward and wanted to go back to the rear? Instead, I said, "I'm OK, lieutenant."

The lieutenant took a look at us and said, "I'm keeping an eye on you two. Report back to me tomorrow and we will see how things work out. Right now get out of here and let the medics do their job."

"Thank you, sir," we both replied. This incident caused Benson and me to pull together, not knowing then that it would bond us for life, however short or long it would turn out to be.

After that day, I swore to God that I would never take another life. Who was I kidding? It was not up to me.

October 2, 1969

Mom and Dad,

We've been sitting in the middle of this rubber plantation all day so I thought I would write a few lines. Not much is new. I would like to see that guy that told me "Time goes by fast out there." He lied. It drags on by. Everybody here has opinions that they pass off as information. Everything is "I heard" or "They said," or "Some guy over in 2nd Platoon heard," Who is running this show anyway? Like I said in my last letter all we're doing is securing the area. There is a little village about 500 feet down the road. There is a lull in the ground fighting like "they say" in the news. You said Richard told you something about air support. That's true. Every time we go out there are two or three helicopters flying around. They have rockets and machine-guns on them. In that fire fight we were in, a helicopter first spotted three VC in the area. He fired a rocket and marked the spot for us. The bombers came in and dropped their load. When we finally went in, most of the VC were dead, deaf, or dying. Mom, these dead guys don't look real. What I didn't tell you is that when we found all of that ammunition and rice, it was buried in a mass grave. They were actually hiding it for future use. We had to dig it out with shovels and the smell was so horrendous as to make everyone sick. I stuck my shovel in and came up with a hand. I couldn't do it. This place smells worse than the stockyards of Vernon. It smells of death and burning shit. I guess you get used to it. The mud, the rain, everything becomes a way of life. At night I find peace. I have great buddies. We spend time talking about our homes and friends and family. Sometimes we forget where we are and it's as if were just on some big camping trip. You see, this isn't that bad. Even as I write this letter, there are two helicopters flying around the area to make sure nobody sneaks up on us.

I'm in good spirits. The only thing I worry about is you and how you are doing. I hoped you don't worry too much. The worst thing here is not being able to keep clean. I'm always dirty. I'm glad you have been writing. Your letters aren't boring. I hope I don't upset you when I tell you about the fighting, but you must understand that it hasn't bothered me.

Love,

Fred.

Time was dragging on, and without the adrenaline rush of battle, we were getting bored. The LPs and APs had stopped and once again, we were lulled to sleep.

So, one day, when the lieutenant announced that he needed two volunteers to go to Lai Khe and pick up a new track I didn't give it a second thought. This would mean traveling alone without the safety of the troop. It seemed like a suicide mission to me and after killing that kid I didn't give a shit if I lived or died. I yelled out, "I'll go, sir."

Dizzy gave me a weird look with that lazy left eye and walked over to where I stood. "You fucking crazy?"

"Yeah," I said.

"Me, too." He looked at Cutter and said in a loud, clear voice, "I'm going with Fred."

An Loc was right off of Highway 13 and that took you right into Lai Khe. The trick was to hitch a ride with some convoy and head on in. With signed paperwork, Dizzy and I went out and hitched a ride with the 707 Transportation Company heading our way. We jumped aboard a deuce-and-a-half driven by some psychopath.

His name was Rudy but he liked to be called Ruby—after Jack Ruby, who killed Lee Harvey Oswald. He had some kind of mental fixation with the image in the Dallas police station that we, as a nation, saw live on TV. He said Jack Ruby brought us all together. He was crazy but he was a hell of a driver. We got on his wild ride with a bowl of weed. There must have been more than thirty vehicles in that convoy and they were all cowboys. We sped down that highway like a fire engine on its way to a burning house.

The Vietnamese mainly rode motorbikes and bicycles with the occasional small car. These guys drove within inches of pedestrians and cyclists and always took the right of way. Honking our horns and never braking, we swerved around people until we got out of the populated areas.

Once clear, we worried more about ambushes than Ruby's driving. Every other vehicle in the convoy had a mounted .50-caliber with a gunner and a loader but this was scarcely the 11th Armored Cavalry, and sometimes Diz and I were grateful for the speed and daring that Ruby displayed. It was a bumpy ride but we got so high that we felt we were on a Sunday drive.

I leaned back in the seat and looked out the window. The scenery barely changed as we hopped from small village to small village. The engineers had cut a clearing of 200 meters on each side of the road to prevent ambushes. They were ruthless in destroying homes and shops along the way. Uncle Sam's version of eminent domain.

I looked over at Ruby. He was a rail of a man, almost tubercular with a screwy, thin mustache that covered part of his upper lip. His uniform was clean and his boots shined. His eyes were glassy blue set in a long pale face.

"Where you headed and where in the hell did you guys come from? You're filthy." He started a conversation that I hoped would make the ride a little easier.

"We're from the 11th ACR and we've been living in the jungle," I responded.

"You ever kill anybody?" he asked.

"More than likely," Diz said.

"Me, I just drive but I'd like to know what it feels like to kill somebody. We've been hit about a dozen times."

"What do you do when that happens?"

"I just drive through it all."

"Well, just drive us to Lai Khe and we will be just fine," I said. He was starting to irritate me. I had just killed a kid. I straightened out and leaned forward.

"You don't want to know what it feels like to kill. Be glad that you drive a truck and sleep in a bunk bed at night in the rear."

"And shower every night," Dizzy added. Diz looked at me and grinned a wicked little smirk, his lazy eye looking sideways. He and I were high and the hot wind blowing through the open window felt good. In the field, we never drove fast enough to have the wind in our faces.

There were countless people like Ruby in Vietnam. They never had to fire a weapon or watch a brother die or get critically wounded. They were necessary components of the killing machine, moving men and material from point A to point B. Maybe this guy drove the machine-gun parts to the helicopter that brought them out to us in the jungle. I don't know. It was too big for me to put my head around. He was just a guy that got drafted and wound up through no special talent or connection to be a fucking truck driver instead of an infantry man. Such was life.

"How much longer is it to Lai Khe?" I asked. I was feeling better about him. The weed helped my mood.

"About two hours."

"Then what?"

"You guys are welcome to stay with us at our barracks. Half the company is always on the road so there is plenty of room." I looked at Dizzy and he nodded.

It was dark when we entered their yard. It was a freight depot much like a civilian operation. Ruby pulled into a slot and we grabbed our weapons and followed him inside a building. Inside of the bay was a hubbub of commotion. There was a chow hall down the corridor and Ruby gave us the choice of hot chow or a shower. We both opted for the shower.

My god. It had been at least three weeks since we had had a shower. And that didn't really count because it was only hot water from a bucket. This was a real hot-water shower. We stayed in it for about twenty minutes. Getting the layers of grime off our bodies couldn't have felt any better. We were grateful for this new, scrawny friend. He found us some clean clothes and we put them on. Of course they were too big but they were clean and smelled fresh. He showed us the mess hall and we filled our plates to the rim. We rammed down the food like there was no tomorrow.

Then came the beer, television and the weed. Man, these guys had it made. Ruby showed us to our cots and we sacked out and slept like babies. In the morning everyone was gone and Diz and I were hungover, but clean.

We went to the chow hall, had breakfast and sat and tried to remember where the 11th ACR liaison was located on the base. We were walking around trying to find it, and had gone about a quarter of a mile when a Jeep drove by. We were confused when it slammed on its brakes and backed up to where we were. It was a full bird colonel. And he immediately started bellowing at us for not saluting him.

"Did you see me?" he screamed.

"No, sir," we chimed in unison.

"You need haircuts and your boots are filthy!" He was ready to burst and his face turned a deep shade of crimson.

"Who's your commanding officer?" he demanded to know.

"Capt. Riddle. We just came in from the field, sir," I said. This asshole was starting to get to us.

Dizzy stared directly in the colonel's eyes and said, "If we saluted you in the field, you would be dead, sir."

This took the colonel over the top.

"I'll have your names and ranks!" he shouted, "and Capt. Riddle will get a full report of your insubordination!"

"Begging the colonel's pardon," I spoke up, "we didn't come to Lai Khe to get haircuts or get our boots shined but to pick up a new track. If you let us proceed we will be off your base by noon."

"Stay out of my sight. It's soldiers like you who give this man's Army a bad name." With that he stormed off.

The encounter with the colonel brought up a good point. Being in the field gave us plenty of freedom to grow our hair long and not worry about the spit-and-polish atmosphere that was so prevalent in the rear. No wonder Ruby had on a clean new uniform and polished boots every day. He had guys like this to contend with.

I looked at Dizzy and said, "Let's find Blackhorse and get the fuck out of here." We scurried off to find the offices of the 11th Cav.

XI
Deserters in Time of War

Around 1 p.m. that day Dizzy showed the clerk our paperwork and told him we were here to pick up a new vehicle. They couldn't find the track in the Lai Khe inventory and calls were made to the big base camp in Bien Hoa. We were told we would have to go to there to pick it up.

"Can you get us there, sir?" Dizzy asked.

"I believe there is a flight scheduled for 1430. That would be cutting it close, but it will take you back to Blackhorse," the lieutenant said, as he wrote us up some travel documents. In a matter of minutes we had our travel orders to Bien Hoa. There was a C-130 on the tarmac when we arrived. The chief warrant officer checked our orders and told us to take the magazines out of our M-16s. What did he expect us to do? Hijack the plane to Cuba?

On our final approach to Bien Hoa, I looked out the window and saw how vast Bien Hoa really was. It was like a small American city sitting right in the middle of Vietnam. Over a dozen units called this home as did the 11th ACR. Here were our dentists, doctors, pay clerks, and postal headquarters. The main supply quartermaster was here and we vowed to get new uniforms that fit and had our names sewn on them. This was the happening place. We went to motor pool and they took us right up to the new Charlie Three-Four.

"I'm going to need a few days to finish it up," the OIC mechanic told us. We looked at each other and laughed.

"We're in no hurry," Dizzy told him.

"Take your time," I said.

"OK, let's see. Today is Tuesday. Come back on Thursday and you will be all set."

That sat really well with me and Diz. In Vietnam when they gave you an inch and you could take a mile, you took it. We had two days to party and that was all right with us.

"Sir, we need to get word back to our troop about what the holdup is. Can you get in touch with Capt. Riddle of Charlie Troop and let him know we are delayed?"

"Listen. Just walk over to the communications bunker and tell them what you need. They'll fix you up."

We could hear Riddle on the radio shouting at the radio operator that they had their heads up their ass.

Now it was time to look for a place to crash. Blackhorse City was big and we had cheeseburgers on our minds. We made our way over to the mess hall and ordered burgers, fries and Cokes. We sat down and smiled at each other.

"This is fucking great," Diz said, as I chomped on my meal, happy as a kid, and sat back in the chair.

I looked around me and said to Dizzy, "This is going to be boring or a blast depending on who is in right now. I don't want that colonel riding our tails."

Dizzy frowned and lit us cigarettes. "What do you want to do, then?" He handed me a smoke.

"Hang out at headquarters? No, that's really boring," I said.

"If only Benson and Jenkins were here with us we could really get down. I don't want to go to the Enlisted Men's Club like we did last time we were here," Dizzy complained. And there it was! An idea was born.

We went to the supply sergeant and asked him to hold onto our M-16s, flak jackets and helmets for a few days. He was happy to do it. We put on our boonie hats and even though he didn't want to join us, we went and had a cold beer at the EM.

Because we were bored and frustrated, Dizzy and I decided right then to abandon our posts during time of war and sneak out of the perimeter that afternoon and go AWOL. We would go to Saigon. We were in Bien Hoa, only ten miles or so from the capital city of South Vietnam. If we stayed a few nights, nobody would miss us.

"You know, we could be shot for this," I told Dizzy.

"What are they going to do if they catch us? Send us to Nam?" Dizzy replied.

"Diz, I think that we can really do this. Our track won't be ready till Thursday, and so what if we don't show up until Friday? No one knows where we are or what we're doing." I was getting excited.

We reconned and found a weak point in the perimeter. Dizzy and I waited for the changing of the guard at the post entrance and slipped under the wire. We made for Highway 1, the route to Saigon. God, it had been so long since I had seen any civilization. I heard they had live music and girls, girls, girls!

We started hitchhiking out in the afternoon sun and for about half an hour had no success. Hitchhiking in Vietnam! What a trip. A car finally slowed and stopped. It is a red Peugeot and we looked inside and saw two Catholic nuns in the vehicle. They were wearing the traditional black habits that I was familiar with growing up in Montebello. Their wimples barely cleared the ceiling of the car.

The one sitting on the passenger side looked cautiously out the window, recognized our uniforms, smiled and said in a lovely French accent, "You would like a ride to Saigon?"

"Yes!" we both screamed.

We tumbled into the back seat. As we fell into the car, the dust and smell of mold arose to greet us. The floors were littered with old newspapers, in English and in French. The headliners were torn and the spring in my seat jetted out of the upholstery, making my seat very uncomfortable. I settled in for the ride.

The nuns' English was limited but understandable. We quickly comprehended that they worked at an orphanage near the waterfront in Saigon. Apparently, they made this trip twice a month. We had just come in from the field and, though showered, were saturated with the pungent odor of the jungle floor. Fuck it! The nuns didn't care. They were happy to take us to Saigon.

They didn't notice the .45-caliber handgun I had concealed in my waist band, or maybe they did, but they had been here a long time and I am sure it was no big thing to them.

Freedom! God, that car ride! We sat in the back seat and I swore to Diz it felt like a '56 Chevy racing down the highway. With the wind blowing in our faces, Diz and I were instantly transported back to our hometowns.

A huge billboard advertisement of a Negro shaving appeared on the left side of the road. We came to discover that the shaving cream was heavily advertised all over the city. The shacks of Bien Hoa gradually disappeared into the outer reaches of a city as the suburbs of Saigon came into view.

As we sped down Highway 1, The Pearl of the Orient started to come into focus. The road widened a little and became more crowded as we approached the center of the city. The poverty that masqueraded as the suburbs consisted of rusting corrugated shacks and trash heaps with shit so nasty-smelling that I gagged. I never gagged in the field except when I shoveled through that shallow, mass grave to pick ammunition from the decomposing corpses, and of course, more recently, when God let me shake His hand.

That was my first impression of Saigon. What a country. The nuns drove a few miles more and pulled into an orphanage/hospital. The people living in the rusted shacks that edged up to the nuns' compound were refugees from villages destroyed from the air. Dizzy and I looked at the collateral damage our air war had produced.

Collateral damage. What a fucking, sanitary term for the infliction of undeserved pain, suffering and ruin. Calling it that, I thought, was the Army's way of keeping us from having a conscience, for how could we otherwise do what we did?

But I did not come to Saigon to search for my soul; I came here hoping to forget I had one. These nuns were saints and we were monsters. It was good that we parted ways when we did. I did not want to see this and Diz must have had similar thoughts. He was getting nervous, his left eye jumping in its socket and he said, "Let's *didi mau*, man. This place is giving me the creeps."

"Indeed." We walked for about twenty minutes toward the bright lights of the city.

"You know, the French called this 'The Paris of the Orient,'" said Diz, trying to lighten the mood.

"They also got their asses handed to them on a platter at Dien Bien Phu and made the good decision to get the fuck out of here."

We walked for a while without speaking, just taking it all in. The architecture was Parisian, of course, and by the time we had humped a few miles, we were ready to catch a pedicab, a staple of Saigon. It was just a homemade bicycle contraption with a seat up forward and a no-nonsense driver you couldn't see pedaling from behind. I did not like it and neither did Dizzy. *Face toward enemy*; isn't that what the Claymore said? It was very uncomfortable for us to have this guy pedaling the cycle behind us. We couldn't see his face; I felt for my .45. He was surely a Vietcong at night and a pedicab driver during the day, memorizing government buildings and GI billets.

We looked out at the street and saw the Saigon warriors. They were everywhere. These were the guys who kept the war effort going through resupply and logistics. There were cooks, clerks, medical personnel, you name it. This was part of the great American War Machine that spat out people like Diz and me for the constant cannon fodder in the field.

Well, we would take over their world and show them what a real fighting man was.

First things first; we were out to have a good time. We looked back over at the pedicab driver. After about half an hour's ride he dropped us downtown on the notorious Tu Do Street, known for its old French, decadent nightlife. Bicycles and motorbikes jammed the narrow streets. The French worked hard at making this the "Jewel of Indochina," but their machinery must have been working overtime: a thick layer of pollution spread out around the city, hugging it like a smoke cloud.

Another unforgettable sight were the white mice, the local police who guarded and patrolled the downtown. They were called white mice because of their uniforms, white shirts and pants. Their hats were short-brimmed white head coverings that looked like the ones worn by the old-fashioned dairy man. They also wore white gloves and they directed traffic from raised platforms in the middle of the street.

Diz and I gazed at the bright neon signs announcing "Dancing Girls." Evening was upon us. Tu Do Street was a wide avenue with beautiful trees lining the boulevard of bar after bar with the occasional opium den. Saigon was a city of commerce and the product here was sex.

Each joint was full of bar girls wearing miniskirts, high heels, and see-through blouses. They swarmed like flies about us and staked out the sidewalks. They lured men into their bar as effectively as flames lure moths. There were fine facades and fancy French cuisine, and bars with provocative names that would comfort G.I.s with tiny slices of home. "Soul House" catered to blacks, and cowboy bars like "The Big Creek Corral" catered to cowboys, and of course, our favorite was the "Hippie Heaven."

Wasn't that exactly what we were looking for and longing for? A small piece of home? Dizzy and I migrated to the Hippie Heaven, and all its implied pleasures.

Me and Diz entered a dimly lit room with the predictable girls and rough-looking bouncers lining the doorway. A Filipino band was playing a song by the Jefferson Airplane. As we entered we were immediately set upon by a perfumed mob of bar girls who rubbed their warm soft skin up against our battle-hardened bodies.

They quickly sized us up, speculating how much cash we had in our wallets by what kind of watch we wore.

We could sit with them if we bought them each a drink. We came to know this as Saigon Tea, which was nothing more than colored water and cost $2.50 each, a stiff price.

Dizzy and I took a look around. The place was a smoky dive. Mama san walked up to us and said, "GI, you want girl?" We looked at each other and smiled. Yes, we would have beer and women.

"What do you have, Mama san?" I asked.

"I have girl love you long time. She have too much love, GI, too much love." She brought out two girls, one who looked like she was still a teenager and the other one looked around 25. That was old to us. They smiled and cooed and I couldn't help but notice the fear come over the face of the young one, directed toward Mama san.

Dizzy said, "Let me have the older one."

I said, "Have a go at it. Give me Baby san."

So with that we started the night in Saigon to end all nights. We started drinking the Ba Moui Ba beer of Vietnam. It was horrible tasting shit that actually had formaldehyde in it. Still at the table, I looked up and noticed a white mouse standing in the doorway. Mama san quickly got up and walked up to him and handed him an envelope.

"Oh, I see that this place is protected," Dizzy said.

"It appears to be. I don't see any Army pigs around. Let's stay here."

And we did. The more beer we drank the better it tasted and the prettier the girls became. We chatted but it was not like being on a date with Mary Jane or Betty Lou. These girls were pros. We were just two of the hundreds of soldiers they had entertained in that joint. The band played "Proud Mary" and the lead singer butchered the lyrics with his heavy Filipino accent.

"Let's dance," I told the girl I was with. I wanted to feel like I was home in a Hollywood nightclub but this just didn't feel right. The more I tried the harder it was to enjoy myself. I discovered that I could not escape the clutches of the war even when far away from it, listening to music with female companionship.

This exercise in futility came to full fruition when Dizzy leaned over to me and said, "Let's take the girls to a room."

Yes, I thought, but one price was for companionship in the bar, and another if we plodded off to a room. "How much money you stay one night?" I asked the one I was with. I didn't even know her name. What was her name?

"Sorry," I said, backing up. "What is your name? I am Fred and this is Dizzy."

"Deezee and Phed. I am Suzie," she smiled. Her lipstick was smeared and for the first time I took a good look at her face. She was five feet two or so and very skinny. She wore a mini-dress with high heels and black stockings. She had ample breasts and her shoulders were slumped forward. Her face was full of makeup covering some nasty pockmarks and her cheeks were highlighted with rouge. There was a beauty mark on her chin and she looked tired and older than I had first imagined.

Dizzy's girl was double all that and carried herself with a false grace that derailed any notion of innocence. These were hard-core working girls. Dizzy's girl was called Lola. The dream of being back home was completely erased. I was still in fucking Nam.

Oh well. Let's make the best of it, I thought.

"Yeah, Diz," I said. "Let's see what this is going to cost us." We negotiated a price and settled in to get drunker. We accomplished that mission by 11:30, paid Mama san and walked out into the hot, sticky night air. Dizzy and I stumbled down the street following the girls to a cheap hotel room. We were noisy and loud as we climbed the stairs to our room. We almost knocked the door off its hinges as we kicked in the door. The lock did not break. The girls were laughing now and Dizzy and I were finally feeling comfortable with them.

"Lola," Dizzy called out, "go get us some Cokes." He handed her a few dollars and she sauntered out the door. I sat on the bed with Suzie and tried to kiss her. She pushed me away ever so slightly. She was waiting for her partner before the festivities would begin. I realized this at once and went down the hall to grab some ice. Dizzy had a bottle of cheap Vietnamese whiskey he had lifted from the bar. When Lola re-entered the room, Dizzy tripped over his own feet and knocked over a lamp. I laughed.

I got four glasses and poured us all a drink. As we sat there getting to know each other we smoked cigarettes and tried to understand each other. The girls spoke very rudimentary pidgin English and Diz and I only knew a few choice Vietnamese words. Dizzy was so drunk that he chipped a tooth with his glass. As he wiped the blood from his mouth, he and stood and yelled, "They're trying to poison us with ground-up glass! They're goddamn VC and she put glass in the Coke!" He reached around and slapped her on the face, screaming, "Bitch!"

He was out of control. I tried to grab him to calm him down. This was one of the first urban myths we heard when coming over to Vietnam. The Vietcong women would put razors between their legs and try to poison you with ground-up glass. He reached into my waist and pulled out the .45 and started waving it around in the air screaming, "Fucking VC cunt! I'll kill you!"

Both girls started screaming and crying as Dizzy's rage turned uglier and uglier. "You cock-a-dile me! I cock-a-dile you." The noise in the room reached hysterical heights and soon the hotel manager popped his head in the door and turned around and ran back down the hall.

Dizzy pushed the pistol into Lola's ear and commenced to shouting, "You're trying to kill me! Kill me! You fucking VC trying to kill me. I'll kill your ass right now!" He waved the pistol in the air again and screamed.

"You crazy son of a bitch!" I yelled. "That's your tooth. We got to get out of here now! That guy went to call the cops."

We were out the balcony within seconds and hit the ground flying. We could hear a faint siren getting louder as we turned down an alley. There were people sitting outside their back doors washing dishes and doing laundry. Some of the men were playing board games. We ran through the hanging laundry, knocking over chessboards and causing havoc everyplace we ran. I came to a corner and turned left. Dizzy was on my heels, still waving the gun around like a madman. I stopped.

"Put the fucking gun away ... or better yet, give it back to me!" I was pissed. I knew that we had to stop running and act normal or we would be popped by the white mice. I somehow got the message across to Dizzy, who was slowly coming down off his bad trip.

"OK, Cal. I'm sorry," he mumbled, and gave me back my gun. People were still staring at us as I tucked it in my belt. I dug my nails in his arm a little deeper than I needed to and led us off.

"Don't be sorry. Just stop acting stupid. Not only did we not get laid, but they got most of our money," I sighed.

Just then an alley door opened three spots down and we could hear drunken laughter and jazz music. Two Aussies smoking cigars looked our way and the taller one shouted, "Hey, fellas, was that you two causing all that ruckus down the street?"

By this time the adrenaline rush had sobered us up a little, and I walked over to them.

"Howdy," I said. "I'm Fred and this here is Dizzy. He proved tonight what a crazy motherfucker he is."

"Come in, come in, my friends, and welcome to the Australian Army's Fifth Aviation Headquarters, such as it is. More a drinking club, if you catch my drift. I'm Gordon and this is Philip."

He didn't need to ask twice.

I looked over my shoulder and back down the street. Couldn't see any mice scurrying around, but it was best to get out of the street.

"What's happening?" I asked. Dizzy and I were quite sober now, after all that excitement. Gordon reached behind us and slammed the door shut. He was a giant, heavyset man with an unkempt Charlie Chaplin-like mustache. He grabbed my arm and I could feel the sweat from his hands. They were small and clammy, prone to small gestures as he talked. He directed us into the hallway away from the door. He had a slight resemblance to Oliver Hardy.

"Bloody awful business going on out there," he said. "Stay here with us a while."

"Where are we?" Dizzy hazily asked, understanding returning to him in chunks.

"We're Down Under," I told him.

XII
Down Under Three-Four

"Indeed! Haha, exactly!" Gordon started to laugh.

"Let me welcome you to the sovereign nation of Australia. This being the embassy, I grant you full pardon and protection. Please feel at home here."

"We ran into some Vietcong," Dizzy said as he sat down on a stuffed armchair.

"Ghastly," Philip said as he joined us.

I turned toward him and said, "No, we didn't. My friend has been too long without a woman and been in too many firefights. Everything is cool. Fucking Dizzy screwed up our whole night out." I was mad and the liquor they plied on us didn't make me feel very good about my good buddy, Darwin Dizzy Anderson.

Gordon looked around and said, "Nonsense! You will both stay here with us tonight and tomorrow we will take you both on a little flight."

We stayed the night with these crazy Aussies and drank pint after pint of ... I don't know what, but it was always, "Another pint, mate?" So we drank till early morning, finally falling asleep on a couple of couches in the big room.

We were awakened by our new friends at around 0700 and treated to bacon and eggs in their big kitchen. As I threw cold water across my face, my senses returned, and while eating a hearty breakfast, I took stock of the surroundings. We were in a great rambling mansion that served as the Australian Embassy with about thirty to forty guys working out of the facility. Gordon was cleaned up and he indeed looked like a top-notch soldier.

"Let's have a fly, then," he said, as he rose from the table.

I had no idea what he meant. Philip turned to me and said, "We fly the bush. In fact, there is a mail run this morning to Ban Me Thuot. Shouldn't take but a few hours time. What's your fellows' schedule like today?"

"Open," I told him. "We don't have to be back at Bien Hoa until tomorrow mid-afternoon."

"Then it's settled. You'll have the time of your life. Ever fly in a small plane?" By now we were calling him Gordo.

"No, Gordo, but it sounds like fun," I ventured.

"Grab your gear and jump in the Jeep back in the alley and we will have at it."

We had no gear but Dizzy and I raced for shotgun in the Jeep and settled in for a ride to the airstrip. Tan Son Nhut was the big American air base in Saigon and the Australians had a small strip on the eastern edge away from the jets and helicopters. The planes looked like WWII vintage and Diz and I looked at each other.

"This is what you guys fly?" Dizzy frowned. Gordo grabbed me by the hand and once again I felt the clamminess of his skin against mine.

"Right. Oh, these shelias will stay aloft forever."

So we clambered aboard, all three of us squeezing in the tight-fitting aircraft. The runway was about as long as a football field and Gordo revved the engines to maximum while taxiing down the grass field. The runway was surrounded by poplar and eucalyptus trees at the perimeter. As soon as we lifted off about halfway down the strip Gordon started yelling at us. We had no idea of what he wanted but he was extremely agitated and was making gestures for us to throw things over the side. We weren't going to clear the trees with the added weight of the third person. I reached down and grabbed a case of motor oil and heaved it. He nodded yes and yelled for more. The plane was quickly approaching the end of the runway and not gaining any altitude. Dizzy tossed a case of C-rations and the nose rose a little as Gordo pulled the .50-caliber machine up out of its mount and threw it overboard. We rose and just clipped the top of the eucalyptus at the end of the runway. The aircraft shuddered. So did I.

"Good job, boys. Well done, well done." Gordo gave us that staccato laugh again. *What a maniac he is, too,* I thought. We climbed to about 2,000 feet and buckled and swayed in the wind. The plane was still overweight and I wondered about taking off again from Ban Me Thuot.

We flew north toward the sea and the view was breathtaking. This was a part of Vietnam that I didn't know. Toward the Central Highlands we flew and soon I was lost in a lush green earth with little villages and hamlets nestled into the rolling hills. I looked at Gordo and saw that he looked at ease. Comfortable in that little cockpit of his, doing what he appeared to love more than anything.

"Is this what you do every day?" I yelled. The prop noise and the wind made it impossible to speak in a normal voice. We had no headsets.

"As much as they will let me. You can find me in one part or another of War Zone C." I realized that there was only one reason for an Aussie bush pilot to be in Nam: this bloke loved to fly. I started imagining different scenarios for Gordo. In one version he was a divorced father of three for whom an armed forces career had been the ruin of his marriage. No, he was a school teacher back home who couldn't afford to fly every day, not even once a month. I started coming up with a third history when a shot glanced off the fuselage. Gordon looked at me and said quite calmly, "Ah, here we are at Ban Me Thuot."

Dizzy said, not so collected, "What the fuck?" His eyes were wild and he had a tremor on his upper lip.

"That would be their 3 p.m. sniper," Gordo said, as he dipped the plane and slid us to the right. I was impressed with Gordo's quick, cool actions. He brought us down gently and deposited us in a corner of the airfield where a few Jeeps were waiting. One of them had a .50 mounted on top and as quick as you can say "Australia," Dizzy and I mounted that sucker and cocked back the arm of the machine-gun. Gordo grabbed the mail bag and deposited his big frame into the other waiting Jeep.

We were off. The long drive to Ban Me Thuot from the airstrip to the villas was along a treeless road, and rounds were now hitting the gun shield and the sides of the Jeeps.

"He isn't their best," Gordon loudly exclaimed.

"What do you mean?"

"If he were their number-one bloke, one of you two gentlemen would be dead by now, I suppose."

"Gordo, you knew about this sniper?" I was incredulous.

"Of course, of course. Everyone knows of the Ban Me Thuot sniper."

"Why didn't you warn us? Why didn't you tell us our asses were going to be targets out here?" Dizzy let loose a spurt of rounds at the enemy ghost.

"Thought you boys were looking to have a spot of fun. They are more of a nuisance than anything else. In my eight months here no one has ever gotten hurt. You should relax and enjoy the scenery." He jostled around to make himself more comfortable and a sniper round flew in the window across his face. The bullet missed his nose by an inch and slammed into the Jeep's inner wall.

That morning, good old Gordo lost a case of motor oil, some C-rations and a .50-caliber machine-gun but he got all his mail delivered. And, to his credit, none of us left our brains on the seats of those Jeeps.

The ride back was uneventful and we returned to their home airstrip after 6 p.m.. It was still hot and humid with a trace of a breeze breaking through the windows back at the embassy. If we stayed in Saigon another night, it was time for Dizzy and me to start thinking of where to stay. This time it was Philip who insisted that we spend another evening in their quarters. It seems Philip was an amateur magician and he insisted on putting on a show for us.

"Nothing fancy, just a few odd tricks," he begged. "I understand Deke appropriated a live chicken. You must stay for dinner and a show. The boys would be terribly disappointed if you passed it up; they've been plucking feathers all day."

The embassy had the feel of a fraternity house, with Gordon as the real leader. As we sat down on a long oak table, Deke asked the Lord to bless us, especially the two Americans He had dropped off on their doorstep. Most of the Aussies knew from our tête-à-tête that we usually ate and slept on the jungle floor. This was a big treat for us and we toasted pints once again and got lost in rambling banter.

"So, Gordon, was today a typical day in your mission over here?" I asked as I leaned over to get the mashed potatoes.

"No, no," he shook his head. "We keep things quite a bit livelier than that. Wouldn't you say, Philip?" Philip turned and started laughing.

"Don't let him get started. We should never hear the end of it. Gordo is plenty nervous on the ground, I hear from my sources in Ban Me Thuot."

"Hear, hear," Gordo raised his pint and shouted. "To our two American friends' quick action on the machine-gun."

"As I recall, Gordo came this close to a new hole in the head." I held my hand up with fingers one inch apart. And so it went for the next hour, our combined experience growing in danger with each telling. Our courage rose with each man complimenting the other. Oh, Mary! We soon were drunk again. And as is the case with drunkards the world over, we swore an oath of solidarity and sloppily pledged our undying love for one another.

We were saved from further embarrassment by Philip, who still wanted to do his magic tricks. Dizzy and I could barely hold our eyes open, so Philip seemed like a world-class magician. He did card tricks and he even pulled a bunny from a hat as we watched, amazed. Dizzy asked him if he could make him disappear. Philip pretended not to hear him, for as I was finding out again, Diz was a pretty mean drunk. Before it escalated, we passed out on the shared cushions.

In the morning, when Gordon heard of our plan to hitchhike back to Bien Hoa, he would have nothing to do with it. He insisted that we let him fly us back to base. We quickly agreed and took that same old airplane right into the heart of 11th ACR territory.

It was raining hard when we landed, and Dizzy and I jumped clear of a puddle, only to land in mud. It didn't matter to either one of us, as we knew we were on our way back out to the field. We went and retrieved our weapons from the supply sergeant. I knew Squires, the supply clerk, from in-country training. I teased him that top was going to make a special trip to the rear to grab his ass.

"Where have you two been?" he asked.

"Nowhere. Why? Did someone ask?" I said.

"Nobody asked. It's just that I knew you two were here and I haven't seen you around in the last two days."

"We've been running errands for the captain," Dizzy lied. We told him that we needed to go check on our new track and grabbed our rifles and hightailed it to the motor pool. We went right up to the officer in charge and he remembered us.

"All ready to take her for a test drive?" the lieutenant asked.

"Yes, sir." I looked at Dizzy and he gave me a nudge to jump in the driver's hatch. This was the new Three-Four, for Christ sakes, so I *should* be the first to drive her.

"Go ahead," Dizzy said. "Pop her cherry, Cal."

I hit the starter button and it started right up. Dizzy jumped behind me and sat down, threw his head back and started laughing.

"You paid dearly for this bucket, Cal. You can drive it all the way back."

I pulled to a stop, jumped out and walked over to the lieutenant and inquired, "How exactly are we supposed to get this vehicle back out to An Loc, sir?"

"Seems to drive just fine to me," he said, a small smile forming on his mischievous face.

"Lieutenant, you know just what I mean. There is a lot of real estate between us and the troop. At least mount a .50 on the cupola and maybe a .60 or two in the rear," I demanded.

"Tell you what I'm going to do for you," — he sounded like the world's sleaziest used car salesman — "I will mount the .50 and give you one .60 plus 1,500 rounds of ammo."

"Let me talk to your manager," I uttered under my breath.

"What's that?"

"Fine, fine," I said. "We will take you up on your generosity."

"Good. Come in the office. I have paperwork for you to sign."

I signed here and I signed there. I signed off my intention to sign. I had him authorize the weapons and stuffed all of the paperwork into an ammo can and drove on over to the regimental armorer. He outfitted our track and as he did we paid another visit to my man, Squires, over in supply, and we each got uniforms and three pairs of socks. Finally! As a matter of fact, we went on a little shopping spree and decided to add an entrenching tool, toothbrushes, soap, candy, and some soda. Squires also gave us handfuls of writing paper and envelopes and pens. We stashed these away in another ammo can.

When we got back to the track, we found the weapons installed and we had a surprise waiting for us. The guys in armor had taken a brush to a can of white paint and inscribed in bold letters "C-3-4".

"Yes siree, buddy! You're back in business!" Dizzy shouted. It was midafternoon and by the time we fueled up and gathered up a few more things it would be too late to hit the road for Lai Khe. After topping off, we headed back over to Squires' hooch to pick up some helmets and flak jackets that we had forgotten.

"You guys expecting to drive all the way to Lai Khe with just the two of you?" Squires asked.

"We will find out tonight what they expect us to do," Dizzy said, as he stowed the last piece of spare track on the rear of the vehicle.

We drove back to the motor pool and Lt. Patrick (by now we knew his name) walked over and said, "She sure looks like a beauty, all painted and dolled up with her guns glistening in the afternoon light."

"How fast can we run her?" Dizzy asked, not catching on to Patrick's attempt at poetry.

"You can run around 35 miles an hour with these new shocks we got in. She'll do 50. I would stay around 35 for the first 200 miles. What do you have, a 550-mile trip to Bien Hoa and another 150 to Loc Ninh? I don't envy you two, but mechanically you will have smooth ride." He turned and I could see his heart was heavy, for all he could think of was that we were on a suicide mission.

"Take a case of oil and a new set of tools. I don't want my beautiful creation busting down in the middle of the jungle and you eating it because you didn't have the right tool."

"Thanks, Lt. Patrick," I said. He was a good man and there were too few of them in this man's Army. I would think of him often.

We finally went and checked in with the sergeant, who had the good fortune to have the last name of Major. To be a sergeant major was a pretty big deal, as far as ranks went, but Sergeant Major was just a noncommissioned officer in charge of the rear area. All those times being addressed as Sgt. Major, he started to imagine it really *was* his rank and not a fluke based on his last name, and he played it for more than it was worth. To say he had a big ego would be an understatement.

We showed up for a small little hello and good-bye and he started reading us the riot act.

"Why did you maggots fail to report to me on Tuesday, the day you arrived? Instead, you show up with your transition papers for me to sign after God knows where the fuck you've been and what you've been doin'! You've got to be kidding."

"We've been hanging over at Bravo Troop, Sergeant, and if you must know, Lt. Patrick over in motor pool was aware of our presence at all times."

"When you report to my base you report to *me*, understand?"

"Understood. Sorry for the mix-up."

He was a petty little man, full of himself and mean-spirited.

"Your orders indicate that all involved should expedite your mission. If that wasn't in writing I would have you both pulling KP for the two days you went missing. I can't hold you here any longer, so give me your paperwork and I'll sign it and let you be on your way." He took a deep breath. "There is a convoy leaving at 0500 for Lai Khe. Just find a spot and jump in. Nobody is going to argue about having two extra guns on the road."

It was still raining and as a parting gift on our way out, we trampled over his nice flower garden in front of his hooch. We ran to the chow hall and tried to dry off during our meal. We ran into Squires and told him that we had forgotten to get ponchos.

"Come by around eight and I'll set you up," he said.

"Thanks. Let's find the party," Dizzy said, as we finished our pie and ice cream.

"I'll follow you," I said.

He led me down a path behind the showers and toilets to an empty hooch. We walked through to the other side and found five guys kicking back in a little shack they had fixed up to live in. They had music blaring from the stereo and a few lit pipes floating around the room. There was Lou, the mail clerk, Joe, from the motor pool, and Squires, the supply clerk. I didn't know the other two.

"What's up?" I said, as I entered the shack.

"This is Hawk and Spinner from Air Cav." Squires pointed at us and said, "Fred and Dizzy."

Hellos were exchanged by everyone there and the pipes were smoked and I lay back on an empty bunk.

"You the two going out alone tomorrow?" Hawks asked.

"We will find a way," Dizzy said, as he started into a coughing fit. "Good shit," he choked.

Squires turned and smiled. "Imported from Thailand via Mr. Hawks."

"Thank you, Mr. Hawks," I said, trying to keep my train of thought. "Major told us about a convoy leaving at 5 a.m. We will be waiting then, at the main gate."

We crashed out in their shack that night and slept restfully, finally no booze in our systems. Dizzy's wristwatch alarm went off at 0430 and we made our way over to the mess hall which was just opening, and grabbed some coffee while Lt. Patrick warmed Three-Four's engine.

When we hit the main gate, we were greeted by a big convoy with well over 100 vehicles, everything from gas tankers to deuce-and a-halves to Jeeps. I waited by the gate until enough space had passed so I wouldn't be near a tanker in case of a direct hit. They were big targets and I did not want to be next to an explosion.

We settled in the line and it took a good ten miles before the serpent was up and running at full capacity. I found it easy to hit 35 mph and keep driving straight. The new hard rubber of our tracks met the pothole-filled Highway 13 with an incessant thud and a relentless churning-up of the angry road. It created its own rhythm and as long as we were moving at a decent clip it sang out to us in the mild morning. I checked my watch against Dizzy's and said, "Should hit Lai Khe by noon." I turned back and saw that Dizzy had set up in the cupola behind the .50 and that was as good a spot as he could have.

We slowed, and the highway changed its pitch and song. We were coming to a stop. We hadn't even logged 50 miles and we were already slowing down because of some broken fanbelt up the line. I jumped ahead about forty spaces and found a new position behind a forty-footer flatbed truck. We got out to stretch our legs. I walked over to the driver of the big truck and asked him if this was normal.

"Hell, yeah, it is. It's always stop and go, stop and go. With this many vehicles we'll be lucky to make it there by 1600."

"No good," I said, more to myself than anyone else. "What if we strike out on our own?"

"Not recommended," he quickly replied.

The engines started up and down the line and I jumped back behind the steering rods and started our own engine with a rush of adrenaline created by my crazy thinking.

"Did you hear all that shit, Dizzy?" I asked my partner.

"Yeah, yeah," he said. "What are you planning on doing about it?"

"I think it's safe enough to venture out on our own, don't you?" My patience was wearing thin and this idea was beginning to take ahold of me. I was ready for anything.

"Whatever you think, man, it's your show," he replied with no hint of sarcasm.

"On the next stop, we break ranks," I said, and jammed the gearbox into drive and slipped out to the side of the road. The second breakdown occurred at 1017 and Dizzy and I never even thought about slowing down. I gunned the engine and swerved around sixty vehicles with the sole intention of putting some daylight between them and us. I opened the engine to 50 mph and put a 500-yard gap before I even slowed down to take stock of the situation.

This was it. We had left the safety of the convoy and were on our own. The area we were in was a lightly populated amalgamation of small villages held together by bicycle shops, iron works, and various other small, private businesses. The villagers did not look threatening as they went about their daily routines. I pulled the track up to a small store.

"What's up?" Dizzy asked.

"I need to find a guitar. The one Jim Gaines bought me burned up with the old Three-Four." We crawled down and entered the shop. The interior was dimly lit and very dusty.

An old woman sat at a stool behind the counter eyeing us suspiciously. She was more concerned that we were going to steal than she was for her safety. She smoked a pipe and wore a black bandanna that covered her wrinkled face and dirty hair. Her teeth were stained black from the betel nut that most women her age were addicted to. The plant was a mild narcotic that the locals used to get some relief from their daily suffering.

In such a populated place off the main highway, the people struggled to live their lives with as little impact from the war as possible. This was not a country hamlet that fell easily into the hands of the Vietcong. There was much more stability here than one would guess. I bowed and asked her if she had any guitars for sale. Most of the people that I had met up to this time could speak pidgin English well enough to conduct simple business transactions. She was different, as she did not understand a word I said.

"Guitar, guitar," I repeated. Then I started to pantomime playing the guitar. She smiled and nodded her head. I pointed to my eyes and shrugged like I did not know where to look. She got off the stool and walked into the back of the store and returned in a minute holding a green-hued guitar wrapped in plastic.

"Ten dolla."

Oh, I guess she knows some English after all.

"Five dolla," I said, holding five fingers in front of her face.

She shook her head violently and repeated, "Ten dolla, GI. No can do five dolla."

I took the guitar from her and unwrapped it. I played a C chord. It was out of tune and God-awful sounding and hard to play. Just like my first guitar. I pulled seven dollars out of my wallet and held the money up and said, "Guitar numba ten, Mama san. Numba ten."

She scowled at me and grabbed the money and the deal was done. Dizzy managed to secure two Cokes, and the cold, bubbly soda sure felt good as it went down my throat. We climbed aboard the new Three-Four and I pulled out, heading north once again. Now I finally felt complete. My whole world had gone up in flames back on September 6. Now I had new clothes, paper, pens, and a guitar. I was a very happy trooper as we set out in the afternoon dust.

We passed Phan Thiet and drove straight through My Tho and reached the outskirts of the Nha Trang turnout and I finally stopped. Exhausted and filthy, I looked up at Dizzy's dirty face and smiled, "Whadda ya got to eat?"

He jumped off the cupola inside the track and came back out with some C-rations. "Spaghetti and meat balls, with peaches and pound cake for dessert?" he said, as if he were having me over for tea.

I was starving and we still had no idea how far we were from Lai Khe. We opened the engine compartment and lay two cans of spaghetti on the manifold and closed the cover. We drove for another half hour until we were sure our meal was ready and pulled off the road once again. Dizzy wrapped his shirt around the cans and pulled them off. With the P-38 can opener he opened our dinner, and like monks, we sat and ate in silence.

I knew that the last hour of our journey would be the most precarious. In those 40 miles we would have to leave the populated areas and head into the jungle. This is where Charlie liked to play. Dizzy wanted to smoke a bowl and I begged off, asking him to please keep his wits clear too. I would need Diz on that .50 if the shit hit the fan.

He complied.

We drove out of the last village as the sun started to sink. An hour would do it if I could keep our speed at 40 mph; we would drive in darkness if I couldn't. I turned on the track's headlights. We flew down the highway and bounced heavily when I hit potholes. The clearings on the sides of the road were not kept clean of debris and I searched frantically for a sniper or a Vietcong with an RPG.

We were exposed.

Dizzy swung his gun to the left; we both thought we had seen movement there. No shots rang out and he swung the barrel to the right realizing that in case of an attack he was our only defense. Around the 20-mile marker Dizzy unexpectedly opened up with that bad boy .50. His shots rang through the leaves and slammed into trees 1,500 meters away. I froze up inside and hit the gas harder and got on the com.

"What is it?" I asked, shaken.

He answered with a twenty-round burst. "Out there!" he yelled into his mouthpiece.

I turned and spotted an RPG flying by our rear. I had outrun the rocket by ten feet. It was a squad of VC spread out on our right side. Dizzy's quick thinking had saved our ass and we were quickly leaving them in our wake. Good thing we didn't smoke that bowl. They had not had time to plan a proper ambush. They had not expected a lone vehicle to be barreling down the road at 50 mph. That was our surprise for them.

Our surprise came with a loud violent explosion some 500 meters to our rear. While we had been engaged with Charlie the convoy had been gaining ground on us and now a tanker full of fu gas had just been blown by that same squad of VC.

A firefight started up behind us. I had no illusion of turning around and going to their aid. They had their own gunners who could take care of the enemy. We would hunker down and continue our getaway.

When we finally reached the gates of Lai Khe the sun had fully set. There was no one there to welcome us. We made our way over to the same hooch we had slept in just days ago. We laid our heads on the bunk and fell into deep sleep. In the morning we went over to the communications bunker and got Capt. Riddle on the radio. The troop was still in An Loc and we reported our own status.

"Three-Four Delta, this is Six. Congratulations on making the Thunder Run in one piece. We will be in present location for ten more days, get out here tomorrow … break … I need your guns in Third Platoon … Over."

"Roger that, Six. We will rendezvous your position by 1400 … Out."

We had our orders and we were good to go. Having taken care of business, we headed for the chow hall for coffee and breakfast. The morning resupply choppers were warming up their engines on the helipad across the ravine. The windsock, filled from a light breeze from the south, indicated good flying weather.

"Wish we could just take a bird back," Dizzy sighed.

"I know. We came out here in the convoy with the 505th Transportation Company. Maybe we should go check with them and see what they have running that way. Beats going at it alone," I said.

Dizzy jumped to his feet and said, "Great idea, let's go look up Ruby and them guys."

We left straightaway and walked almost the distance of the perimeter until things started to look familiar. I went into the bay and asked, "Anybody here seen Ruby?"

"Who's asking?" a gruff staff sergeant wanted to know.

"We're looking for a convoy headed past An Loc today. We met him on our way down here," I answered.

"Nothing going that way today," he replied, almost gleefully. He stood up and approached us with bad attitude stamped all over his face.

"Look, we made friends with some of your men a few nights ago," I said. "Hung out in this very bay for a night of drinking and telling stories. If you see him tell him Fred and Diz came looking for him."

"Tell him yourself. He's in the Cam Ranh Bay field hospital with burns over thirty percent of his body." He paused. "We got hit up there yesterday and his truck is still smoldering. He's lucky to be alive."

"Fuck," Dizzy said. "Give him our best. Did you lose very many men?"

"Enough!" the staff sergeant shouted, and we both could smell the booze on his breath. Nine in the morning and this lifer was drinking and ready for a fight. It reminded me of my encounter with those two racist white guys back when I was an FNG.

Dizzy and I excused ourselves and left through a side door.

"Shoots down that idea," said Dizzy.

I grabbed him by the arm and he stopped. "We were always in it alone, Diz, and you and I got to make it solo back to the troop. Feel comfortable with that?"

"Fuck, yes. We made it from Bien Hoa, didn't we?" It was a statement rather than a question. I agreed.

"Let's pick up the little things that we forgot to get, like C-4 and grenades. Load up and head out around noon."

We went to the armorer and supply sergeant and picked up the sundry items that we had missed in Bien Hoa. We had only one .60.

We went to a hidden corner of the motor pool and commandeered the missing item to make our matched pair. Now we were complete. We looked around base for some bodies headed back out to the field that day and found Jimmy Castillo and Roger Turner, who were scheduled for that evening's chopper flight out. We asked them to complete our crew and they accepted without hesitation.

Now we had our full complement of gunners on the sixties. At 1150 I rolled to the front gate of Lai Khe, they opened it, and we were gone.

My throat was parched and I grabbed my canteen and took a big swig of the still-cool water. I splashed a little on my face and grabbed the mouthpiece and cued the mike: "Six, Three-Four Delta."

I repeated this several times, and finally I heard the statically scratchy voice of Capt. Riddle answer, "Three-Four Six, go. Over."

"Six. Three-Four is Oscar Mike. Repeat, Three-Four is Oscar Mike, over." Oscar Mike meant "on the move."

For his part, Riddle's voice held not a trace of concern as he said, "Roger. Six out."

We moved down the road at a steady clip, slowed only by the giant potholes in the pavement. In some areas the pavement disappeared completely and we drove on hard-packed dirt. The mud never had an opportunity to congeal on the road, as it was sloped to run the water off on the sides.

We passed no villages or hamlets. We saw no remnants of civilization. We just moved steadily like a freight train running in the country. I looked over my shoulder at Jimmy as he manned the left-mounted sixty.

Being another Chicano from California, Jimmy and I made it a habit of sharing our boxes from home. My father used to go to *tortillerías* and have them triple-wrap the tortillas and my folks would send two dozen or so along with canned refried pinto beans. Jim and I would get some C4 and pop holes in a coffee can and warm them on the makeshift stove. That was a little piece of heaven that we were able to enjoy in the bush.

Jim and I had some great times in the hobo woods and outside of Quon Loi. He got stuff sent to him from home, too, and we always took care of each other. I was glad to have him on board.

Roger was a black kid out of Chicago. He and Benson were real close so that made me Roger's friend, too. This was a veteran crew and as we chomped up some more dirt and dust we moved forward with confidence and competence.

Only Dizzy and I had radio contact with the troop. We moved at a steady clip while Jimmy and Roger checked our flanks. Diz and I kept a clear focus on what was to come. Some 40 minutes into our trip we approached the first village. This had been held off-and-on by the VC for the past three years.

"Hey, man, you better slow down," Dizzy said, with no radio etiquette. Fuck it. It was only the two of us on a closed circuit frequency.

"Say what?" I asked.

"Looks like some friendlies," he announced. I looked ahead and saw some grunts walking single file down the highway. They were part of the Big Red One, 1st Infantry Division. Lai Khe was their base camp and they were coming in off a two-week hump that probably took them up around the Cambodian border where Charlie Troop was. I slowed down as we passed them.

What first appeared to be a squad quickly became a company and they shouted to us as we crept by, "How 'bout a lift?"

We yelled out to them and saw how happy these motherfuckers were, heading in for a hot shower and a real bed. They had earned a hot meal for the countless patrols they had been on. I wondered how many men they had lost. I drove up to the captain and half-heartedly saluted him. He was a well-built man with a ruddy complexion and a mermaid tattoo running the length of his left arm.

"Morning, sir."

"Morning, trooper. Where you headed?"

"An Loc. How's the road? Are you coming from there?"

"An Loc, eh? Well, young man, we found the road to be open.

There is a little activity outside of Loc Ninh but you probably know, there always is," he replied.

"Yes, sir. Thank you, sir. We'll make it OK. Have a good stand down."

"You got it, trooper. Keep your wits about you and enjoy the scenery. Beautiful country this is. Too damn bad we got to blow it all apart to make it right." He looked over our crew.

"Always look out for your men, son. That's the way I look at it. Someone keeps an eye out for me and I look over my men and we come out of this damn 365-day tour in one piece."

"Yes, sir," I replied, as I gave the track a little bounce and off we went on our journey. He stayed staring at us as we pushed ahead and gathered up speed. I wondered again about how many men he had lost. Oh, well. Herman had always said it's a mean old world.

XIII
The Big Hurt

I was always reeled back to that dark day whenever I thought of Herman. I tried not to, but I saw his face everywhere. I had to force myself not to think of him, or I couldn't function. I had seen a lot of death and gravely wounded guys and could put it behind me, but still, when I thought of him, it always left me fucked in the head.

I drove that track for another hour and a half while the dust blew on our faces and turned us reddish in that late morning sun. It started raining. Easy at first. Just a drizzle, but then with a crack the sky blew open and poured rain on our heads, and Jimmy and Roger started calling for ponchos to cover their weapons and I yelled at them for thinking of such a foolish idea.

"We're in the middle of nowhere, man, and these fools want to cover the sixties," Dizzy said into my earpiece. I pulled over in the rain and stopped.

"Straighten this shit out, Diz," I said into my mike. As far as rank or authority went, Dizzy had the most time in country. Sitting in the cupola behind the .50 technically made him the track commander so I looked for Diz to pull rank and restore some sanity.

He grabbed the poncho away from Jimmy and said, "These weapons work just fine in wet weather, brother. Do we have a problem?"

Jimmy smirked and let go of the poncho and said, "We're good, Dizzy." Jimmy tried to laugh it off as some kind of joke. He picked up the poncho and pulled it over his head. We all broke out our ponchos and put them on, for it was pouring monsoon rain.

The rain fell everywhere, turning everything to mud. Mud! Well, we fucking loved mud! Fuck! We were back in the jungle and it seemed like we never left. The memories of our night in Saigon were washing away with the rain. What a reality check we received with the rain and mud. Settled, I drove back to the center of the road and tried pushing the engine to get more speed. As I accelerated, I looked up at Dizzy and said, "Tough crowd."

Dizzy laughed at this remark. "Better check with the troop. We're halfway there, by my watch."

"You make the call," I said.

Dizzy jumped down inside the track and changed frequencies on the radio. He got back up on top and said, "Eagle One Three Four. Eagle One Three Four," he repeated, and waited a few moments. A lot of scratching noise filled our ears. He tried again, "Eagle One Three Four."

"Three Four, Three Six. Over." It was Lt. Cutter on the horn.

"Roger, we are halfway home, lieutenant. Over," Dizzy said.

The lieutenant answered with, "Roger that, Three-Four. Glad to have you back up and running. When can we expect your presence? Over."

"We should be seeing you around 1500, break. We have full complement of crew on board. Over."

"Roger. Copy that your boat is full and all oars are in the water. Over."

There it is. All oars were in the water and we were rowing hard. The track started to slide in the mud. I eased off on the pedal and slowed down a tad.

"Easy does it, Delta," Dizzy said into my ear.

I moved around in the seat and tried to get myself comfortable. I had been in the hatch for two days and was getting antsy. "Eat me!" I told Diz. I thought it might be time to take a break. "Let's stop here."

Dizzy nodded and I pulled over to the side of the road and killed the engine.

Jimmy got the canteens out. Roger started looking through the C-rations for a meal and Dizzy and I stretched our legs and looked around. It was quiet. I suddenly realized that it had stopped raining. We were so used to the rain that we never noticed the abrupt nature of the monsoon, its ebb and flow, its starting and stopping with no warning.

Roger found the C-4 and lit a cooking fire and threw on some franks and sausages to cook us all lunch.

"My man, Roger," I said, as I sidled up to him. Tensions started to leave us and for once we felt like a crew. Untested by fire, but still a crew.

"How you like your franks, Cal?" Roger asked.

"Hot, baby, hot. I love my franks red hot. Gimme what you got. But I'll take my franks red hot," I sang a bluesy little tune to him. He smiled and Jimmy laughed and Dizzy slapped me on the back. We pulled out our brand-new mess kits and Roger served us our meal. We removed our ponchos to eat more comfortably, and commenced to chow down while chattering loudly in the stillness of the bush.

Jimmy heard it first.

He put down his plate, stood up and pointed to the sky. We all raised our heads and saw a small biplane, like an old Kansas cropduster, approaching from the east. It was spraying a dirty-looking liquid, and the son of a bitch kept spraying as he passed right over our heads.

"Cocksucker!" Jimmy yelled. By then the plane was gone and we started wiping that shit off our faces and exposed skin.

"What the hell was that all about?" Rodger asked no one in particular.

"Ever see that before, Cal?" asked Dizzy, turning to me.

"I thi—"

Amazingly, no one heard the shot. The bullet bounced off the gun shield and ricocheted off of Roger's mess kit. We were fast. We threw down our shit and hit the track, Jimmy opening up on his .60 before I could get the engine started. Dizzy brought in the .50 and I pulled away before the sniper could get his second round away, which hit the side of the driver's hatch with such ferocity that I almost blew a gasket.

I had a millisecond to decide if I should turn in on the sniper or hightail it out of the kill zone. With no command structure to answer to I could make the call myself, and decided to skedaddle the fuck away instead of engaging the enemy. I don't know what the LT would have had me do, but I was my own man and the decision was mine to make. We ran away to live to fight another day, or at least, to live.

What a bad shot that sniper was. As Gordo would say, "If he was their number-one bloke, you gentlemen would be dead now."

That's right. We escaped without a scratch, the only casualties being the brand-new mess kits we had just scored from Squires. As we hummed along, I found a T-shirt or a rag under my seat and wiped away from my forearms more of whatever shit that flyboy had unloaded on us. It felt like an overdose of mosquito repellent, but a real shower was less than an hour away. I had endured worse.

We made it to An Loc without further incident. When we first saw the troop, we came in along First Platoon's edge of the perimeter. Dizzy had called the captain ten minutes before, and they were expecting us. We pulled into where Third Platoon was bivouacked and I parked the baby between Three-Three and Three-Five. Jimmy and Roger high-fived us and went to their vehicles for the early evening. The troop had come in early in anticipation of our arrival.

Dizzy and I were besieged with hugs and cheers fit for heroes. I had left the encampment a baby-killer and returned a rock star for making the Thunder Run solo. Jenkins and Darnel gave us a cold soda and Jenkins told me that Capt. Riddle had put in the paperwork for Dizzy to get his sergeant stripes and take over as commander of Three-Four and, yes, of course I could stay on as the driver. I toasted Dizzy and congratulated him on his promotion.

He started moving his belongings over to Three-Four and we split the night up in two shifts of guard duty. After everything we had been through a night of little sleep seemed a minor inconvenience. In the morning we would have our own crew. We were home, and all thoughts of Saigon stole away with the daylight as darkness filled the sky.

I sought out Benson before calling it a day. "What's happening, brother?"

"Same old same old," he said, as he slapped my palm and we high-fived and low-fived and did that crazy jungle handshake.

"You OK?" he asked.

"Had a crazy night in Saigon with the Diz and he almost killed a couple of whores, but nothing to write home about. You all right with that kid shit?"

"It bothers me some when I think of it." He let the air out of his lungs, and did not inhale again for what seemed a lifetime. "I try not to think about it much."

"That's all I thought about on the Thunder Run," I said. "God's going to kill my kids. I'm going to hell. I swear, Benson, I will not take another life. I'm done with the killing. I'm driving from now on and Cutter can kiss my ass if he doesn't like it. I'm finished." With that said, I left Benson to ponder the matter.

That was the extent of our conversation about the kid. I was convinced now that Benson felt he fired the fatal shot and I was equally sure that I did. Who knows but God? I now saw this was the demon that would haunt both our lives to our graves.

I walked over past Clementi's vehicle. He was drying some new ears he had gotten while we were gone. The platoon had had a minor scuffle with some guerillas last night and Clementi had harvested the ears for his ever-growing necklace. It disgusted me. I vowed to myself to get out of the field and into that Special Services band I had heard about in Saigon. I had been working on Capt. Riddle to let me go and try out but he wanted to keep as many men in the field as he could.

That week we started digging trenches. We were going to be here a while and the CO wanted the perimeter to be fortified with trenches. The resupply chopper brought out a slew of sandbags and we filled them with the dirt we dug out. Billy and Benson excelled at this backbreaking labor. They dug a trench six feet deep. Like gravediggers, they worked day and night to manufacture the best fighting position of the troop. Dizzy and I helped out but those guys did the bulk of the work.

After three days it was complete, with dugout benches surrounding the hole. The roof was plywood covered in sandbags stacked three feet high. Mighty fucking impressive. Guys came from all around the troop to inspect this modern engineering achievement. During all that digging and stacking of sandbags I felt something in my back snap. When I got blown out of the driver's hatch I knew I had hurt my back but I didn't make a big thing about it. Nothing was broken, no blood. I should have said something.

We had been in An Loc for almost six weeks, through September and October. At the end of September, a company of grunts from the Big Red One joined us. There were rumors of a heavy buildup of North Vietnamese Regulars. M Company of the First Infantry Division spread out between our vehicles and took over our bunkers and fighting holes. It was our gift to them. By Halloween the bunkers were being used by crew members not on guard duty to sleep in. Creature comforts adorned the giant bunker we had worked on. We had canteens and extra ammo and C-rations stored in there.

On the day before Halloween, my back went into a spasm and I couldn't move. The pain was more than I could bear and I lay sprawled out in the track unable to get up. We stayed in that day and I was grateful for that. Lt. Cutter thought I was faking it to get back to the rear. I could not find a comfortable position to lie in and I went sleepless that night, unable to pull my guard duty. Jenkins let me slide and Cutter gave me the dirty look as he came to inspect me.

"Call the doc," he told Jenkins, and he did. When Sykes came to inspect me I just lay there and he gave me a shot of morphine. That did not help. To Cutter's mind I was trying to get over; he glared at me and walked away.

Just then a loud explosion ripped through our NDP. Fire sprang up on a track in Second Platoon. Three louder, concussive detonations rocked the track and men went running in every direction. I could not raise my head up to look at the commotion but I could hear yelling and screaming coming from the wounded.

Dizzy hit the .50 and the perimeter opened up. There were flares popping above us and the trip-flares around us were going off like crazy. Henderson came running by and saw me lying there, not moving.

"Rivera!" he yelled and came running over to me. "Get up! Get to the bunker!" he screamed.

I could not move and *bam!* another rocket hit a track, blowing it sky high with all crew members cooked in the blast.

"The gooks got our positions laid out. You got to come with me," Billy said, exasperated. We now added crying to the cacophony of sound on the battlefield, as wounded and dying men called out to their gods and mothers to save them. Another explosion and more shouts of "Medic!" rang out to my heightened sense of hearing.

"I can't move, Billy," I cried. Henderson grabbed an infantryman who was close by and they picked me up. I screamed in pain. As they carried me off the track and into the bunker I felt like I knew hell. Never could anything in my life equal the anguish I was feeling. They finally plopped me down on the floor of the bunker. It was raining hard and about six inches of water had accumulated on the floor of the dugout. I lay still and slowly opened my eyes as they adjusted to the darkness of the hollow. I could make out Billy, Jenkins and Cutter.

I felt something on my chest and moved my eyes down and saw two giant rats settled across my stomach. I could not move. One of the rats turned and moved toward my face. He stared at me as if demanding to know what I was doing in his home. To him I was just a meal. Cutter looked down at me, aghast at what he was seeing. He leaned down and in an act of compassion, swiped those motherfuckers off my body.

"God damn, Cal, you're *not* faking it, are you?"

I looked over at him and said, "With all due respect, sir, fuck you."

His face flushed and he turned to Henderson. "Get him on the next evac."

That was the last time that I saw Lt. Cutter. For six months he had been my platoon leader. He had bravely led us in countless firefights. Unlike Capt. Riddle, Cutter had lived with his men in the jungle and mourned the men he lost. Now our relationship had ended as quickly as death.

I lay in the mud and watched him march off to issue more orders to try to keep his men safe. I would not miss him.

Sykes came and pinned a note on my shirt and an hour later they brought a stretcher and put me on it. Two grunts carried me through the blaze of burning vehicles. I bounced amid the acrid smell of burnt rubber and flesh, each bounce turning the roar of the battle engulfing the men of C Troop into my own naked hell.

When I reached the Medevac chopper, I was shoved into the middle slot of a three-stacker rack. The whirlwind of the blades spattered rocks and dust up inside the helicopter. The crew medic read the note on my shirt and injected me with morphine. He helped the door gunner secure the other casualties in place. As before, the morphine had little effect on my pain.

Above me was a grunt from the 1st Infantry Division who had a catastrophic chest wound. His blood spilled over my body in a steady drip. I could not move. The chopper rose and I turned my head sideways and surveyed the scene below me.

It was chaos.

At least five vehicles were blown or burning and as we moved higher in the air the men looked like ants after a kid lights a fire to an anthill. The guy above me moaned. Now the blood flowed a little faster. It was pissing on my neck and chin. He started sobbing. The medic attached an IV to the poor guy and sprinkled a yellow powder about his wounds. I was miserable but grateful that I at least was in one piece.

I don't know how long the flight lasted. It was chaotic and I was more worried about the guy above me than anything else. Now he was crying out some woman's name. His wife? Girlfriend? I knew he was dying. The medic knew this as well and he soothed the kid by rubbing his good side and running his hand through his hair.

I felt the chopper start to descend and looked out the open door at a familiar sight, the billboard of the Negro shaving. Things started to look familiar as Saigon came into focus. Wow! Back again so soon?

We landed at a pad inside the Third Field Hospital. A group of orderlies and nurses were at the pad to greet us. They took my severely wounded comrade down first. A priest started administering the last rites as a doctor started giving him CPR. As they rolled him away I knew I was witness to another death. When they finally got to me, two orderlies grabbed my stretcher and put me on a rolling gurney. The guy at my head looked down at me and said, "Hey, man, didn't you go to Montebello High School?"

"Class of '66," I whispered.

"Me too! I'm Tom Fuentes. Remember me? You used to hang out with Scott Siedman and Lance Goto, right?"

"I remember you," I mumbled.

"Yeah, so how you doing?"

I passed out from the pain.

XIV
Third Field Hospital

When I came to I was in an ambulatory wing of a hospital with about twenty other patients. I was still in incredible pain and unable to move my legs or arms. Flat on my back I looked around at the green walls and black and white linoleum on the floor. Someone was screaming, "Get me the fuck out of here!" A few others were yelling obscenities and still others were lying still in their beds like me, either sleeping or too fucked up to be moving about. The fluorescent lights flickered on and off. In the distance I could hear a radio playing Tommy James and the Shondells' "Crystal Blue Persuasion."

A nurse came up to my bed and said, "Well, look who's awake. You gave us a little bit of a scare."

"Where am I?"

"You're in the Third Field Hospital in Saigon. Can you fill out this intake form?"

"No, ma'am. I can't raise my arms or hold a pencil. I feel paralyzed," I said.

"That's OK, sweetie. We can do it together," and she proceeded to ask me a list of questions about my medical history. Finally she came to next of kin notices.

"Who should we notify about your wounds?"

"Am I wounded?" I asked, startled by this question.

"Your injury, then. We won't know what's wrong with you until we perform some tests."

"Just let me write my mom and dad a letter when I can."

She agreed and I lay there thinking about everything that had happened. The last thing I remembered was Fuentes. The fact that he saw me lying covered with blood and had the audacity to ask me how I was meant that these people were really ignorant or had no concept of what transpired beyond these walls.

It was November 1, exactly halfway through my year-long tour in the jungles and bush of this god-awful country. My best friend had died in my arms. I had lost a lot of good buddies and friends. I had killed many men and been shot at countless times. Now I lay still in this hospital bed wondering what it was all about. Survival had been my aim and I was halfway there. I wondered what awaited me the next six months.

They took me to X-ray.

The first four days of my hospitalization were full of tests, X-rays, scans and then finally a doctor came and stood at my bedside.

"How did this happen?"

"I don't know, Doc, I was digging bunkers when all of a sudden my back popped. It hurt like hell and I couldn't move. Next thing I know I wound up here." I tried to move into a comfortable position and winced with pain.

He shoved an X-ray in my face. "It looks like someone took a hammer to your back. You have major disc problems in the lower spine. No way this happened from digging. So what else has been going on? Have you suffered any traumatic injuries prior to this?"

"Does getting blown out of the hatch of a track count?" I said mockingly.

He grabbed the X-ray from my hands and wrote something in my chart. "Your back is in bad shape. I will recommend light duty for sixty days. I'm going to give you some pills for the pain. If it keeps hurting, come back and see me. Take it easy on these pills; they're not M&Ms." He smiled. He shook his head and walked over to the next bed.

The next week was full of physical therapy. Gradually I regained the use of my arms and legs and was able to compose that dreaded letter to my folks.

November 6, 1969

Dear Mom & Dad & Sis,

By now you're probably worried because you haven't heard from me in so long. I'm sorry I haven't written. You'll never guess where I'm at. I'm in Saigon at the Third Field Hospital. Remember I told you we were building bunkers and filling sandbags? Well I injured my back doing all of that and they dusted me off by helicopter to Saigon. I'm feeling OK now. But it really hurt for a few days. I will be here about three more days than I'll probably go to Bien Hoa for a few weeks. If I play my cards right this might get me out of the field for good. I just can't believe Saigon. This is a regular hospital with hot running water, American girls, the first I've seen in a long time. It's a regular modern city. When I first got here I was all dirty and unshaven and this American woman and her husband wanted me to go stay at their house and take a hot bath and eat a home cooked meal. I had to turn down the offer because I was going to be admitted.

I'm watching T.V. and writing this letter. This is the first night my leg hasn't hurt. I guess you should keep sending my mail to the same address. Most guys just get their mail when they go back to their unit. You know I still haven't been back in the heavy fighting. Being here is nice but I'm going to forget how to set up trip-flares and Claymores if they don't send me back out pretty soon. There's this old papa san here getting a big kick out of Batman on TV. This hospital has Vietnamese civilians in it. There are some children in the next ward. Well we heard the news about the 11th Cav. Leaving Vietnam in 1970. Our Lt.

called a meeting and told us not to get our hopes up too high.
I hope it's true. Have the kids received their dolls yet? I hope
so. This is going to be bad because I won't get any mail while
I'm here. I'll probably be out of the hospital by the time you get
this letter. Mom you just don't know how happy that package
with the tortillas made everyone on the track. Jimmy is from
California so he has eaten Mexican food before, but Roger (the
gunner) is a black guy from Chicago and you should have seen
his face when he took a bite of that chili. We made a tortilla-
warmer by punching holes in the top of a saltine cracker can
and placing plastic explosives inside of it. That's how we warm
all our food but the burritos came out beautifully. Well, I'm
going to enjoy the TV now so I guess I'll quit. Don't worry I'm
not hurt that bad. It's just a sprained back. I'm feeling really
good now. I miss everyone very much. I'll write tomorrow.

> *All my love,*
> *Fred*

After three weeks in the hospital I was released. It was my
responsibility to get back to Bien Hoa. I had no idea how to do that. It
was a sunny morning and I found myself walking alone through the
wide, tree-lined boulevards. It was a pleasure to walk again after three
weeks on my back.

I didn't know if I was healing or if it was just from popping
the M&Ms the doc had given me for the pain, but I felt a lot better. I
walked for about half an hour and gradually worked my way into the
downtown area where Dizzy and I had spent the night. I passed by the
bar where we had drunk and saw two Air Force guys walking my way.
Their uniforms were clean and freshly starched. I asked the shorter of
the two, "How do you get to the USO?"

He gave me the once-over and said, "Where you coming from?"

I was clean but my clothes were dirty and still full of blood.
My hair was longer than the military liked to have it and I had the

beginning of a good little beard. I must have been quite a sight for it was the larger of the two who answered, "You're headed in the right direction. Keep going till you see the traffic circle with the Tomb of the Unknown Soldier. Make a left and it will be two blocks down on your right. You can't miss it. It's usually really crowded for late breakfast." He stared at me for a minute. "Did you get wounded, or what?" he asked, puzzlement filling his face.

"It's more like *or what.* This isn't my blood on the shirt."

"Oh, OK, man. Sure. These things happen. We've never been in combat."

"What do you do?"

"We work at the air base here in Saigon. We do jet maintenance."

"Sweet," I said.

"Good luck," he said, and the little guy gave me the peace sign. I gave it back to them and walked on down the road looking forward to breakfast at the USO.

The Saigon USO was bustling with guys from all four branches of the service. There were sailors, airmen, Marines and Army dudes hanging around the three pool tables and eight picnic tables they had set up inside a cool, well lit-hall. A counter with three short-order cooks behind the stove was full of breakfast orders. Everyone was in a good mood and there was much laughing and singing along with the jukebox. I immediately felt at home. I ordered a cheeseburger and fries and waited patiently for my food.

A guy from the 1st Infantry Division pulled out a stool next to me and sat down. We struck up a conversation and he told me about how he got out of the field a month earlier and was now a driver for a general in Saigon. He lived in a barracks that had been converted from an old hotel, and he told me that his duty was a piece of cake. He looked at my Blackhorse patch and shook his head, "We worked with you guys a lot over near Lai Khe," he said.

"I don't miss it one bit. You can take that fucking war and shove it up Nixon's ass." We started in on my fries.

"There's a lot of good jobs here in Saigon if you're in the right place at the right time. You're going to have to clean yourself up first if you want to hook up with somebody here."

I thought about this for a minute and took a bite of my cheeseburger. "Have you heard of Special Services?" I asked.

"Yeah, sure. It's an outfit over on Binh Dinh Avenue. That's the headquarters of the Command Military Touring Shows. The general that I drive for goes there all the time."

"Can you take me there?" I asked, trying to mask my growing excitement.

"Like I said before, brother, you're going to have to clean your act up. But sure, I can take you there tomorrow. Meet me here at 10 a.m. and I'll hook you up."

"What's your name?"

"Toxy French," he said, and I felt my life and fortune turning with this golden opportunity. If I could just get my face in front of whoever was in charge I was sure I could play bass well enough to get into a band. *I better get started,* I thought. The USO had a shop called The Supply Sergeant, and I went and got me a new shirt. They also gave away toiletries and I got the shaving kit and cleaned up my face and brushed my teeth. I was feeling pretty good.

Then to find a place to stay until my big meeting tomorrow morning. I walked back over to Tu Do Street and checked the alleyways looking for the Australian Embassy. I came across the back door and found it unlocked. I walked inside hoping to see someone I knew. I found Deke sitting at a desk sorting through mail.

"Well, well, well. If it isn't my old friend Fred, the American. How are you, mate? You're looking dapper this morning. Come to visit us?" He said this without missing a beat on his sorting.

"Hello, Deke. How are you? Is Gordo in?" I asked as I found a chair.

"Gordo took a flight to your favorite holiday spot, Ban Me Thuot. He should be back in a few. Relax. Tell me what brings you back to Saigon so quickly?" He rose and came up to me and shook my hand.

"I've been in the hospital for the last three weeks and I was wondering if I could bunk with you guys tonight. I have a big appointment tomorrow," I said, stretching the truth. I had no such appointment, only a dream of a chance for change.

"Of course! You're welcome here, mate, for as long as you wish to stay. How is that bloke, Dizzy? Quite a character, he is."

"Well, we had a little too much to drink that night," I said sheepishly.

"Not to worry. We all get pissed from time to time. Speaking of which, you look to be too sober. Care for a drink?" he asked, as he started pouring one for himself.

"Thanks, but no, Deke. I'll just wait for Gordon and the other fellows if you don't mind. In fact, I want to check things out in the city. Just wanted to book my room, if you know what I mean."

"Indeed. Dinner is served at 1800 if you can make it back in time. I promise a meal you won't easily forget."

"Thanks." I left through the front door and walked over a few streets and found an open marketplace. I walked through the stalls and found the exotic smells intoxicating. This was the first taste of a city that I would come to love. I bought some souvenirs. I asked a Marine where the PX was and he told me it was a few miles away in a part of town called Cholon.

I grabbed a taxi and told the driver to take me there. He did, and when I walked into the store, I was amazed. TVs, stereo equipment, washers, dryers, and even fucking refrigerators were for sale. Who bought this shit? I felt like a hick on his first trip to a big city. There was so much stuff here as to make a combat trooper reel. I couldn't believe the array of goods on display. I bought a 35-millimeter camera and lots of film and stood in the check-out aisle with a wide-eyed look of amazement. If I were to tell Dizzy or Benson about this place they wouldn't believe me.

What really blew my mind was that everyone was so clean. There was no mud even though it was raining hard. I picked up my bag and hurried out to catch a cab to go back to the heart of Saigon. The drive was a shocker. We passed through areas of abject poverty. This was the Chinese district and they were treated as second-class citizens. Apartment building after apartment building filled the passing scenery. Manufacturing shops polka-dotted the apartments that were full of three or four families living together. There were no big factories; they ran businesses out of their homes. Countless small enterprises could be glimpsed inside the doorways of the lodgings, from rattan furniture-making to batik printing to tailoring, or making sandals from tires discarded from the war machine.

Shoeless and half-naked children ran among heavy machinery, their hair and clothes covered with dirt and grease. Old men sat on their haunches smoking opium while others, heavily under the influence, slept in doorways as the children scurried about them. Skinny, ragged dogs roamed the streets in packs, rummaging over trash heaps in the gutter. A resentment swept across my being as I watched a scene that played out every day.

I arrived back at the USO and started using my camera. There was a line of guys waiting to use one of the three phones they had set up to call the States. I found my place in line and struck up a conversation with the fellow in front of me.

"You been in line long?"

"About an hour and twenty minutes. It's not too bad today."

Shit! What day was it? What time was it in Montebello, California? I thought about this for a few seconds and decided that whatever the time, my parents would be happy to hear from me, given the last letter I wrote to them told them I was in the hospital. They had no idea what was going on over here. I better call.

It was called a MARS station. I forget what the acronym stood for but it was a decent, cheap way to call the United States from Vietnam. I picked up the receiver and gave the operator the number I wanted to call and waited. Halfway around the world the phone rang in the bedroom of Art and Marina Rivera. It scared them to death, having a son in Vietnam fighting a war, and it crossed my mind that if they got a call at an odd hour in the morning they would be sure it was bad news. Someone picked up the phone on the second ring.

"Hello?"

My eyes misted over as I heard her voice. This was Mother— the one the boys and men cried out to as they lay dying.

"Mom? It's Fred."

"Oh my God, *mijo*! How are you?" I could hear her calling out to my dad in the darkness, "Arthur! Arthur! It's Fred!" I heard him stumble around and make his way to the other room to pick up the extension.

"*Mijo*. Where are you? Are you hurt?"

They were both on the phone now and I was overwhelmed with emotion.

"I'm fine. I'm at the USO in Saigon and they let me call home. Sorry to wake you but I had the chance to call and I took it. Don't worry about me. I just hurt my back. I'll be fine with a little rest."

Memories of childhood swept through my mind and that quiet little suburb of Los Angeles seemed like heaven to me—right now out of reach, but with luck, I would one day be there again.

We talked for about five minutes. I don't remember exactly what we said, but by the end of the phone call we had assured each other that we were all fine and in good spirits. We were looking forward to my homecoming in six months and that word, homecoming, finally became a reality that seemed obtainable.

Yes, I was halfway there.

We said goodbye, and as I hung up the phone, I realized that I was weeping. Could I finally drop my guard? Better not. Better to keep sharp till that day comes when I am sleeping in my own bed once again.

I went back to the embassy just in time to see Gordo and Philip before dinner.

"Fred, my friend." Gordo reached over and shook my hand. "The prodigal warrior returns. I understand you want to bunk with us tonight. Well, that will be no problem. We have *beaucoup* room. How about some supper?"

These guys just loved to eat good food and drink tall pints of ale. I sat down and Deke served me a wonderful meal. He shopped every day at the open market and used nothing but fresh Vietnamese ingredients. I had never had duck before and the taste took me back to Thanksgivings spent with my family. The sauce was intoxicating.

After supper I told them everything that had happened to me, everything I had done, and I told them of my oath never to take another human life. Gordo took this with the seriousness that it demanded. He knew I was seeking redemption, or at the very least, I was seeking forgiveness. But from where? From whom? My old God had failed me.

"I just want to get rid of the pain inside."

"It was a chance shot, that kid was. You had no idea it was a child."

"It doesn't change the fact that he is dead by my hand," I said. I studied his face. He was about forty-five years old, with gray around his temples and a small scar below his left eye. His eyes were blue and seemed to carry great wisdom. I paid close attention to what he said next.

"Out in the bush, everyone is the enemy until proven otherwise. Stop blaming yourself, mate. You're a good man and you don't have to carry the burden of that guilt with you everywhere you go. There is a certain sadness to your face that was absent the last time we were together. Pull yourself together, man.

"Realize that bad things happen in war. Bad things happen to good men and I would hate to see it ruin your young life." He moved around in the overstuffed chair and shifted his frame into a comfortable position.

"I appreciate the kind words, Gordo, but they don't lessen my pain." I looked him dead in the eyes and saw his face darken. He looked lost in thought and seemed far removed from the scene.

"You know, I killed a mother and her child," Gordo said. "Shot them down in front of the entire village because I thought she was going for a weapon. I'm sorry for this and I try to live my life making amends for that deed. I don't punish myself but I try to have it make me a better man. I believe it has. Shit happens every day in this country that would make a decent person sick. We are part of history, good and bad. Best to just do your job and be of service to others."

He took a heavy breath and let it out slowly. He got up and took a few steps toward me and hugged me right in the middle of the room. I felt warmth spread throughout my body. Cutter and Riddle never talked to me like this. For the last six months they had been the men I looked to for advice. Now this foreigner was confiding in me. He opened a channel that I could take for real guidance.

"You're a hell of a bloke, mate. Keep your head above the fray and you'll make it all right."

I decided to lighten up on myself. I told them that I was a musician before the war and about my planned trip to Special Services tomorrow morning. This excited Gordon and Deke.

"See, a path is opening up for you to help you fulfill your promise never to kill again. You can kill an audience with your guitar but it will soon be no more war for you. Good show. Good show."

He fumbled for a smoke. "I understand it's quite difficult to get in. We transport the musicians all the time. Perhaps we will see you out there."

"Thank you, Gordon." I didn't really know how to thank him for what he did for me, but I did feel relief. They all wished me luck and we turned in early. I was glad to see that they didn't carry on every night the way they did when Dizzy and I last saw them. These were decent men, all volunteers to fight with Uncle Sam against the communists.

In the morning I showered and trimmed my hair and met Toxy French at 10 a.m. at the USO. We had a quick breakfast and he looked me over and said, "You clean up nice, man. I almost didn't recognize you when you got here. Are you ready?"

We got up from our table and walked out to his Jeep. It was raining—not hard, but enough to make the ride in the open Jeep uncomfortable and wet.

We passed by big two-story homes. Some were French-built but more often than not it looked like Any Town, USA. This is where the upper class lived. I thought about how the people living in these homes had the most to lose if the North Vietnamese were one day successful at taking over the country. There must be real fear behind those doors.

We came to a mansion along the boulevard. Toxy told me that he could not stay and wait for me. I told him I would be fine and he wished me luck. I gingerly walked to the front door and rang the doorbell, which was answered by a sergeant E-5. His uniform was clean but unkempt. Wrinkled and hanging loose on him, his uniform looked two sizes too big.

He smiled and said, "Can I help you?"

"Yes. I'm looking for a job."

"What? You're in the Army. You just can't go around asking for a job interview like a civilian. You go where they send you," he replied.

"I know, it's just that ..."

"We couldn't use you unless you are a musician," he interrupted.

"I *am* a musician."

"Well, we have no openings right now except for a bass player."

"I *am* a bass player." This was working out beyond my wildest dreams. I stood erect with new confidence, and I could hear the cogs turning in his head.

"Let's see how good you are. Go down that hallway and go in the third room on the left. There is an audition going on right now." He pointed out the direction with his hand and then swung it around to shake mine.

I walked down the hallway and found the door ajar. I opened it wide to reveal four musicians—all Army—sitting around shootin' the shit. The drummer sat behind a new set of Ludwigs, and there was a wall of Fender Showman and Bassman amplifiers.

"What's up?" the drummer asked.

"The sergeant sent me in to audition on bass."

The guitar player grabbed a bass and handed it to me. Wow! A brand new Fender Jazz Bass, just like the one I had at home. I picked it up and immediately set out to tune it. That impressed the band and I wondered what kind of talent they had just seen.

I looked over at the singer with total confidence. "Anything," I said.

"How about a twelve-bar blues in A?" he asked.

I looked at the drummer and said, "Count it off."

And just like that, my life was saved and forever changed by "Johnny B. Goode."

XV
With the Solemn Oath

We played the kind of music I had cut my teeth on. I came up playing the blues and rock and roll, and as strange as it seemed, I found myself playing music with a group of guys in an air-conditioned studio in Viet-fucking-Nam! We played for three hours and before they said anything to me I knew I was in the band. The music came and flowed so easily between us. The chemistry was there between the drummer and the bass player and we became instant friends.

His name was John Fortuna, and he was from New Rochelle, New York. I told him that the only person I knew from there was Dick Van Dyke. He smiled and his mustache curled up over his mouth and his cheeks glowed with a kind of tenderness. It was the hippie look, I guess. He possessed that warmth that I missed from my friends at home. Well, to me it seemed that John and I had been friends forever. The sergeant came into the room and asked them how it had gone.

"We got our man, Keith," Larry the guitar player answered. Marvin, the singer, agreed, and the NCO asked me to please come to his office. I high-fived the guys in the band and left with Sgt. Askins.

"You're in a combat unit, aren't you?" he asked, as he pointed me toward a chair.

"How can you tell?" I asked.

"It shows. I don't have very good luck getting you guys off the line. I just want you to know that. The commanding officers of fighting units don't give men up so easily. Now, those guys you just met are cooks and company clerks. They've never been on the front lines. They're in for a shock because we send bands out to places where it is too dangerous to send civilian entertainment. Fire bases, landing zones, small encampments. For you it will be a walk in the park. Not so for these Saigon warriors. If your company commander gives you up, and remember I said *if* he gives you up, I would want you to look out for your band mates."

"Can do, Sgt. Askins. But I feel you're being way too pessimistic. I just got out of the hospital and I have a note for a couple of months of light duty. The CO will have no use for me for a while," I said, believing that this just might work.

"Good. It's a three-month temporary duty. I'll give you a set of orders and if your old man signs them you'll be with us. Good luck."

I grabbed the papers and left without saying anything to the other guys.

It was a beautiful, hot day, and I decided to walk back to the USO. My leg felt fine and I wanted to exercise it. My back hurt, so I took one of the pills the doctor had given me.

It took an hour to maneuver my way back. Around 3:30 I sat down in the club and thought about everything that had just happened. I was blown away. I ordered another cheeseburger and sat with a Marine from Baltimore. I told him my story and he was moved by my vow. He told me that I should get my ass back to base camp and show them my orders. He was right, but how was I going to get to Bien Hoa? Gordo! Of course. I walked straight over to the Australian Embassy and found Gordon lying about reading a magazine.

"Good photos?" I asked.

"No, no, no. It's not that type of rag, now, is it?" He looked like I had hurt his feelings.

"Sorry, didn't mean to imply that you're some kind of idiot. Say, Gordon, do you think you could hook me up with a ride back over to Bien Hoa?" I asked.

"Right now."

"No, when you get a chance or have something to do over there," I said.

"I meant *right now*. You can see I'm not doing much of anything. Let's have a go at it right now."

"You're outta sight, man." We jumped in a Jeep and made the trip to the airport. It was a perfect day for a flight. Not a cloud in the sky, as we had a much less eventful takeoff than our first one. Thirty minutes later I reported to Sgt. Major. I showed him my paperwork and asked when I could see Capt. Riddle.

"He's due in next week."

"I have orders for him to sign," I said.

"You're mine till he says otherwise."

"Sorry, Sarge, but I got a note from the doctor that I have light duty for a month. I just got out of the hospital."

That pissed him off. He couldn't fuck with me like he wanted.

"Well, stay in the area while you wait for him. I don't want you wandering away like you did last time you were here. I don't like all that sneaking around."

"Fine. Am I excused?"

"Get out of my sight," he snarled. I walked away toward the supply tent looking for Squires. I found him sorting through boots.

"What's up? Back so soon?" he asked.

"Yeah, I love it here. I want to be just like you when I grow up, and stay in the rear."

"Aw, man. Don't give me all that shit."

"No, I mean it. You have a cool job here. Everyone is just envious, that's all."

"Yeah, well, I know that a bunch of guys have resentments toward me and I live with it," he said.

"Hey, Squires, come on. Quit it. I love your ass, man. Now can you hook me up with your man Hawks again? You holding? Let's go top off." Squires dropped the boots he was holding and smiled.

"I believe I can handle this. Follow me." He led me down that

crooked path to oblivion. I had a week to wait for Capt. Riddle and I
was square with Major so why not spend a day in the zone, I thought.
I was learning that being at war has its up moments. By dinner time I
found it hard to walk in a straight line. Squires and I stumbled to the
chow hall and saw Hawks still in his flight suit. He was walking in the
other door. We walked over to him.

"Rough day?" I asked.

"Hey, Fred, how you doing? They told me you got dusted off a
few weeks ago. Paralyzed or some shit."

"I fucked up my back bad. I couldn't move for a few days. Got
me a sixty-day profile and I'm trying to go TDY with Special Services,"
I told him.

"Good luck with that, brother. So you going to be here a while?
It's movie night tonight," Hawks said, as he set his flight gear down
on a table. I told him of my intention to get back to Saigon ASAP. The
three of us enjoyed a nice meal together. That evening we found some
lawn chairs and sat around an outdoor screen to watch John Wayne
in "Green Berets." We all laughed at the silliness of the film with an
overaged Wayne leading the charge.

The rear consisted of guys like Squires and Hawks. It had the
guys from the motor pool and the company clerks. Dental assistants
and other medical workers made up a big part, but the largest group
by far were the transients. I was a transient waiting to find out my
destiny. Olgovey and Jenkins were in the rear for personal problems.
Jenkins' mother was dying and they were trying to get him home.
This is where the record clerks shined. Moving paper and generating
orders were their specialty. It took a lot of diverse people to make
Charlie Troop run. Olgovey was there to see a dentist and have a
molar removed.

Choppers left for the field every evening, transporting men and
equipment and supplies out, bringing wounded and dead back in. We
had a busy heliport. On the second day Hawks asked me if I would like
to go out on a mission with him.

"By the border?" I asked, not really wanting to visit that shit hole.

"No. To the troop. I've got to ferry Olgovey and a few others back out. Come on, it will be fun." Hawks had that pilot devil-may-care attitude, and it was contagious.

Jesus, I can get Riddle to sign my orders and be back by dinner. I thought. "Is Riddle there?"

"Is the Pope a Catholic?"

"Sure. Fuck yeah, I'll go. I can see the motherfucker if you wait for me."

Around 3 in the afternoon I stopped by the armorer and picked up my tools of war. I met Hawks out at the helipad and he reached out and helped lift me up into the helicopter. As we rose, he tilted the sticks forward and we took off to the north. He lifted to about 2,500 feet and leveled off. I was excited, and all I could think about was getting that goddamn signature. We were off to see the wizard. Would he release me? I was a good gun with *beaucoup* kills. Could he spare me?

We landed 200 meters from the perimeter, where they had carved out a nice little landing zone. Hawks kept the rotors turning as I jumped out and made my way straight over to headquarters. I asked for the old man and Clementi told me to wait a while he went into the communications bunker and looked for him. Capt. Riddle came out, adjusting his eyes to the sunlight.

"How are you, son?" he asked, knowing I had been dusted off.

"I'm better, sir, but you can improve my situation dramatically."

"How's that, troop?"

"I spent three weeks in the hospital and the doctor gave me a profile of sixty days light duty. I have a chance to go TDY with Special Services if you will release me for three months."

"Three months? But you said yourself you'll only be down for two. Why should I give up one of my best drivers?"

"Thank you, sir, for the words of confidence. But I may never be any good to you. You know the nature of back injuries, and the doc says I screwed mine up real bad. Have I ever let you down, Cap? You know it's been my goal since day one to play in a band. If you release me I promise to make it up to you when I come back. I hate to beg, but I will. Please, Captain, it means a lot to me to play music."

He looked at me sideways and said, "You ain't fucking with me, are you boy? When does this all start?"

"Immediately," I lied. "I've already been accepted into the band. I just need your permission."

He took the paperwork from my hand and looked it over. He reread it and finally signed his name on it. My heart rate rose.

"Make us proud, Fred. Strut that Blackhorse patch all over Vietnam and make us proud."

"Yes, sir!" I almost shouted.

I gave him a quick salute and ran back to Hawks' waiting chopper. This time I scurried up without any help and sat there and thought, *I'm never coming back out to the field no matter what happens — so help me God!*

XVI
Somebody Pinch Me!

And with that, Hawks lifted off, leaving Dizzy, Benson, Darnel and all my friends to fend for themselves. I said a quick prayer for them and felt conflicted leaving like this with no goodbyes.

As we rose to 500 feet, I looked down and saw the tracks breaking bush to set up their NDP for the night. This was a task I knew well and I was overcome by a sense of grief and guilt for abandoning my friends in the mud.

For me it was all roses.

Hawks and I said nothing to each other during that ride. We returned to Bien Hoa and I realized that I had forsaken everything that I owned. Gone again were my guitar and new clothes. I needed to hit up Squires in the morning but no need to worry about it right then. I had three weeks before I needed to report to Saigon.

I wanted to get out of Blackhorse fast in case Capt. Riddle came to check on me. I bunked with Squires and Hawks again that evening and in the morning, after breakfast, I followed Squires to his supply tent and picked out three new uniforms, socks, underwear, and T-shirts. My boots were pretty ragged and I asked him for a new pair to complement my new attire. I took my three shirts to the tailor in the village to have my name sewn on them. I went to the steam bath and sweated all the dirt and grime from my body. I went to Mama san and had a manicure and pedicure, and a much-needed massage. I went to the base barber and had a haircut. I was going to Saigon and I insisted on arriving in style.

As I packed my duffel bag, I remembered all the good times that we had had in the field. I remembered dropping acid with Herman. I remembered the day I meet Dizzy. I recalled with fondness the nights spent with the brothers, Benson spouting on about the Black Panther Party and arguing with Doc Lewis about the social ramifications of Johnson's Great Society.

I looked down at the bracelet made from Herman's bootlaces that I was wearing and missed him so much. I picked up a few more items at the small PX and I was ready. I asked Hawks if he could fly me to Saigon.

"Where you want to go?" he asked.

"Do you know Tan Son Nhut?"

"Yeah, I can get you there tomorrow."

I figured I could catch a taxi from there to the USO. I was using the USO as my base of operations as it was near the Australian Embassy. I also knew how to get to Special Services from there and, more importantly, they made the best damn cheeseburgers this side of Bill's Paradise in Montebello.

When I hit the ground at Tan Son Nhut, the sky was pouring rain in biblical proportions. I thanked Hawks and we said our goodbyes and I went into the terminal building. It was awash with activity. Everyone was coming or going and the noise from the jets was deafening. I hurried over to where the taxis were parked, and jumped in the back seat of the first one that I saw.

"Take me to the USO," I told the driver.

He turned around to face me and asked, "You new to Vietnam?" I realized that I looked like an FNG with my new haircut and sparkling clean and pressed uniform. I fit right in with the guys who made up the rear.

"No, I am new to Saigon."

He turned back and started to drive. "You like girl?"

"I'm fine. No, thank you." I had had my experience with the whores of Saigon and they did not interest me right now.

"You like smoke-smoke?" he asked, not giving up on me. I considered this for a moment.

"What you got, Papa san?"

"Me got numba one smoke-smoke, GI." He reached over the seat and showed me a pack of Carlton cigarettes. I was intrigued so I bought a pack. I sat in the back seat and was amazed by how the weed was packed professionally inside a brand-new pack of cigarettes. I pulled the cellophane wrapper off and opened it to find perfectly rolled joints with filters. *Amazing!* This was a world more attuned to my days in Hollywood.

He dropped me off at the USO and I walked in like I owned the joint. The girl behind the counter recognized me and I told her, "I'll take the usual."

She popped a burger on the grill and I turned to look over the scene on the street. I relaxed. Everything I had done after being discharged from the hospital had been a hustle. I had hustled the Australians for a place to stay. I had hustled Special Services and my commanding officer to get in that band and it had brought me here, alone with nobody to report to until the second week of December. That was when rehearsals started for the tour.

It was only the third week of November and I needed to stay out of trouble and out of the command structure's eye for three weeks. I could do it. Just keep my head down and stay with Gordo and the guys. I ate my cheeseburger and felt a peace fall over me.

There was not the constant tension of the enemy. There were no big guns firing off in the distance. No B-52 strikes nearby. It was peaceful. The rain was nothing but an inconvenience as there was no mud to contend with and everywhere I looked, I saw happy, smiling faces. They were untouched by the horrors of war, here.

Sure, there were Vietcong agents running freely around town, but they hardly carried out any actions. Apart from Tet last year, the war had not entered Saigon. I could see why it was called the Pearl of the Orient. I decided that I should run over to Binh Dinh Avenue and take care of business with Askins.

I paid for my lunch and considered my financial situation. I had about 100 bucks on me but I knew it was going to be a hassle getting paid once I went TDY. I would work that out with the sergeant. I arrived at Special Services soaking wet, having taken a pedicab. I was conserving my money, so there would be no more cab rides. Askins met me at the door and was surprised to see me back so soon.

"Well, how did it go?" he asked.

"I've got the old man's signature right here, Sergeant."

"Oh, just call me Keith. We run things a little informal around here. Good job. I thought it would be weeks before I heard from you," he said, moving toward his office.

I followed him and took a seat. I pulled the dry paperwork out from under my shirt and handed it to him. "I'm no good to them with my back the way it is. I had to go back out to the field to get his signature."

"Good job," he repeated. "Let me tell you, as I indicated before, this is not without danger. The Command Military Touring Show sends entertainers into places where we can't send Bob Hope and Ann Margret. Can you imagine sending Raquel Welch to a fire base? These will be small audiences, but very starved for entertainment."

"Don't worry about me. I can handle it. I've been working up by the Cambodian border the last four months. By the way, Keith, when do we start, and where will I stay?"

We sat in his office for over an hour and he laid the whole thing out for me. I would be staying at the Metropole Hotel ten blocks away from the USO toward the Cholon district. I would have a roommate and be given a *per diem* for food. I was welcome to eat at any of the various US or allied establishments scattered in the Saigon area. Being unsupervised, we were expected to always carry ourselves in a military manner and not embarrass the Special Services with unruly behavior. There was a 10 p.m. citywide curfew enforced by the MPs.

"I don't want to get a call in the middle of the night with someone telling me that you're in the brig. You understand, you will be terminated." He reached into a drawer and pulled out a badge.

"Wear this on you at all times. It lets the MPs and officers know that you're one of us. You are going to have a lot of spare time and it really makes some officers pissed to see their subordinates walking around like they've got nothing better to do. Know what I mean?"

I stood across his desk. "Listen, Keith, I'm already checked out of my unit. As far as they're concerned I'm on duty with you. Now, I have a place where I can stay, but when do you think I can check into the hotel?"

He looked surprised.

"Well, now, why did you go and do that for? I'm just kidding. I'm from an infantry unit myself, the Fourth Infantry. This is my fourth month of TDY. I know you wanted to get out of the field the same way I did. Let me put the paperwork in. I'll figure out some way for it to work. And Fred?"

"Yes?"

"Don't fuck this up. These chances come around maybe once in a lifetime—if you're lucky. Out of the hundreds of thousands of men who have served in Vietnam for the last ten years, only 500 have made it in the Special Services. Don't push your luck."

I considered his words carefully. I had been a lucky mother-fucker so far and I might be pushing my luck by trying to get the hotel room early. Oh, well, I had put it out there. Let's see where it goes.

There were no cabs waiting out front, so I humped it back to the embassy. Thank God it had stopped raining. I arrived at the front door just as Philip was arriving with groceries, and I opened the door for him. We walked into a hearty aroma of another of Deke's super suppers. Gordo was in a jovial mood and I joined them for another meal. At supper I told my friends about what was transpiring, how I felt as I had stood in the field for the last time and about having three weeks to fuck around.

"Well, of course you know you always have a place here with us," Gordo said. "Congratulations on your new career."

I liked Gordon tremendously, and I told him as much. "I don't know what I would have done without you guys. You've made me feel at home here right from the start. I'll be happy to earn my keep around here doing KP or any other chores you might have for me. I appreciate your generosity, Gordo."

"Nonsense! We're glad to have you around. You're part of the family now, mate. Deke has no need of a helper in the kitchen. The bloke is doing a grand job, don't you say? Here is what you can do. Johnny has a guitar. Perhaps you could give us a little concert later?"

"It would be my pleasure," I said, as I finished my glass of wine. Later in the evening, as Gordon was smoking his pipe, he came and sat down next to me.

"You're looking much better. You're not carrying that heavy burden on your sleeve anymore."

"It shows?"

"Yes. I'm glad to see you happy. You're too young to carry the world on your shoulders." He put his hand on my shoulder and said softly, "You know, I have a son at home who is about your age. How old are you?"

"Twenty-one."

"Sam is nineteen. Close enough." He drew back his hand and picked up his pint and took a swig.

"You have a family, then? What brings *you* to Vietnam? I was drafted, but you volunteered." I was curious.

"The army is my life. From my great, great, grandfather to the present, a Fenton has always worn the uniform. As far as Vietnam is concerned, well, it was the only war in town. I'll retire after this tour. I love flying every day and this allows me to do it."

"I'll bet it does. That was a crazy flight you gave the Diz and me. How is Ban Me Thuot?" I asked, remembering the sniper fire.

Gordo got animated and almost fell out of his chair when I asked him about Ban Me Thuot. "Ha ha. They still haven't found that bloody sniper, but as I told you, he has yet to hit anyone."

"Well, he came close to hitting *you* that day." I laughed.

Johnny and Philip appeared with the guitar and I played a few songs. It was not a cheap box; it was a Gibson and it sounded great. As I played, more and more guys came around and sat in a circle. We partied and carried on late into the night, and when we got ready to hit the rack Gordo came up to me and said, "It's nice to see you again, Fred. Thanks for the splendid concert."

In the morning, after a hearty breaky-breaky (that's what they called breakfast) I hurried out to Special Services. I left the embassy's phone number with Keith and made my way back over to the USO. I called home again and told them the good news. They were so happy that my mom started to cry.

"Oh, honey, Saint Jude is watching over you," my mother cried into the phone. They were still making the weekly pilgrimage to Pasadena every Wednesday. Without fail, rain or shine, tired or not, they had religiously kept up their end of the bargain with the Almighty and He had certainly been a God of his word. I thanked them for their prayers.

After I hung up I looked around me, in a daze. Talking to them made me super homesick. I tried not to be resentful, but I thought about all of my friends who had deferments and were escaping service. Most of them had college deferments. Well, I had read Camus and Sartre and the Russians. Were they any smarter than me? I had been with a band that was signed to Mercury Records. Our album was released on the day I was drafted. We had played with all the big West Coast artists: Jefferson Airplane, the Grateful Dead, Buffalo Springfield and others.

My guitar player, Kent, was drafted on the same day I was. Our manager tried to get us out of the draft by sending us to a psychiatrist to get a note saying that we were queer. We arrived at the induction center in downtown Los Angeles together and proceeded to take a battery of tests. When I spoke to the Army psychiatrist I guess I just wasn't that convincing, and before I knew it I was being sworn into the Army.

They believed Kent. He got out.

I was whisked away on a bus for an all-night drive to Fort Ord, near Monterey, California. The yelling and screaming and abuse started that morning and they particularly liked to fuck with me because I was a long-haired hippie. It was a nightmare of surreal proportions and the bubble of hope burst when I sat in the barber chair and watched as they cut away layer upon layer of hair and finally shaved my head.

I looked ridiculous. That was the coldest, most helpless state I had ever been in, the desperation matched only by my nightmarish experiences in Vietnam. It was there that I surrendered to the Kafka-like experience that was the US Army. To say that the following six weeks of training was anything less than hellish would be an understatement.

I was what you would call flabby. That, combined with the intense physical training along with the constant hazing by the drill sergeants made me yearn to be anywhere else but there.

Even Vietnam ...

I surveyed the street. I decided to take a walk, as it was still early and I had so much to explore. I walked over to Tu Do Street and saw many servicemen drunk and causing scenes outside of the girly bars. As I approached the first skirmish I heard a tiny voice say, "Hey, *cabrón. Tienes dinero?*" Surprised, I looked over and saw a small girl around sixteen sitting on a stool.

"Did you just call me a *cabrón*?" I asked incredulously.

"*Sí, señor*," she smiled.

I laughed at this and asked, "*Hablas Español, hermosita?*"

"Perfectly," she replied in proper English.

"How did you know I spoke Spanish?"

"I could tell. You have those high cheekbones."

"You sit here studying Americans?"

"Only the interesting-looking ones," she flirted. "I speak French, Italian, Spanish, and English. Oh, and of course Vietnamese and Mandarin."

"Of course," I replied. "You must come from a good family to have that much education. Why aren't you in school right now? And what are you doing in such a bad part of town?" I scolded.

"I'm here with my friend. He makes his living shining shoes. Do you want a shoeshine?" I looked down and saw a kid of about twelve years old squatting with his shining gear at his side. I took a few steps to get into the shade and took a good look at him sitting there. He was dressed in rags. His feet were surprisingly clean and so were his hands and face. He looked up at me and smiled.

"Shine shoe, GI?" she asked, on the kid's behalf.

Well, why not? I was trying my damndest to be a good soldier, for three weeks, at least. When I told him to go for it, he looked to her for a sign, and she nodded to him, and I realized he was mute. He took out his cloth and whipped my boots down and the girl showed me some bracelets and charms that she had for sale. She was wearing Levi's and a striped blouse. She wore her long hair up in a bun, in contrast to all the long-haired beauties that dotted the street.

She told me that her name was Thieu, and that she lived with her family nearby. I introduced myself and we fell into talking about Saigon while I sat on a tripod stool and the kid buffed my boots. I told her I was new in town and she insisted that she take me and the kid to the zoo.

"There's a zoo here?" I asked.

"Of course we have a zoo. We also have an opera and an orchestra."

"Can I usually find you here?"

"You can find me up and down Tu Do Street. I sell my jewelry here because after a night with a strange lady it's remarkable how some men feel that they have to buy their wives or girlfriends a gift. I make a lot of money here."

Thieu and I made a date for the next day to visit the zoo. I was skeptical about its existence and looked forward to seeing it. As we chatted, the day wore on and she made her sales on the street.

I could see what she meant about business being brisk, with hungover soldiers and Marines sauntering around in misery. They purchased diamonds and gold bracelets, spending anywhere from five to seventy dollars. I made a mental note never to fall for that bar girl scene again. It just brought misery and pain. Why hassle with it? It was a pleasure to stand there and talk to Thieu all day and before we knew it, it was half past four in the afternoon.

I had to resist the temptation to speak to her in pidgin English. She was so proper, a sweet, young French-Vietnamese girl and I looked forward to our date. As the day ended, I excused myself and headed on over to the embassy. As usual, Deke had prepared a luscious supper. I took my place along the long table and looked around and didn't see Gordon.

"Where's Gordo?" I asked.

"Gone to Cam Ranh Bay," Philip intoned.

"What's he doing up there?"

"Taking a man to hospital," Deke replied.

I missed my old friend that night. I was eager to tell him about my new street friends and fill him in on my adventures. He discouraged me from visiting Tu Do Street, but I always let his cautions slide down my back.

After dinner, Johnny brought out his guitar, but before anyone asked me to play, I excused myself for a few minutes and walked out into the alley. I was eager to try one of those Carltons I had purchased and thought this a perfect opportunity to burn one. I lit up and watched an old lady empty a pail of water into the alley.

She glanced over her shoulder and I moved into the shadows. She spit out a big piece of betel root. It was a root that the poorer Vietnamese were strung out on. It blackened their teeth and stained their mouths a deep red. Though legal, it was frowned upon by the upper and middle classes. She didn't see me and I drew another puff of smoke into my lungs and was surprised at how smooth the weed was. I proceeded to get wasted on three pulls of the joint and my eyes went out of focus for a minute as I struggled to breathe.

Wow! What good shit this was. I missed Dizzy and the guys and wasn't sure if I should let the Aussies know I was smoking weed. I had never seen any of them getting high. They were drinkers and probably down on stoners. I should keep the Carltons hidden and enjoy Deke and the gang for what they were, I thought.

I made my way back inside and picked up the guitar. I started playing and lost myself in the music. The Australians really liked the songs I had learned for Jim Gaines. We enjoyed another lively night together.

In the morning, right after breaky-breaky, I walked out into the rain toward Tu Do Street. As previously arranged, I met Thieu at the Brodard Café, where we sat and ate ice cream while we waited for the kid. Thieu had explained to me that he lived on the streets down by the waterfront. He didn't have a name, and we just called him "the kid". He was a scruffy-looking child and he showed up right on time. We were off for the zoo.

As we entered through the wide gates, I was pleased to see the ivy covered walls and well-kept gardens. I recognized the indigenous trees and shrubbery, carefully sculptured and recently washed by the rain. Thieu grabbed my hand as we exited the cab and said, "I told you. We are a cultured people."

"A very old culture at that," I said. "Why don't we take the path on the right and make a big circle." I studied a map. I got my camera ready and asked her and the kid to stand in front of a beautiful floral display. Next to us was a young family with five daughters dressed in very colorful clothes. They were brimming with smiles. As I took their photo, I was taken aback by seeing such a joyful family in a country where war was never more than a few clicks away.

Looking at the father, I realized I was seeing what the middle class looked like in Vietnam. I tried to imagine what he did for a living. He'd really be out of place in the small villages and hamlets where there was only poverty and despair. I thought about the two disparate worlds miles apart from each other and yet so very close.

Thieu was excited as she pointed to the monkeys and chimps. "Have you ever eaten one of them?" she asked playfully.

"You're kidding, right?" I played along. "That's what American soldiers live on out in the jungle. How do you like yours prepared?"

"With hot chili sauce," she said, laughing.

The sun came out from behind the clouds and the light shone on her face. I studied her face and she appeared a little older today. To my eyes, all Vietnamese had young looking faces, but I could tell by the way she carried herself and conversed that she was older than she looked. I got curious.

"How old *are* you, Thieu?" I knew you're never supposed to ask a woman her age, but she was not a woman. She was a young lady.

"Twenty," she said. "Why do you ask?"

"It's just that yesterday I thought you were only about sixteen. You have a very pretty young face," I said, as I watched her blush. Today she was wearing a white *ao doi*, the traditional Vietnamese national costume. It consisted of tight-fitting silk tunic worn over pantaloons. She was ravishing and it felt great to walk together holding hands.

We visited the lion's den and the tigers. When we reached the petting zoo, I gave the kid some peanuts and watched with joy as he had fun feeding the animals. I bought some popcorn and we caught a taxi to take us back to Tu Do. It all seemed so normal. It all seemed so pleasant.

I hurried to the embassy, hoping to catch Gordo before supper. I found him sitting in the parlor smoking his pipe while filling in blanks on the crosswords on the back page of the Stars and Stripes. No pipe, but except for that it could have been my dad, and it was so much like home, I wanted to walk into the kitchen and raid the fridge for leftovers.

When Gordo saw it was me who entered the room, he put down the paper and smiled, patting the chair next to him.

"Everybody tells me that I missed another great concert last night. I was, how shall I put it, *detained* in Cam Ranh Bay," he chortled.

We were happy to see each other and he extended a hand and I shook it with pleasure.

Words started speeding out of my mouth. "Gordo, I must tell you about a girl I've just met. We went to the zoo today on a kind of date and I really like her a lot. She speaks perfect English and five other languages. She sells trinkets on the street and hangs around with a mute kid, she—"

"Slow down, mate, slow down. You're getting way too excited. Calm down and tell me all about it." Gordon laughed.

I spent the next half hour telling him all about Thieu and our day together. He was happy for me and said, "Ah, love springs eternal. But clarify something for me, though. The mute kid. Is the boy her brother?"

"No. He's a street urchin. He lives over by the waterfront. I guess they just look out for each other."

Gordon loaded his pipe, stalling to get his words right. "You might be getting set up. The girl by herself, that's one thing, but ... What did I tell you about going around Tu Do Street, Fred, my boy?"

"Oh, Gordo. Don't be such a prude. I've been in combat, for Christ sakes. I can handle a few drunks."

"It's not the drunks I'm worried about; it's those women and unsavory Saigon cowboys.

Saigon cowboys were the Hell's Angels of Saigon, if you could call a preppy freshman an all-star quarterback. Instead of Harleys and Indians, they rode around on scooters. *Scooters!* They were pale and thin and apparently not good enough to be conscripted into a South Vietnamese Army that scooped up every male between the ages of seventeen and forty. We laughed at them as they picked on old women and children.

I dropped the subject. I wouldn't let anyone, even Gordo, spoil my budding feelings about Thieu. Something good had happened to me in these suburbs to Hell, and I just wanted to make it all so much bigger and last longer by telling Gordo about it. I did not realize how much I craved his approval, until I did not get it.

By now I had learned two things in Vietnam, and this was the first: Let go of things quickly. Easy to do this time, thanks to Deke, who had just prepared another incredible supper. For all I knew, it could have been the monkey Thieu and I joked about at the zoo, but it was delicious. I had never tasted food like this. It was a mix of traditional Vietnamese cuisine, everything that smelled so fresh and good from the wet market, mixed with that gutsy, Australian outback flavoring. Each morsel dissolved in my mouth and the aftertaste lingered just long enough to make me want more.

But the *other* thing that I learned was that things that you *do* let go of quickly never stray very far, and come back in their own time, and in their own way, and almost always with vengeance.

I wasn't even through the meal before suspicion about Thieu crept into my heart, and I was angry and hurt that Gordo put it there. I did not play the guitar that evening. Nor did I look Gordo in the eye until lights out.

XVII
The O.D. Circus

The next morning I got a call from Keith Askins, asking me to come in to see him that afternoon. I left the embassy and decided to kill time by exploring the waterfront. It was sunny and hot. The humidity was spiking and I longed for some rain to cool things off. I found that if I continued up Tu Do Street past the bars and Maxine's Supper Club I eventually would reach the river.

The river traffic was heavy that morning, with freighters and barges navigating the sharp elbow turn that the river took at this juncture. There was a strong stink of rotting fish along with the usual smells that came with the decaying docks. Garbage was piled high in places and I was reminded of the first day Dizzy and I had in Saigon. It seemed like such a long time ago. The humidity made it all smell worse. I sat there thinking for an hour about Thieu and what Gordo had said before getting my camera out and taking some pictures. An old beggar made his way slowly toward me and lifted his shirt to show me his wounds.

"VC die me!" he said. "VC die me!" And he lifted his shirt higher and I saw the horrible burn scars that he wore with bitterness. He was trying to elicit my sympathy by telling me he was shot by the Vietcong, and of course, he did. But I also wondered if people I had maimed in a failed attempt to kill them were doing the same thing, somewhere. I handed him a dollar and realized this guy was only in his forties. Man, I sure had trouble telling these people's ages. Suffering definitely made a person look old beyond his years, but what about Thieu? I thought she might be *younger* than what she looked. I was glad I had been wrong and we were only a year apart.

I wanted to talk to Thieu some more. Fuck Gordon. He was *wrong* about her and I did *not* need his permission to go to Tu Do Street. I marched in that direction just to show him I could, but I decided that it would be more prudent to go see Sgt. Askins and find out what he wanted. It still wasn't raining and so I passed up an empty pedicab. It was still early.

After about twenty minutes into an hour's walk it started pouring. Of course it did. That's the way things worked over here. I made it to his office soaking wet and out of breath from running. He took one look at me and started laughing. "Well, sorry to laugh, but you look like something the cat dragged in. Don't despair; I have good news. You can check into the Metropole Hotel tonight. Your roommate will already be there waiting for you. Do you know where it is?"

This was good news. After last night I felt like my friendship with the Australians was running thin. It was a good time for me to move out on my own. I assured him that I knew where it was and he handed me a voucher and told me it would be good for a month's stay. I thanked him profusely and asked when rehearsals would start.

"I'm not quite sure. We still have another member to add. We want it to be a five-piece band and the fellow we're waiting on still has not gotten his commanding officer's approval," he said with a frown. "But I can let you go pick out a bass to borrow so you can get your chops back up."

I liked that idea very much. He took me to the equipment room and I tried several basses until I found the one I wanted. It was a brand-new Fender Jazz Bass. I asked Keith to call me a cab and as we waited for my ride, we talked about music and clubs we had both worked in. The conversation was just getting interesting when my taxi drove up. We said our goodbyes and, throwing my bass in the back seat, I sat up front with the driver.

"Metropole Hotel," I said, and at once I was whisked away on another adventure.

I arrived at the hotel and went up to the desk clerk. I showed him my paperwork and he wrote my name in the register and gave me a key. I moved my stuff I had taken with me from the embassy and saw my new roommate, John Fortuna. As we had in the studio, we started talking and felt totally at ease with each other. He was tall and rail thin with the greatest bushy mustache I had seen in Nam.

"I'm excited about this band thing," he said. "I've been playing drums since I was ten years old and I never in my wildest dreams thought I would be playing in the Nam."

"Where is your normal hang?" I asked.

"I'm stationed in Da Nang. I'm a cook. How 'bout you?"

"I've been living in the jungle." I didn't feel like going into detail and he didn't push. We soon found out that we both liked getting high, and we spent the evening getting to better know each other. I like him from the start.

The day quickly came when we secured our fifth member and started to rehearse. I had managed to stay out of trouble during these last three weeks. I knew the city pretty well. Thieu and I had been visiting museums and had caught a few films in Vietnamese. She laughed at my attempt to speak her language. I had yet to meet her family. She had two little brothers and her mother. Her father had been arrested as a subversive two years ago and they had not heard from him since. They were sure he was dead but she always spoke of him in the present tense. Hell, maybe he was still alive.

We walked many miles each evening holding hands and enjoying one another's company. She would close up shop each day around 5 p.m. and we would go to Maxine's or the Brodard Café and have dinner. Our relationship was growing and she was all that I could think about when we were not together.

I know she felt the same about me and one night while we were walking hand in hand she stopped and turned toward me. She stood on her tiptoes and planted a kiss on my lips. I felt like a schoolboy, but it was a grown man who put his arms around her and embraced her little frame, and held her still for a few moments.

"I love you long time, GI," she said, only halfway joking.

"GI love Vietnam girl," I replied, in pidgin English. She twirled away from me like a ballerina and laughed that cute little laugh of hers.

We never spoke of this again.

We each knew the pitfalls that awaited American-Vietnamese relationships. They were almost all doomed from the start. Both governments frowned on such liaisons and I was leaving on tour in two weeks, and for home not long after that. What would happen to our love affair? What would happen to her when Saigon fell? We all could see the inevitability of that day. We were losing the war but no one spoke of it, like no one spoke of her father being dead.

December 8, 1970

Mom and Dad,

I'm really sorry it's been so long since I've written to you. I had to go to the field to pick up my stuff and have the CO sign the paperwork to release me. I stayed out longer then I wanted to. I'm so glad to get out of there. The troop went back up to Loc Ninh.

I've eaten nothing but steaks since I've been here. We practice in a studio at the Special Services compound. They have all new Fender equipment and the studio is air conditioned. The compound is a block from the Presidential Palace. The American Embassy and everything is close by. I'm taking a lot of pictures. I'm staying in a hotel downtown. The room is air conditioned and I have hot running water, a shower, and even a refrigerator. My room has a balcony where I can sit at night and watch all the people and the traffic on the street down below. I'm having a great time just being able to sleep late and relax. This is better than an R&R.

My leg and back still hurt but I'm afraid if I go to the doctor and he puts me in the hospital, I might miss the tour and I'll have to go back to my unit. It doesn't hurt that bad. I think it's just from all the walking around I do taking photos. I'm going to take it easy and I bet it will be OK. Please don't worry. I will be getting $4 a day plus $40 to buy civilian clothes to wear on stage. The four bucks a day is for food. It amounts to $120 a month raise. I don't know if I'll be able to call home again. I had to wait four hours today when I called. Everyone wants to call home for the holidays.

Did I tell you about the Life reporters? We picked them up and took them on a MEDCAP mission. MEDCAP is when we take doctors into isolated villages to look at the people. We set up around the village to protect the doctors. Well, they took a bunch of pictures of us. I hope they use them. That's about it for now. Have you been receiving my allotment checks each month? If not, tell me so I can straighten things out. I love and miss you very much. I know the next ninety days will go by fast for me because I'll be having a good time. When I go back to the field I'm only going to have 100 days left in the army. God bless you.
    Love,
    Fred

I stopped by to see the Australians a few times a week, never letting them know how I felt after what Gordo had said. I brought Thieu with me on several occasions and they fell in love with her. She charmed them with her quick wit and intelligence. Her impeccable table manners impressed Deke. Philip was taken by her knowledge of six languages and they spoke freely in French at the dinner table. I guess nobody expected someone so refined in a place that was busy falling into the abyss of war.

Gordo took me aside one evening, and I figured it was to scold me for hanging out with her, after all his warnings.

"She's a great catch, Fred. I'm happy for you," he said.

"But what?" I asked.

"No buts, this time mate. No, no, no. I just want you to be the happiest bloke on the planet. Thieu is a beauty in every way. What are you going to do with all this?"

"My intentions?" I thought hard about this and settled deep within the cushions of the overstuffed chair. I had been too quick to judge Gordon, *Gordo,* but just as quickly his fatherly influence was winning me over again.

"I'm confused, Gordo," I said. "I leave on a three-month tour in a few weeks and after that I will be returned to my unit to go out and continue fighting this fucking war. I'll only have 100 days left at that point. I can't take Thieu home with me. What do I do?" I pleaded.

"Son, you do what is right with that little girl. You ask her what she expects from this relationship and you don't lie to her and promise things that you can't deliver. A lot of women are looking for a ticket to a better life in the United States. You tell me that her father is in prison and that means that her family is being watched. It is no democracy here, just a brutal dictatorship run on greed and graft. *Of course* she wants to marry a bloke like you and leave this shit place post haste. She'll probably want to bring her whole bloody family with her."

He was watching me, to see if any of this was sinking in. "Do you know what true love is?" he asked.

"I think so. I've had two girlfriends back home."

"You're just a baby in the ways of love. Don't get angry with me again but you are nothing but a virgin when it comes to matters of the heart."

I kept my mouth shut. I knew he was right. As scary as it was, I would have to have a heart-to-heart talk with Thieu and do it soon.

Just not tonight.

I thanked Gordo for his wise words and went and joined my gal on the couch. We listened to some jazz and R&B records and when Wilson Pickett hit the groove she asked me to dance.

"Musicians don't dance," I protested.

"Sure they do. They make the best dancers. Come and have some fun," she laughed. I stood up and everyone started clapping their hands to the beat and I broke out in the Twist and Mashed Potato. I took a shot of whiskey to loosen me up and moved my body in time to the music, as Thieu grabbed my hands and then released as she flew across the room. She threw back her head and swayed to the music. Her long black hair flowed this way and that, and everything that was beautiful about this country was beautiful in her. She was laughing the whole time when I took her waist and moved her in and out. When the song was over we collapsed on the couch in hearty laughter. The next song was a slow "Dock of the Bay." I stood and offered her my hand, leading her to the center of the floor. I put my arms around her tiny waist and she held me tight. We moved back and forth and side to side, lightly swaying to the snap of the snare drum. Two and four. Two and four; the beat rattled on.

And then, a deep and lasting kiss. *Thank you*, Otis Redding.

Gordo was right. I had not been with many girls and I was amazed to find myself lying to her, saying, "I want to marry you and take you home." Oh shit!

I heard Gordon's voice in my head. *Don't lead the poor girl on.* I had opened up the floodgates. I walked her back to Tu Do around 7 p.m. and when we reached her stand, I stopped and looked at her.

"Look, about what I said. I have never been in love before. I'm not sure that I know what it is. We have only known each other four weeks." I kept stumbling, backtracking.

She sensed my retreat. She lowered her head and her voice when she spoke. "If I stay here, I will die."

She turned and started packing up her boxes. I stood in the pouring rain for ten minutes trying to figure this out, hoping the rain would wash away my latest travesties. It was too much for me. I returned to the hotel.

She was probably right. In the course of a single evening I offered and withdrew a chance for her salvation. There it is.

I met John Fortuna for a nightcap across the street. I had found John easygoing and, more importantly, he had a nonjudgmental ear. We had become close the previous two weeks. Living together for ten days, he had come to know everything about me and I about him. We had spent every night smoking Carltons and talking about everything under the sun. Or should I say stars. We sat out on the balcony as I told him why I showed up soaking wet.

"The words of a horny man," John said, when he heard about my blunder. He saw me grimace, and he turned to me and added, "I don't mean to be cruel, man, but you brought this shit on yourself. What you were saying, and what she was feeling — that's not love; that's desperation."

We each took another draw.

"In the long run, we have more serious stuff to talk about tonight," he said, changing a subject that could have no happy outcome.

"Yeah?"

"Yeah. We sure are playing crappy songs."

"I know, man. Nothing hip," I said. Once again, I let something go that would come back before I was really free of it. Like Charlie, waiting until my guard was down.

"Let's talk to Mike and the guys tomorrow and see what we can do. It's just a matter of Mike learning the lyrics."

At the morning rehearsal we cornered Mike and Larry, the guitar player, and told them about how unhappy we were with the song selection. Larry immediately got defensive. "Just give me the record. I can learn anything."

We soon discovered that Mike's taste in music was the real issue here. We gingerly asked him if we needed to do so many show songs and standards when our audience obviously leaned more toward rock and roll. He was taken aback. "Well, why didn't you say anything sooner? We're pretty set on our song list."

"Maybe we can learn a few Beatles songs off their new Abbey Road record," I said.

John jumped in, "*Come Together, right now. Over me.* That really grooves. 'Something,' and 'Here Comes The Sun.' All good stuff."

Mike, Marvin, and Larry jawed on it. John and I didn't realize it at the time, but lines were being drawn. It would be the two hippies, Fred and John, against the Three Stooges, Mike, Marvin and Larry, from then on. They, with the very conservative musical tastes and John and I with the balls-to-the walls rock-and-roll attitude. We were in a fucking war zone and adrenaline was the drug of the day. Nothing tame or lame for us.

John and I were not afraid to mix it up, so in the end we learned those three new Beatles' songs and two by Cream off "Wheels of Fire." We rehearsed every day with the weekends off. Askins was a cool boss and he let me bring Thieu to rehearsals. The Three Stooges thought me crazy for having a Vietnamese girlfriend, but John thought it was really cool, and, in spite of what he told me—calling it all testosterone poisoning—he was a romantic and often accompanied us on our little dates to museums and gardens.

John was a great photographer as well as a kick-ass drummer, and I traveled to the PX with him to have his film developed. On the ride to the PX he told me about a new thing that he had discovered. *OJs.* Opium joints. They came prepackaged the same as Carltons but under the brand name of Montclair 100s. I told him I would be interested in that and for him to cop some when he got the chance. I didn't meet up with Thieu that evening, preferring to hang out with John in our room, listening to a cassette tape that one of his friends had mailed to him. We stripped down to our skivvies in the night heat and humidity and smoked the Montclairs. Our high was peaking, when suddenly there was a knock on the door. Being paranoid, we flushed the roaches down the toilet and checked each other's eyes.

It was the bellhop.

"Mister Fred. You have a visitor." I bolted upright and grabbed my shirt off the chair and quickly got dressed.

"Who is it?" I asked.

"A girl. Rules state you cannot have girl in your room, Mister Fred. Must talk to her outside. Yes?"

"Yes." I grabbed my key and made my way down the three flights of stairs to find Thieu standing in the lobby, crying and distressed. The kid was with her.

"What's wrong, Thieu?" I asked, worried about her, and pretending I didn't know the answer.

"You never came by," she sobbed. "I waited and waited until after 6:30 and you weren't there."

She faced me like an armed Claymore. Face Toward Enemy.

"Oh, Thieu, I thought we had discussed this. You cannot have illusions that we are anything more than friends."

But really, we had never discussed anything. It was just me, telling her the way it was, and I was about to do it again.

"I can't always be at your beck and call. I have a band getting ready for tour, and John and I have been working on songs tonight." I put a hand on each of her sloping shoulders, to keep her from making herself any smaller. "It's going to be like that from now on. You have to get used to it. It doesn't mean I don't care for you any less. Just give me the freedom to change plans from time to time."

The kid looked at me, all-knowing. Him, I couldn't bullshit. I was glad he was a mute.

Thieu was scaring me with this behavior. She imploded, detonating before my very eyes. I tried to pass it off as a hormonal thing, but Gordo was right; I was still a novice in the ways of the heart. I calmed her down and sent her home. John had come down to close ranks, and gave the kid some money and they left quietly.

John said nothing to me as we trudged back upstairs and went back to work on the songs, but my heart was just not into it. I was worried about the monster I had created. John picked a few chords; I picked shrapnel from my soul. Fucking Claymores.

December 13, 1970

Dear Mom and Dad,

Just a short note to say I'm fine and having a great time in Saigon. This is just like a fantastic vacation. I've taken a lot of pictures. The drummer and I go downtown every night and enjoy the people and the city. I'm going to the museum tomorrow. I don't even have much time to write because john and I are always going here and there. The band is coming around nicely and I'm so happy to be playing again. I am very happy so don't even worry about me anymore. Well I got to go. Hope you are all fine and in as good of spirits as I am. I love you very much and miss you. Say hi to my sister and the kids.

Love,

Fred

The tour was set and we were to start in the southernmost section of the country down in the Delta, a place called Soc Trang. We were all excited, and on Christmas Eve John and I decided to celebrate with the opium joints. He unpacked them from the Montclair packs and crumpled up the foil and the cellophane and threw it in the trash. Once lit, we wasted no time in smoking it down to the filter. The smell was sweet and pungent and I could tell at once that I was smoking something much more powerful than marijuana. When Johnny put the pack down, I grabbed it and took out and lit another cigarette.

"Are you crazy, or what?" Johnny stared into my eyes.

My eyes were on fire. I was more loaded than I had ever been in my life.

Then it hit me.

Hot, hot flashes followed at once by the bitter cold shaking of a man strapped to an iceberg. In addition to all of this, I felt nauseous and I felt like someone was taking a hammer to my head. While I could still speak, I turned to Johnny and muttered very calmly, "I think I'm overdosing on this dope."

I tried to stand, but fell. My head was about to explode from the pain. I crawled into my bed and shouted, "John! Do you hear me? I'm OD'ing or having an allergic reaction to this shit. *Do something!*"

I lay there alternating between extreme heat and excessive cold. All the while my head would not let up an iota of the pain and I tucked up into the fetal position.

"Oh shit!" I had walked off countless battlefields without a scratch, only to find myself reeling from a tiny, blossoming flower.

"*Jesus!* John boy! Get me to a hospital!"

He was loaded, too, but he seemed to be holding it together.

I was not a lightweight when it came to the world of getting high. I was angry at myself for lighting up that second joint. I should have left everything alone but, no, I had to always drink, smoke, and do all the vices with more gusto than the average guy. Who was I kidding? The average guy would not be smoking opium in the first place.

"Shit, Fred!" I knew he must be paranoid about getting in trouble if the authorities found us together this fucked up. But I also knew he'd come through for me, anyway. "There is a first-aid clinic across the street. Most guys go there to be treated for the clap but there are real doctors there. I saw one walking out this morning."

"*Please.* Take me there," I begged.

John collected my ID and wallet. He put my orders in an envelope and walked me down the stairs. I felt like I was going to lose my lunch on the second landing, but made it to the street OK. I put my arm around his shoulder and let him guide me across the street, avoiding motorbikes and cyclists and some very aggressive pedestrians. When we reached the waiting room, John decided that he had fulfilled the best-buddy end of the bargain and scampered away before anybody could make a connection between the two of us, and I was cool with that. A first sergeant who I suppose was the head nurse handed me a medical history form and checked my vitals.

"What seems to be the problem?" he asked. I could hear Christmas music playing out of a radio in the examination room.

"I believe I'm overdosing on opium," I said, with the utmost attempt at clarity.

He looked me over. "Pretty wild Christmas party?"

"Not at all. In fact, I forgot what day it is. Is it really Christmas Eve?" I felt myself fading again as another crew of doctors and nurses swarmed to my side.

"Let me get a blood sample. How did you ingest the opium?"

"I smoked it. How long do the effects last?"

"It varies with each person's tolerance. I'm not so certain that's what we're looking at, however. The blood test should lead us in the right direction. Want me to dim the lights while we wait?" he asked.

I don't know if it was just because of the holiday season or if this sergeant was just a super nice guy. Whatever the case may be, he kept me from having a bad trip and made a miserable experience a little less stressful with his nonjudgmental behavior. After a little over an hour he returned and asked, "Been taking your malaria pills?"

"Not since I got out of the field. Nobody has issued them to me here in Saigon," I said, as my head throbbed.

"Well, the good news is that you're not OD'ing from opium. You have malaria."

"Thank God," I muttered under my breath.

"How's that?" he asked.

"Blood, yeah, I was talking about how the mosquitoes drank my blood. I get them high and they give me malaria. How fucked is that? I'm leaving on a tour in two days. Can you just give me some medicine?"

"Sorry, man, but you're going straight to the hospital. You're going to have to postpone your trip for a week."

"You've got to be kidding me! Sergeant, this is a matter of life or death."

"You bet it is. That's why I'm admitting you. You won't be able to function out there anyway, till all this passes. Look at it as a holiday rest," he said, trying to lift my spirits.

And so on Christmas Eve, 1969, I was readmitted to the Third Field Hospital in Saigon. My run of incredible luck had reached its end. I ran into a block wall at over 100 miles an hour and I was crushed.

December 26, 1969

Dear Mom and Dad,

Sorry I haven't written but I'm in the hospital again. I was admitted on Christmas Eve with malaria. I'll call you as soon as I get out. The doc says I might possibly get out tomorrow. It was a slight case of vivex malaria and nothing to worry about. I feel fine now. There were four guys from my troop here. The troop moved from Loc Ninh to Bu Dup which is closer to Cambodia. They made contact the first day. I'm glad I wasn't with them. They said it was terrible. My band went to Canto today to play for four days. The rhythm guitarist is playing bass and I'll rejoin them when they come back. Well I better get some rest. I love you both dearly and miss you.
Fred

The start of the tour came faster than I had expected it to. Don't get me wrong. The band was ready. We had an hour's worth of material worked up and we had long since put the finishing touches on our arrangements. John and I had gotten used to living among the people. Eating their food, going to their museums and taking a ton of photographs had been the way we passed the time. Now I lay flat on my back again in almost the same bed and certainly the same ward as before. I looked over the Christmas cards sent from fifth-grade schoolchildren in Ohio. They were handmade holiday cards that doubled as get-well cards. They were cute and lifted my morale up a few notches thinking about the girls back home. The older of my two nieces was around that age. Suddenly I heard a commotion at the nurses' station.

There was much screaming and shouting and if I listened hard enough I could hear a tiny voice calling out my name.

"Where is Fred? Where is he? I want to see him right now," Thieu screamed, as if someone was hurting her.

"Ma'am, if you will just calm down we will let you see your husband."

Husband! What had she told them? My headache suddenly exploded like a B-52 raid. I never in my wildest imagination thought that I would make Thieu a war bride. Did she think I would bring her and her family over to the United States? Did I set this in motion with a single kiss and a few words, misspoken? That was an accident, like that kid waking up in the jungle, babbling.

I saw that kid, whose name I had already forgotten, who woke up talking in his sleep and was punished with a bullet in the head. Wait? Did he take it in the head or was that somebody else? I couldn't focus. *Herman? You still got my six? Herman, I need you, man.*

I took a deep breath and sat up in bed just as they brought her in the ward.

"Your wife is here to see you, buddy," the nurse said, as she brought Thieu into view.

"She's not my wife," I said, too late, as the nurse had already left to attend to another patient.

"Not my wife," I mumbled to the empty hospital walls.

"Fred!" She charged over and threw herself across my chest. "What happened to you? I went to visit you for Christmas and John told me you were here, but he was packing, getting ready to leave on big trip. He didn't tell me anything!" She sat up and I kept her at arm's length when she leaned in on me again. She was trying hard to hold it together, but when she slipped into pidgin I knew she was losing it.

"Thieu," I said, as I pulled the covers up to my face, "you always knew that I was going to leave you. There should be no surprises there.

We've only known each other for about three weeks and here you are telling these people that you're my wife. You are not my wife."

"It was the only way they would let me see you." She jerked her body upright and started crying. "One day you will just get up and go and I will never see you again. Is this what you want?" She cried into her hands.

Just then the nurse popped her head in and asked of Thieu, "Is everything all right, sweetie? Can I get you anything?"

"Can *I* have something for anxiety?" I asked, only half kidding as my head pounded.

"I'll see what the doctor says." She disappeared again.

My mind rolled back two months ago to when I was in the field. Things were easier there. I was missing the adrenaline rush that came with walking the thin line of insanity. Everything was crystal clear out in the jungle, where I constantly carried an M-16 locked and loaded with the safety off. If I had the Thieu problem in An Loc I would have put a round in her head and walked away. She would be part of a body count that I could abandon like the butt of a cigarette and move on.

What? What the fuck was I thinking!

Had I really turned into what the Army wanted — a trained killer who could take a life and think nothing of it? I had done a lot of shitty things in my time over here. My body count was respectable and I even killed a child. A *body count? Respectable?* Had I really turned? This thought scared me more than anything had ever frightened me in my life.

I pointed my words toward the helpless little girl before me, and fired. "You have to leave. Wait until I get out of the hospital, and we will talk. Right now, Thieu, you have to leave."

I said this in a tone so cold that I had trouble believing it was me speaking. As the words found their mark, I closed my eyes, and in that darkness I searched for any signs of life in that littered battlefield of my soul, anything decent in me that might still have survived, and was devastated to see that I, indeed, had really turned.

I opened my eyes and saw only Thieu, standing, trembling now, by my bedside. I did not love her. She was just a hostage I had taken.

"You have to leave. Now."

XVIII
The Coward's Way Out

What an experience this was turning out to be. The band returned to Saigon after a few days in the Delta ironing out the kinks. John told me it was a drag without me there. He said I had left him alone with the Three Stooges and he would find a way to get even with me. We weren't scheduled to go back out until after New Year's. This was good news as it meant that I could celebrate New Year's Eve with John. I still had not decided what to do with Thieu so I did not include her in our plan.

Word on the street was that the Rex Hotel was the place to party on New Year's. This week also found the five of us shopping for band uniforms. In an unsurprising three-to-two vote, it was decided that we would have a tailor make us striped pants and silk shirts in matching purple to wear on stage.

Outvoted, John and I could only laugh at these ridiculous clown costumes. In a *surprising* move, though, John and I found a majority to honor my Christmas Eve shenanigans and name the band the O.D. Circus. The Stooges thought that it referred to Olive Drab. It was John's and my private joke.

I avoided the Tu Do Street district and did not see Thieu. But, by chance, I ran into Gordo and Deke at the wet market.

"I heard you had malaria. Thank God. I was afraid it was Deke's cooking. I came straightaway to the hospital when I heard — Christ, we all did — but you had checked out by then."

I was hoping he had not heard why I had checked myself in.

"I don't know what you see in opium. Come by for some good Australian beer to flush it out of your system."

Shit.

"I suppose you know all about Theiu, then."

"Your wife?"

"Ah, Gordon. I just don't know what to do. She's young. I am, too, I'll grant you but you don't see me carrying on like that," I said.

"She is playing for more stakes than you are, my friend. She is playing for her life. I told you before that you're her ticket out of here. Oh, I'm sure she has strong feelings for you, but in the end, you are just a path to a better life. Did you set down your intentions like I told you?"

"Only half-assed."

"Back in Australia, or stateside, breaking up with a woman can be a process, something you edge into, in fits and starts. You don't have that luxury here. It's an event, not a process. You do it, and it's done. Anything less is cruel."

Hard to let go, hard to let go, but Gordo was right. We agreed to meet later and flush the opium out of my system.

I snaked my way through food stalls and vendors, some under the shade of makeshift tents, some squatting on a blanket with whatever they were selling before them, over to Tu Do and found Thieu selling her own wares outside the Mumbo Jumbo bar. The music inside was blasting but I caught her attention. She smiled as if things were all right and we moved to a spot where we could talk, away from the noise.

"I missed you," she said. "Are you feeling better? You still look pale."

"I'm all right," I lied. "It's been crazy," I lied again.

She grabbed my hand and asked, "What are we doing for New Year's Eve?"

It was as if she had never come to see me in the hospital.

"We need to talk," I quickly said, "about us. You have to understand that there *is* no we."

She let go of my hand and turned her face. When she turned back to look at me, a monsoon began to well up in her eyes. "I'm sorry about the hospital. I was afraid of losing you so quickly. Everyone loses people quickly, here. Everybody. Every day. I hear stories."

And one of those stories was mine. And mine … and mine … and mine. I lost so many, so quickly. I did not want to hear her talk like that. I didn't want her to be a human being I could understand and relate to. I had watched as my comrades, friends, were torn apart, and dead before they hit the ground, or died cradled in my lap. Yes, I knew all about losing people.

Thieu I would lose, by choice, by my own hand, and not to the greed of some hungry bullet, or a piece of shrapnel the size of a BB.

"I'm sorry, but that's where we are headed. You know that I will go home. I can't plan a future that includes us. There is too big a gulf between our worlds. I like you. I like you a lot and have fun being with you and doing things together. Can't we still at least be best friends?" The coward's way out.

"I would like that very much," she said, fighting off tears, sensing a reprieve from the inevitable. I saw how beautiful she was and saw the slow spiral of the bullet trained on her heart. I, too, became tearful. Maybe there *is* something left of my soul.

We hugged each other, and now that I had crushed any expectations of a future together she found the grace to step away, wipe her eyes, smile and say, "So how about New Year's, buddy boy?" My heart raced with joy and I wondered if I was throwing away a good, happy, love-filled life.

"The Rex Hotel," I replied.

I had supper with the Aussies that evening, and under Dr. Gordo's supervision began to flush the remnants of opium out of my system.

"Things feel a lot better getting the whole truth out there with Thieu," I said.

"If you never have to slink around rubbish heaps of lies you're a happier man for it. Another weight has been lifted from your shoulders. Keep shedding the burdens, Fred. I'm proud to call you a friend," Gordon shook out the ashes of his pipe, refilled it, and lit it up again. As an afterthought, he said, "In this place, sometimes it's better to be in love than to *have* a future."

XIX
The Colonel and Jack Ruby

New Year's Eve came, and John, Thieu and I went to the party at the Rex Hotel. As we arrived at the front door I heard someone call my name. I looked around and saw Toxy French, the general's Jeep driver, waving at me from the vehicle. I excused myself from my friends and walked over and shook his hand.

"You know, if I hadn't met you I would most likely be back out in the field. That lift to Special Services opened so many doors for me. I just want to thank you for being friendly to a guy that needed a friend," I told him.

"Not to worry, man. Glad to see you got a job in the rear. Real sweet. Good luck, and have fun tonight," he replied, and was gone.

The party was in full swing when we arrived. They had an open bar and a magnificent banquet spread out for the guests. The band was playing tunes from all eras of modern American music. Thieu asked me to dance and before I knew it I was sweating on the dance floor. The girl loved to dance. John came up to me and said we should serve ourselves some food before they ran low. I agreed and grabbed a reluctant Thieu from the dance floor and went and stood in line for the food. I had my eyes on the jumbo shrimp.

"Great party," Thieu said to Johnny.

"I thought it might be fun. There are a lot of reporters here. Check it out—David Brinkley is making the rounds," said Johnny. "I was going to shake his hand, but he was holding a drink."

At midnight we stood in the terrace on the roof and watched the fireworks light up the sky. I concealed my shame to be standing there celebrating with civilians and officers on a world holiday, as I thought about my buddies still out in the field. It was a regular Fourth of July show and I watched in wonderment and remembered the night the Special Forces blew their fu gas. I hoped for a better year in 1970. It was already starting out beyond my wildest expectations. A tour with a band!

Just like in the World.

As the night receded, I walked Thieu a few blocks from the Rex, to her home, where I had never been.

There was no goodnight kiss. I was not sure why.

John and I stayed in our room on New Year's Day, hungover from the party. The next day we left on tour. I finally got around to writing a letter home.

13 January, 1970

Dear Mom and Dad,

I'm fine but this tour is really hectic. Yesterday we landed in Ban Me Thuot and nobody knew we were supposed to be here so these Air force guys took us to their Villa down town. Ban Me Thuot is the provincial capital of this province and it's real nice. We couldn't get out of here today because of bad weather. Everywhere we go we are treated like Kings. And the band is really sounding great. Our lead singer is the best I've ever worked with. He's one of these guys with 13 years of voice training. He has a fantastic ear for music. Well I haven't written because of the frantic pace we have been going. We have been all over the Delta and now we are in the Central Highlands. We played in Nha Trang two nights ago and it has the most beautiful beach I have ever seen. The water is so clear. You can't imagine what a fantastic experience this is. Tomorrow we go to Cam Ranh Bay

for 4 days then up to Da Nang. I won't get any mail until we get
back to Saigon so if you sent me Bobby's address, I won't get it
in time. I don't know what else to say except that I love you and
miss you. I have 135 days left in the Army. I haven't been sick
since I got out of the hospital so don't worry about that malaria.
I feel great. Here's a picture at Soc Trang in the Delta.
        Love,
        Fred

When we first hit the road we started at the southernmost tip of
South Vietnam. We were gradually going to work our way up to the
DMZ but we often found ourselves back at Saigon. This was our base
of operations. It took a few shows to hit our stride and start playing
with cohesiveness. We traveled by helicopter, airplane, and Gordo and
the boys ferried us over to Ban Me Thuot.

The Three Stooges were all based as clerks in Saigon. I had been
to Mike's building once and his quarters were about as nice as they
came in the city. They were a little put off with the traveling. Johnny
and I thought it was a gas. John had been a cook up at Da Nang. He
was looking forward to our show there in front of his friends and I had
a cousin stationed there. The trick was going to be finding him on that
sprawling base.

Of course, the Three Stooges freaked out over the famous Ban
Me Thuot sniper. I didn't tell them about him until Gordo had landed
the plane. I had already made that run and knew the hazards of the
Jeep ride to headquarters. Larry almost shit his pants as the first
round glanced off the rear of the Jeep. John and I laughed our asses off
watching how scared those guys were. To them they were at the front
and in a perceived battle.

This sniper meant nothing to me. Gordon had already proven
to me what a bad shot the guy was. Some day that sniper would get
lucky. As I had learned in the beginning, they were patient and single
minded, but the five members of the band made it out of Ban Me

Thuot in one piece. We eventually made our way up north to Da Nang where my cousin Bobby was stationed.

January 18, 1970

Dear Mom and Dad,

Well here I am in Da nang. It's kind of a bummer because the water is off limits due to rip-tides. We are staying at the R&R center at China Beach. The last time I wrote you we were in Ban Me Thuot. After we left there we played at the 6th Convalescent Center in Cam Ranh Bay. It is right on the beach and it was the best crowd we've played for. They gave us a whole ward to ourselves to stay in. Then on the 15th we played for the Special Forces group. Cam Ranh Bay is really a beautiful place with the ocean and mountains all around it. Like I said before, they treat us like Kings and I'm having such a great time playing and traveling around. Tonight we played at the Special Forces Camp outside Da nang. Everywhere we've played for the Special Forces, they have really appreciated it. Tomorrow we go to Quan Tri which is up by the DMZ. Then we come back to Da Nang for two days then it's back to Saigon. I haven't gotten any mail since we left Saigon because they keep our mail there. So I won't know how you are or what's new until I get back there. I hope you are all fine and not worrying about me because I am fine and having a great time. Pray I get another tour. I don't want to ever go back out in the field but if I have to I guess I will. Has Bobby left for Vietnam yet? If he hasn't, tell him to bring warm civilian clothes because it gets pretty cold here at night. And the Air Force guys can wear civilian clothes. Well, that's about it. I miss everyone very much and I'll see you in 134 days,

Love,

Fred

Staying in that ward by ourselves was one of the ugliest experiences of the tour. By the time we hit Cam Ranh Bay, Nixon was winding the war down. He was withdrawing troops and not sending in replacements. This was the beginning of the end of the war. The morale of the wounded troops was at a low and it seems like everyone was strung out on heroin. Guys would come into our sleeping quarters at all hours of the night in their wheelchairs and gurneys, missing legs and other body parts. They would shoot up dope right in front of us and offer to get us high.

John and I didn't go that route and routinely declined their offers. We were musicians so I guess they thought we were cool and they felt comfortable doing things in front of us.

One such soldier who had given up the war and his life was my old friend Ruby. He was still in the hospital, with burns all over his body and he had found the easy way out of reality.

"It's good to see you, Ruby. Do you remember me?" I asked as one of his buddies wheeled him into our quarters.

"I remember you. How's your buddy, Daffy"

"Dizzy," I corrected.

"Yeah, Fred and Dizzy. What's up?" he asked with a foggy brain. I looked at him and at the scene around the ward and was taken aback. I looked at the burn scars on his face and realized he had deeper wounds to carry than the visible ones. I had nothing more to say to him.

The colonel from the Special Forces heard us perform and he just fell in love with us. He wanted to make sure that all of his troops got a chance to have a show and he extended us out for another four days. We also were scheduled to tape a show on AFVN in the television station in Da Nang. The Three Stooges were worried about appearing on TV. John and I had plenty of experience on radio and television but these guys were amateurs. We showed up to the taping and despite Larry's fear, the show went well. I looked at the technicians and thought, *What a fucking job these guys have.* There was so much involved in supporting a war effort. I felt grateful for my chance to get behind the scenes and out from the main theater. We returned to Saigon to a stack of mail. Three and a half weeks worth of mail cluttered our beds. I looked at John and said, "This shit just makes me more homesick than anything else. What do you miss most at home?"

"Besides my family?" he asked.

"Yeah, what is the one thing that you can do at home but not do here? For me it's hanging around the clubs on the Sunset Strip and being a rock star."

"You're a rock star here," he replied. "Everyone here loves the band. That Special Forces colonel was one of your biggest groupies."

We laughed and I decided to go look for Thieu. *A process*, I reminded myself, recalling Gordo's words. I wasn't ready to let go completely. I grabbed my key from the table and scurried down the stairs to the street. I caught a pedicab and had him take me to Tu Do Street and before I knew it I was standing outside a bar with Thieu. We embraced, and she told me she had missed me. I told her I had missed her, too, and told her all about my adventures on the road.

She laughed about my stories of the Three Stooges and how they were scared of the rough flights we had taken. I told her about every place we had visited. Before long, I had dropped my defenses and fallen back into the trap. All I knew was that I felt very comfortable with that girl. Comfort was hard to come by. We sat talking on a bench in the park when she surprised me.

"I have a business proposition for you," she said.

"What kind of business could I possibly do?"

"You can buy a refrigerator at the PX for under $400. My mom has a friend willing to pay $650 for it. Are you interested?"

"I have to leave again tomorrow, late afternoon. If we do it we're going to need a van or small truck to carry it, but sure, I'm in."

"Why don't you come over to my house for dinner tonight? I want you to meet my mother. You remember the way?"

I went back to the Metropole to talk to Johnny. I arrived and found him still reading his letters from home.

"John, are you ready for a little larceny? Ready to commit a class A felony?" I halfway joked.

"Sure, what do you have in mind? We've broken just about every law here already."

"A little black market operation. I'm going to need you to help me carry a refrigerator tomorrow morning." I liked the mild adrenaline rush of being a black marketeer, like the ones I had seen in the black-and-white WWII films on television. The danger seemed pretty tame. What consequence, if we got caught, could compare to the consequence of being drafted?

This deviant little enterprise was just part of the string of entrails that made up the guts of war. No real discussion about it. It was settled; we would do it.

I showered and said goodbye to John and I found my favorite pedicab driver in the queue downstairs. It is not that I no longer worried that he might be one of the bad guys; I no longer cared if he was. I gave him Thieu's address. He pedaled toward the Central Cathedral and the neighborhood soon changed into tenements. I found her house and paid the driver.

It was a walk-up flat in a nondescript building with plastic flowers decorating the common hallway. I knocked, and the door was immediately opened by Thieu. At once the aroma of garlic, onions, ginger and fish sauce filled my nostrils and I stepped into the world Thieu inhabited with her mother and two brothers.

Her mother stood in the shadows and she was a most beautiful long-haired woman in her mid-forties. I could see where Thieu inherited her grace and beauty. Her name was Lau Xuan and she invited me in to sit on a chair that barely held my frame. I sat and looked around the room.

The apartment was a one-room flat painted that dull hospital green of the Third Field. I looked around and saw a curtain drawn to create a sleeping room. A baby cried from behind the curtain and a very precocious two-year-old ran naked around the front room.

The kitchen area was cluttered with pots and pans, most of them simmering or steeping. A blackened wok was nested over a slight blue flame, and a cleaver dangled on a hook over a well-worn butcher block next to the sink.

"It is so nice to finally meet you, Fred," she said, in perfect English. "You're all Thieu talks about. I understand you're a musician." She poured me a cup of tea. I was embarrassed.

Thieu was dressed in a light pink *ao doi* and her mother wore a beautifully laced powder blue one. I found it easy to talk to her and before I knew it, dinner was ready. We sat on the floor around a small table that was low to the ground and Madame Lau served hot steaming rice with a noodle soup for starters. The food was absolutely delicious. It was better than anything Deke had ever prepared and we fell into quiet dinner talk. I complimented her on her cooking.

"Thieu is the gourmet chef around here. You have to taste her cooking," she said, as if trying to sell me a wife. I took note of it and went on eating.

"She gets that from her father, I'm afraid," she said sadly. "He is the real cook." She made a small ball of rice and passed it through the lips of the two-year old.

"I understand he's a professor," I said, broaching the delicate subject of her absent husband.

"He's in prison," she said softly. "No one has heard from him for two years. We're afraid he might be dead." As she said "two years" she glanced quickly at Thieu. Something she did not mean to say. It wasn't hard to do the math. I startled myself with the thought that the baby behind the curtain was not really Thieu's brother, but her own child. She never let on.

"The government arrested him?" I asked.

"Yes. He's a human rights worker for an NGO and he uncovered some government maltreatment of some indigenous people."

I was amazed at her command of the English language and the brutality of the government that I was sent here to fight for and maybe die for.

"Does the government harass you?" I asked.

"They sometimes watch the house and I think they are interfering with Thieu's career."

"In what way?"

"She has passed her exams for the university, but somehow they keep telling us that papers are either lost or filled out incorrectly. She's still waiting for her diploma."

"That is so unfair."

"The gentleman buying the refrigerator tomorrow is an old acquaintance of my husband. Please don't speak to him of any of this."

"So did you secure a van?" I asked, changing the subject.

"Yes, everything is in place."

"Did he give you the money?

"It's all here." She laid out a stack of twenty-dollar bills and I counted them just to make sure.

"We're all set, then?" she asked.

"Everything is Jake," I said, forgetting that these two women were not American and might not understand the 1940's reference I had just made. But they understood perfectly what I meant, and I rose, picking up my plate.

Thieu and I cleaned up the kitchen, against the mild protest of her mother, and when we were finished with our after-dinner tea, Madame Lau said, "You should spend the night with us, so we can get an early start." She handed me a pillow and blanket from her cupboard, and stepped into the bathroom. I turned to Thieu and raised my eyebrows and opened my eyes wide.

"Mother is a very modern woman," she whispered. "She has an open mind about sex. Please don't be prudish." I bowed to her mother who was now wearing a sleeping sarong, and followed Thieu to her bed. We pulled the curtain shut. She shared the space with her two little brothers. The infant had a cradle, by the side of the bed. The two-year-old had a mat on the floor in the corner. The mother slept on a bamboo mat herself, on the other side of the curtain, and turned out the lights.

I was ill at ease with the whole arrangement. The baby was asleep, but the two year old continued to stare curiously at me while Thieu knelt down and stroked his head and covered him with a light blanket, as I imagine she did every night. In a few minutes, he closed his eyes, and I could hear the rhythmic breathing on the other side of the curtain, as Thieu's mother fell easily to sleep. But, still.

Thieu stood and eased toward me, satisfied that the young one had fallen asleep. "Why do I feel like I have been set up?" I asked, almost mouthing the words instead of speaking them.

She put a finger to my mouth. "Shush. It's going to be OK." She raised her lips to mine and, and I dropped the bedding. We kissed, as we often had before. I never told Gordon, I never told Johnny, but Thieu and I had never made love. I just let them assume that we did.

"We shouldn't do this," I moaned, half-heartedly. "This doesn't change a thing. I'm still leaving on the road tomorrow."

"Haven't you learned by now that in my country you have to live each day as if it's your last?" she countered.

She was right. Of course, she was right. I picked her up and lay her down on the bed as we kissed again. My hesitation vanished as I became intoxicated with her kisses and lost in the curves of her body. I slipped her from the *ao doi* and I kissed her breasts, small but firm. Her nipples were hard as I moved my tongue around them. As my tongue explored the tip of her nipple, she reached down and gently moved my head to her rising and falling stomach. I grabbed her panties and gently slid them down her legs. She sighed. I kissed her all over her body and she giggled when I tickled her thighs with my chin.

Seeing her naked, I realized I had never been with a woman who didn't shave her legs or underarms, but the shock could not break the spell. The sudden slope of her waist made me want to hold her forever. We made gentle, passionate love late into the night.

After we had paused, as lovers do, to feel a deep appreciation of each other, she mounted me and we began again, this time wilder and with an animal abandon I had never experienced. She finally collapsed on my chest, both of us breathing hard and smelling the sweet fragrance of our love-making. This was a woman whom only days before I had actually visualized shooting. I was happy, and, for the first time in this country, I felt peace. We fell into a deep slumber that comes only with the spent energy and exhaustion of a passionate act of love.

Around 3 a.m. the baby started crying.

"Thieu!" her mother blurted, forcefully but not harsh. Thieu quietly picked up the infant and expertly rocked him in her arms. I was completely surprised when she lowered him and placed him to her bosom and started feeding him. Satisfied, the baby fell back to sleep and grandmother came into the quarter to take the baby to bed with her. I did not think to cover myself before it was too late. Thieu slipped back next to me.

"He's yours, then?" I whispered. She turned her back to me and quietly sobbed.

In the morning Thieu served me tea in bed. I lingered as long as I could, wanting to avoid her mother. I could never imagine something like this happening in Montebello. My dignity, Madame Lau's dignity and that of her daughter, I added to the body count.

As promised, a van materialized on the street, the driver handing me the keys. Thieu rode with me to the hotel to pick up Johnny. She looked a lot like her mother. I could not escape feeling that the two of them were complicit in a scheme with farther-reaching consequences than just selling a refrigerator on the black market. They had conspired for me to sleep with the sole daughter of a family that would need some way out when the war was lost, and I ignored all the trip-flares. I dismissed the thought and fear I had of future reports of a false—or real—pregnancy. Thieu looked so pretty, sitting beside me.

As we jostled through the traffic, I didn't feel we were breaking the law or starting a crime spree. It was more like we were doing a favor for a friend. Making the extra money sure would come in handy.

I was running low on cash. I had been living high on the hog eating at Maxine's every night.

We picked up John at the hotel and we were at the PX by 10 in the morning. We found the refrigerator and John went outside to wait for me as I paid. We slipped a guy five bucks to help John load the damn thing and ride with us to deliver it. Pain in my back lingered, in spite of the meds, and there was no way I was going to heft a refrigerator.

Thieu directed us to our destination, a colonial house set behind a courtyard full of blossoming flowers. It was a well-kept garden and it reminded me of the grounds at the zoo. The buyer appeared and tried to help carry it.

"That's OK, sir. We have it," I told him. He gave me a curious look and took a quick glance at Johnny and the helper. He wore wire-rimmed glasses and had on a sweater vest, even in the heat. He was thin as a rail and very distinguished-looking. I figured him for a professor, as he certainly had that scholarly air about him.

"You can make a lot of money doing this," he said. "I have a lot of friends in the market for American goods. They are so much cheaper at the Post Exchange, it is hard to believe. You can mark the price up thirty or forty percent, and they still save money," he said, like a true capitalist. They put the box down in his kitchen.

"Sorry, but I'm afraid this is a one-time deal. I leave Saigon this evening."

He shook his head and frowned. "Too bad. This could be such a great deal for both of us." So he wasn't offering me friendly advice; he was making a business proposition.

I left it open. I was still holding out hope that I could stay in Saigon after the tour ended. "If I make it back, I'll look you up."

That afternoon, while we still had the van we made our way to a C-130 transport plane waiting for us at Tan Son Nhut. We boarded quickly, rain pelting us as we chugged on board. I stared out of the blurred porthole and waved goodbye to Thieu on the tarmac. As we made our way to future exhilaration, the thought I had been choking back all day broke free and took a deep breath: *Could I have gotten her pregnant?* This fear would have to accompany me to Chu Lai, for that was our first stop on this leg of the tour.

February 12. 1970

Dear Mom and Dad,

I'm in Chu Lai and the area here is so beautiful. It is the most beautiful part of Vietnam I have seen yet. It is so green and fertile, full of lush valleys and mountains. We played at two fire bases today and rode out there on slicks. (Helicopters) It was a beautiful ride and view. One of the places was on a mountain and you could see all the way to the sea. We will be going back to Saigon on the 15th and I will know then if I am going back to the field or not. Before I left to come here I applied for a job at Special Services as a driver. The Sgt. said he would let me know. I hope I get it.

I was with my cousin Bobby yesterday in Da Nang. I missed a flight and I hitch hiked to where he lives. When I got there he was asleep and we didn't recognize each other right away. He told me my dad told him he would be looking for a fat Fred and I would be looking for a skinny Bobby. I laughed because that sounds like something my dad would say. I miss the letters from my dad because I really got homesick when Bobby started telling me all the funny things my dad said. Bobby lives in a nice place. He has his own refrigerator and they've got a TV and a little stove. He works nights. He's a foreman at the job. I had someone take a picture of us, all we needed was David.

Well that's about all. I'll try and write as much as I can because I know you're going to be worrying a lot when I go back out to the field. Try not to worry too much. I've got 109 days left and before you know it I will be home. I miss you and love you very much.

Love,

Fred

Time was running out. My tour with Special Services was coming to an end. I also had the end of my 365-day tour of Vietnam in sight. So much hinged on whether I could finagle more time in Saigon. Curly, Moe and Larry were happy for it all to end. They wanted to go back to the comfort and safety of their old jobs. John didn't care if we stayed out. He was game for anything. I carried myself as a worry free, seen-it-all kind of guy, but inside I was churning. I had the constant fear that Thieu would pop the old pregnancy trick on me but moreover I was afraid of going back to Charlie Troop.

Word was that they had just spearheaded the invasion of Cambodia. After all that time of having to stop pursuit of the enemy at the border, Nixon had given us the green light to go in after the bastards. That was the motto of the 11th Armored Calvary regiment: "Find the Bastards and Pile On." I also heard through the grapevine that Capt. Riddle and Lt. Cutter were gone. Rotated out. There were a bunch of FNGs filling the troop roster and I had no idea of who was left in Third Platoon.

I knew that once my feet hit the mud I would be promoted to sergeant. I would rather stay an E-4 and out of the action.

"Dear God, please let me extend with the Command Military Touring Show!" My prayers were unsurprisingly rare but this was uttered aloud with the utmost urgency. Everything had been great on the tour so far. The people loved us and we had our moments of greatness. Things were running smoothly among the five of us when we hit Charlie Two.

Charlie Two was the northernmost base of operations for the American and South Vietnamese armies. You could see the North Vietnamese flag flying across the DMZ and the action was intense, so intense that guys walked around with their M-16s cocked and loaded with the safety off. I knew this kind of thinking and living. A chill went down my spine as I looked at the NVA flag waving in the breeze. I had certainly been this close to the NVA before but this was different. It was as if they were just strutting their shit, walking around in the open.

As we had approached the camp on the chopper, John turned to me. "These guys must be starving for entertainment."

I looked at him and then the gathering crowd. Still aloft, I watched as the infantrymen brought out chairs and tree stumps to sit on. They were getting ready to enjoy the music. As soon as the blades of the bird stopped spinning we broke out our equipment and started setting it up on a low improvised stage. Johnny was so right; these guys were hungry for a little rock and roll to take them away from this place, and the seats were already filling up.

Johnny was tightening up his high hat and I was adjusting the controls on my bass when John caught eye contact with a grunt in the first row.

There was a loud shot followed by three quick moans. The guy went down and we watched as he died with his eyes open, just staring at the stage waiting for the concert.

It was an accidental discharge of a weapon. His buddy's weapon had fallen against the chair and fired the round right into the poor guy's back. There was nothing the medics could do with the mortally wounded man, but they sure had their hands full with the shooter.

He went crazy. Plain and simple. He freaked out that he was the cause of his friend's death. Two soldiers had to hold him down while the medic injected the guy with a sedative. The poor soul had to be medicated and flown out of there along with the body bag containing his friend.

We packed up and left. Whoever said "The show must go on" never played the Winter 1970 Vietnam Tour.

We flew back to Quan Tri a broken band. Whatever the chances of extending our tour were smashed that day. John was devastated. The Three Stooges were whining about it being too dangerous out there. I was distraught knowing that this guy's death had earned me a one-way ticket back out to the field.

Had this been the first time I had seen such senseless killing, I might have felt something for the guy, but I had seen so much, was so drained of any capacity to feel sorrow that I all could feel was anger that the motherfucker got in the way of the bullet, and spoiled our plans.

As soon as we got back to Saigon, I went to see Thieu. She was waiting for me at Tu Do. We went to Maxine's for a nice dinner. I told her about what happened. She was worried about John. He was a very sensitive guy and we all knew that if the poor son of a bitch that got shot wasn't standing there it would have been John who took the bullet. I assured her that John was all right. She asked me what else had happened on our tour.

"Well, we had an interesting thing happen to us at the Black Virgin Mountain. Do you know of this place?"

"Nui Ba Den? In Tay Ninh?" she asked.

"Yes, that's the place. Tons of Vietcong and NVA up in that mountain. We have two fire bases there. There is one at the bottom and one at the top. Nobody ventures between the two."

Working her stand at Tu Do, Thieu picked up a lot of gossip from soldiers. In fact, she learned enough she might have made a good spy.

"It's a very dangerous place. I worry so much about you when you go out."

"Believe me, it's a lot safer than what I was doing before. But let me tell you the story. We played at the bottom base and the show went fantastic. We packed up our gear on a Chinook and headed to the base on top. When we landed on top and started unloading our equipment the wind from the chopper blades caught John's bass drum, case and all, and blew it over the side of the mountain."

"That's unbelievable. What did you do?"

"Well, it's what *they* did. They were an infantry company. I forget which one they were. Anyway, the lieutenant sent an armed patrol down the mountain to retrieve it. It must have fallen at least 2,500 feet but even that small distance was dangerous to travel in."

"No way!"

"Really. John was upset that someone could get shot going after his drums. He played the show but I could see that it had bothered him. He later told me that he would not have been able to handle it if some chump got killed going after his bass drum. He somehow felt responsible for it."

"It sounds like John had a tough time on your road trip."

"It was interesting, to say the least." I called the waiter over for the check. "Are you ready?" I paid the bill and we walked out into the sticky evening heat.

"Let me walk you home," I said, and we walked quietly to her apartment in silence, both of us lost in thought about our future together. It was becoming clear that the clock was running out.

In the morning I swung by Special Services. Keith Askins informed me about the dissolution of the band. He said he was sorry but there was no way to extend me there in Saigon.

"I'll do what I can for you. I'll write you a letter." I thanked him for everything and went to my room to pack.

February 16, 1970

Dear Mom and Dad,

I am going back to my unit so write to me there unless I call and tell you otherwise. The sergeant at Special Services is giving me a letter to take with me asking that I be released to Special Services, but I doubt if it will do any good. Don't get your hopes up. Don't worry, I'll be fine and I'll be sure to write a lot. Start the goodie boxes going again. I am going to send some film home to be developed as soon as I find a post office. Make the prints 3X5 OK? I bought the mute kid three sets of clothes for Tet. It's bad luck to wear old clothes for the holiday. It's like Christmas, New Years, and Easter all rolled into one. Today we went out and ate dinner and he is so smart. We talk to each other in sign language. The Vietnamese girl who speaks Spanish went too. It is such a pleasure talking to her. It's the first time that I don't have to speak Pidgin English with a Vietnamese. She has become a good friend and I will miss those two. I'm also sending the photos I have developed already so that they don't get ruined in the mud. Well don't worry I have faith that I will be home all right. Don't worry; time will go by fast for me in the field. I love you very much and miss you more than ever. Call my friends and give them my new address.

    Love,

    Fred

I had 105 days left in the fucking Army and I had a bad attitude. My parting with Thieu had surprisingly gone better than I ever could have hoped for. She was calm and mature beyond her twenty years. She had resigned herself to her fate. I could not begin to imagine what would happen to her when Saigon fell. She was resourceful. No doubt she would find a way to survive, I thought.

We made love one more time. Even with her knowing I was leaving her, she still pleasured and satisfied me. I'm the one who was the emotional wreck.

I don't know if it was just that I knew I was headed back to the jungle and life-and-death situations, but I fell madly in love with her our last two days together. I promised that I would return for her after the war. Once again, our parting was staged on a military tarmac, with me flying off and her being left on the ground. She remained cool, with just little sobs escaping her breath. She did not cry or carry on like she did at the hospital. She hugged me and told me to watch myself out there, and then blades started to spin. I answered hastily before the rotors blew away all other sound.

"I will," I promised. "You take care of yourself. Keep an eye on the kid." I turned away from her and climbed aboard Hawks' helicopter. We took off straightaway.

I sat back in the seat and looked to the ground. I realized that I had no problem abandoning people. I had left Dizzy, Benson and Olgovey in the jungle and now I was ditching Thieu to an uncertain fate. I don't even think that I had said goodbye to John. I could not help but notice that a big change had happened to me. I popped a couple of pain pills and let my mind drift away from guilt.

By the time I got to Blackhorse I knew that my life was in ruins. When I settled in I started looking into the possibility of marrying a Vietnamese civilian, one I professed to love and yet could so easily abandon. I sought out the paperwork but before I could make any headway the order came down for me to catch the resupply chopper and head on back to the field.

I also sought out Squires in that warren of tents and huts. The new CO was Capt. Gary Clark, but I had yet to learn the new platoon leader's name. Squires would know. He would also know I could use a bowl. The flap to the tent was open, and Squires and Hawks were kickin' back inside.

"Hey, my man. What's happening?" I didn't know which of them said it. I only know it was not Herman and it didn't feel the same. I popped a few more of the pain pills, and before I remembered why I had come, I smoked until I crashed.

I came to and found myself in that smoky haze of burning pot.

"That's the new lieutenant's name." Squires handed me the bong. I took another hit.

"What?"

"Yeah. You asked me the new lieutenant's name," Squires poked me in the ribs and slapped me on the back. "Chapman, Carl Chapman."

"You best be getting ready to hop the flight out," Hawks said.

"I'm good to go," I mumbled.

"Troop's in Cambodia," Hawks said. "*Beaucoup* gooks. Man, it's Dink city out there. I hate flying into that shit."

I readied my duffel bag and grabbed my guitar and slowly stood. I wobbled to the door. Squires took one look at me and blurted out, "Oh, shit, man! You ain't going out there in that condition!"

"It don't mean nothing. I've had my fun. If they want to kill me, then let's go for it. I give up. *Chu hoi, chu hoi,*" I said. We made it to Hawks' bird and he put his flight helmet on and contacted the troop. I swallowed more pills.

"Sorry, man. They're in heavy contact right now. There ain't nothing getting in or out right now. You scored, dude. You have another night with the Hawk."

I was *so* relieved.

"Live to fight another day, eh?" I asked sarcastically.

"You've made it this far. There's no use pushing your luck."

Where had I heard those words before? Askins. That's right. The whole Saigon experience was sounding like a foreign movie to me already. What had it been? Seventy-two hours since I last saw Thieu? Every bone in my body ached for her. How would I feel after three months of heavy combat?

I staggered toward Squire's digs. A first sergeant recognized me and asked when I was going to perform for Charlie Troop.

"The only way I can do that is if the band gets another tour."

"Go pack your bags and go back to Saigon. I'll take the paperwork out to the CO and have him sign it."

"You can do that?"

"Of course."

I doubted that he had that much clout. Tomorrow, I would be heading for the field again. But today I got a reprieve, and a safe way to eat another day off my countdown until I could leave this place.

February 28, 1970

Dear Mom and Dad,

> *I'm still at Blackhorse but tomorrow they want to send me to Tay Ninh because they still haven't done anything about*

my request to work in Saigon. I'm pretty discouraged about the
whole thing I hope to straighten things out up at Tay Ninh. I
saw a friend of mine from Fort Knox today. He came back to
Vietnam for the second time. I can't understand why he did it.
I hate this place. I hate the 11th Cav. In Saigon there is no war.
It's just like living and working in a foreign city. Back here you
always are thinking of the war. Last night three guys were killed
by ARVNs who fired rockets on Blackhorse (By mistake?) Now
the days are going by slower and I'm more homesick than ever
before. I'm in sort of a limbo between Saigon and the field and
I don't like it here. Don't worry too much. At least I'm in good
health and my spirits should lift by finding out exactly where I
stand. I am very depressed but don't worry I'll write tomorrow
and let you know what is happening.

> *Love,*
> *Fred*

I could no longer hide the truth from my family. I was very
fucked in the head. More and more I was coming to rely on the pills
to pull out the dagger in my back, and booze or weed to put me in a
zone where I didn't give a shit about anything or anybody. When I
thought about it, my actions to get the paperwork for Thieu had been
half-hearted. Thieu, the woman I loved and could have shot, was a
bullet I dodged.

XX
The Devil's Deal

That night I walked around the entire perimeter of the base trying to get my head straight. It was an immense complex, miles wide at the thickest part. I was used to walking the streets of Saigon and I just wanted to be alone to think. I passed whole blocks of empty hooches and by chance I turned and entered one of the tents. I thought nothing could shock or startle me anymore, nothing about life or death or even about myself.

But then, passing what I thought was an empty tent, I opened the flap to find a place to lie down for a while, and walked in on Sgt. Major, sitting on a cot with his arm tied up, ready to shoot heroin.

He yanked the needle away from his vein and dropped his works as he attempted to stand too quickly.

"What the fuck are you doing here?" he grumbled.

"What the fuck are *you* doing here?" I answered. My mind was racing and all the street survival skills I possessed took charge and I approached him and yanked the rig out of his hand.

"Oh, Sgt. Major, what are you doing? Your career will be ruined if this ever got out. Your whole world would collapse and you'd never see the light of day from the Long Binh jail."

His body became rigid and he stood and glared. "What do you want?" He was angrier at himself than he was with me and he fiercely stared me in the eye. He asked again, "What the fuck you want?"

I knew the answer. "I want to spend my remaining three months back in the rear, with you."

A plan started falling in place.

"No one need know about this. It can be our little secret and I'll even go to the village and cop the dope for you. What do you say? The captain knows that I have experience in Special Services. That's entertaining the troops. We can take one of these empty hooches and make a little club out of it. I'm sure we could find a pool table around here and a fridge for cold sodas and beer. I could run it."

I was on a roll, running full throttle. My mind was coming up with all kinds of schemes. If I could be a black marketeer, then I could surely be a blackmailer. "Why don't you have a talk with Capt. Clark? You can swing it. You're fucking in charge of this place, for Christ sakes."

He sat down on the bed and I could see the gears in his brain trying to sort this out. He had to do it quickly if he wanted to shoot up while his need was cresting. I had caught him red-handed and he had to come to terms with it. He knew I would not back down, as I had never been one to obey his orders. He also knew my M-16 would be sawdust if I had a notch for every kill.

"You'll make the dope run?" he asked, while I stared him down. "Do you use?"

"I'll make the run and, no, I don't use, so you won't have to worry about me ripping you off. There will be no skimming off the top." I stood my ground, unafraid of what his reaction might be.

"I'll write up some paperwork. There is no need for this to go any further."

I was dripping sweat and my heart beat twice before I realized I had resumed breathing. His full name was Arnold Major. He had seven years in the Army and he was an E-6. He wouldn't make much rank having a noncombat job but he loved running the rear area. He had the clout, too, and I soon found myself with Marty Squires looking around for a pool table.

We found one at Regimental Headquarters and quickly transported it over to an empty hooch closer to Charlie Troop. Squires was happy that I would be joining him and Batty, the company clerk.

"So how did you ever swing this?" Squires asked as we cleaned the dusty hooch and mopped the floor.

"It was my good fortune. I can't help it if I'm lucky."

"Sgt. Major doesn't put up with much malingering. How do you intend to escape the wrath of the old man?"

"I'm going to learn from the master, Marty, *you!*"

We laughed and he put the mop down and took a pull of his canteen and said, "I've watched a lot of guys pass through here this year. Some stayed for a week, maybe ten days max. Major always finds a way to get them back out to the field. That's his only fucking job. Keep them moving and back out to the jungle. I've spent too much time with that man to know you must have offered him something special. You're not going to share it with me, Fred, after how long I've known you?"

"Forget it, Squires. He knows that I have a bad back and anytime I want to play that card I can. The man really thinks I can do a good job entertaining the troops right here in this empty tent. You'll see. It's just the way it's supposed to be. Now, help me get that table in here."

I needn't tell anyone a thing about Arnold and my arrangement. I gave him my word and he gave me this tent, one of the few with a floor in it. It was now up to me to make it work. I wouldn't admit to myself that my fear of the field was far greater than taking the chance of getting caught transporting heroin.

It took a week of hard work to get the club ready. I borrowed (or stole) tables and chairs, and picked up a stereo for next to nothing. The guys sent home for rock posters and everyone stationed in the rear came through with one thing or the other. It turned into a group effort and by the end of the week we were ready to open.

Arnold Major came up to me and asked, "Ready for the big day tomorrow?"

I told him I was, and showed off the club to him.

"You're missing the most important thing," he said.

"What's that, sergeant?"

"You need a refrigerator to keep the beer cold." He took me outside and showed me a small fridge that he had on a dolly.

"You've got to be kidding? Sergeant, that is so cool," I said in delight.

"You can't have a juke joint without the suds." We pulled back the flaps of the tent and we wheeled it into the corner behind the counter.

"It's complete," I said.

"Hey, I have a stake in this place, too. I want it looking sharp when the old man comes in two days." He took a quick glance in every direction. "Listen, after you're done here I need you to take a little trip to the village."

I immediately caught his drift.

"The place is off the main drag where the tire store is. Look for a house on the right with a red door. Do you think you'll have any trouble?"

"Who has guard duty at the gate tonight?"

"Shields and Gardner."

"No problem. I know those guys." He turned to leave and then stopped and fumbled for his wallet.

"Don't worry, Arnold. This one's on me."

I was grateful for this arrangement and I figured that building goodwill with him was a good idea. I was being paid back tenfold. After he left I straightened out the club and made sure there were tablecloths on all the tables. I arranged the mishmash of chairs in the best-looking order I could get them in. I racked the pool balls up and hung the sticks on the wall. I took a step back and was impressed with the fruits of my labor.

I went to my bunk in Squires' hut, since by then I had moved in with him and Hawks. I liked these guys and I wanted to stay on the good side of Hawks so I could catch rides to Saigon with him from time to time.

After evening came, I waited an hour and made my way to the main gate. As promised, Shields and Gardner were posted there.

"What's happening?" I asked Tim Shields, as John Gardner poked his head out of his fighting hole and lit up a cigarette.

"Where you think you're going?" Shields asked pleasantly.

"Well, Tim, if you must know I'm going to go get a piece of ass. It's been a dry spell and I need to mellow out, if you know what I mean?" I said. "Major knows about it and said you guys would not hassle me. I'll only be gone for less than an hour."

Gardner laughed. "Less than an hour? You an old man? I thought a young buck like you would take three or four hours."

"Got to be up early. You wouldn't let me out for that long anyway." They looked at each other and Gardner stamped out his cigarette on a sandbag.

"Hurry up, then," he said, and I walked out into the village.

The village was full of activity. Young men walked down the street holding hands. Mama and papa sans scurried about carrying firewood on their heads and buckets of water on poles stretched out on their shoulders. There was no presence of GIs but that didn't mean I didn't have to worry about the MPs. They routinely patrolled the streets at night looking for ominous people just like me. I walked in the shadows and luckily the intersection I was looking for was not far. I found the tire store and nervously looked over my shoulder. I turned left down a side street. This beat the jungle by miles. I came to the house and knocked on the door. It was answered by an old woman. When she saw me she started jabbering away in Vietnamese to an unseen person behind the door. She moved away still yakking and a small man of thirty moved in from behind.

"Yes?" he said.

"Are you Mr. Kwan?" He was dressed in black pajamas of the countryside and stood holding a lit pipe. The radio played in the background and it was so dim inside that I could not see beyond three feet. He obviously wasn't going to invite me in so I just came out and asked him if he had any heroin.

He smiled and asked me, "How much, GI?"

"Ten dollars." I handed him two Lincolns. He motioned for me to stay where I was and he disappeared into the darkness of the house. Two minutes passed and it seemed an eternity before he returned holding a small paper bag. I looked inside the packet and saw the China white shining off his dim porch light. No more words were said and I backed away and felt naked, unarmed. I scrolled up the bag and put it in my pants pocket. I made a mental note not to ever come without a weapon again and I slid back into the shadows. When I reached the tire store, a Jeep pulled out of nowhere and turned on its headlights.

Cops!

They flashed their lights on and off so I turned and walked over to them. Two MPs stayed seated in the vehicle and the driver asked, "What you doing out after curfew?"

I studied them in their shiny black helmets, sidearms ready in the holster, and handcuffs lying on the seat between them.

"I had to get laid." I shrugged my shoulders and opened my palms. "I stayed a little longer than I intended to, gambling." I was gambling again that they would believe me.

"I just came in from the field this afternoon. It's been a while since I have been with a woman," I lied.

The MPs laughed and the shotgun glanced at the bulge in my pants and said, "Looks like you started gambling before you were finished with the prostitute." I looked down to where the bag of heroin was bulging in my pants.

"I can go back and finish the job."

They laughed again and the driver said, "You're finished tonight, troop. Stay off the streets at night. In case you don't know it, there is a 2200 hour curfew. Dip your dick in the day, OK?"

"Got it, Sarge," I said. "Can I go? They told me to hop in the back and they drove me to the gate.

Shields and Gardner smiled when they saw me being escorted by the MPs.

"Back so soon?" Tim scoffed. They both laughed but I walked right under their noses with a bag of dope and a hope for a better future.

March 12, 1970

Dear Mom and Dad

Well it's already March and I have 79 days left. You're counting until the 27th of May but I get out 7 days earlier. I am in Bien Hoa still and it looks like I am going to stay here. I am running the club selling soda and beer. Well it isn't exactly a club it's just a refrigerator inside a tent. I have a TV and the tent all to myself. So I guess I will just stay here until I go home.

Right now the weather is hot and dry and dusty. It has been like this since the beginning of December and the rainy season here won't start again until about May or June. You asked why some people come back for a second tour. Well I can't understand why they come back to combat units but there are a lot of beautiful places to be stationed. Like Saigon for instance. If I had time left I probably would have extended to be stationed in Saigon. I really had a good time when I was there. I don't have my tape recorder anymore but I can always borrow one whenever I want. Yes I received the tape for Christmas when I was in Saigon. I got a kick out of everyone getting all nervous. Well that's about all for today. I miss you and I'm counting the days.

Love,

Fred

And just like that I was set for the duration. The first week saw the commanding officer, Capt. Clark, visit my little EM club. He thought it was a good idea and when he left I felt as though I had crossed the biggest hurdle. With the old man on my side, Lt. Chapman could not complain. Sgt. Major's and my understanding worked out, as I kept up my end of the bargain and continued to cop his shit in the village.

More and more, I began to rely on Percocet. It gave me some relief from the incessant back pain, but Dr. Jack Daniels and weed did more for the cancerous sense of guilt that had invaded my soul.

To avoid calling attention to myself, I no longer tried to get my M&Ms through proper channels. The pharmacy behind the red door carried more than just heroin. I got to know Arnold Major's dealer; now, he was my dealer, too.

His name was Nguyen Kwan, and I never found out the old lady's name. She treated me the same every time I showed up. She always got excited and started yapping her head off like a small terrier. I didn't know if she liked me or not but Nguyen sure did. I must have been one of his most consistent customers.

Soon he began to supply me with morphine.

XXI
The Endless Rotation

The first chance I had I hitchhiked to Saigon. I crept up to Thieu on her street corner and put my hands over her eyes.

"Guess who?" I teased. She turned around and her eyes glistened and she gave me a wide smile. She hugged me and I lifted her off the ground and planted a giant kiss on her mouth.

"Fred! I knew you would come back. What are you doing here? I thought you were going back out to the jungle." Her face lit up and I could tell her excitement level had risen 100 percent.

"I'm only here for a few days, Thieu. Can you close up shop so we can go somewhere and talk?"

"Of course." She closed the lid of her vendor display and took it inside the Mumbo Jumbo. The mute kid was standing there now and he came over and gave me a big hug. We walked over to the Rex Hotel and got a table. It was hot and humid and I worked up quite a sweat ambling those six blocks to the hotel. Thieu noticed this and laughed. "You are getting out of shape. What do they have you doing over there?"

I proceeded to tell her the story about Sgt. Major and the blackmail I had committed. She was the only person that I had ever mentioned the truth to. She was amazed.

"You took a big chance, Fred. He could have done something bad to you."

I shrugged this off and said, "If you only knew what I was facing in the field you might have done the same thing. No, you *would* have done the same thing. You're a survivor, Thieu. You know your way around trouble."

We caught up on each other's lives and she asked me if I was going to stay with her and her mother. I promised that I would be there by eight. I had to go see my friends at the Australian Embassy. I had disappeared on them without saying goodbye. I wanted to go and make that right. We kissed goodbye and I caught a pedicab over to their place.

I walked into the alley and saw that their door was wide open. I walked through it and found them much as I had seen them the last time I was here. Gordo was taking a nap slumped in the big, overstuffed chair. Philip was reading; Deke was preparing supper. Deke turned, holding a slicing knife and saw me standing in the doorway. "Fred!" Deke screamed, waking up Gordo. Philip put down his book and Gordo scrambled to his feet and everyone in the big room smiled.

Gordo approached and I gave him the biggest hug I could muster.

"Well, well, well, if it isn't our rock star in residence," Gordo joked.

"Gordo, so much has happened. I still haven't gone back out to the field and I'm not feeling right about it."

"Not feeling right? Do you feel like a coward?"

"My friends are in heavy contact and I'm sitting on my ass at base camp. I feel guilty," I said pouring my heart out to the only man left in Vietnam that I trusted. "Yes, I guess that's it. I do feel like a coward. Was it honorable playing in that band? I feel like I just abandoned my friends and went off on this wonderful adventure."

"What do I always tell you? Slow down."

"Ever since Herman died I have not felt connected to anyone here. I feel that a part of me died with him."

"You have a habit of letting your emotions get the better of you. You wear them on your sleeve, Fred. That's one of the reasons you are so special to me," he said, in a calming voice. "Go back to your unit and take pride in the combat that you have seen. It's not as if you've been stationed here for your entire tour. No, I seem to recall you telling me about some hairy encounters on the battlefield."

He motioned for me to sit down on the sofa. I sat and listened. "It's not as if you did something wrong or unethical." His words hit me like a ten-pound hammer. I reeled under the weight of guilt.

"But I have," I told him. I proceeded to tell Gordon about my blackmail scheme. He listened without judgment and when I was finished he smiled and put his hand on my shoulder.

"We do what we have to do, mate. What's that saying? All's fair in love and war?" He gave my shoulder an affectionate squeeze and continued. "You're beating yourself up again. That sounds pretty funny to me. I don't feel sorry for that bloke. He's a hypocrite and a snake. He deserves worse than what you are giving him. Ha, ha, that's a rich one. Please excuse me, Fred, but I think Philip and Deke need to hear about all this tawdry business."

At once the heaviness lifted. Gordo had done it again. I had come to him at my lowest and was ready to walk away holding my head up. God, I will miss this man. He told them the story and they all had a good laugh. I stayed until seven-thirty and told them that I didn't know if I would see them again, as I only had two months left. We exchanged addresses and phone numbers and Deke took several photos of us.

I was happy when I hit the alleyway and started to Thieu's apartment.

When I reached Thieu's place I was greeted at the door by none other than Mr. Choi. I shook his hand and bowed slightly to Thieu's mother and walked into that sweet aroma of cooking food. They said that Mr. Choi had requested a meeting with me, so they invited him to dinner so we could talk. He didn't beat around the bush and got right down to business as the main course was served.

"Fred, it's so good to see you again. I trust you're doing well. I have another piece of business that I would like to propose to you."

"Thank you, Mr. Choi, I am doing well. As far as this business opportunity is concerned, is it along the lines of what we did before?" I asked, already knowing the answer.

"I have a buyer prepared to pay top dollar for a washer and dryer. Have you seen them at the Post Exchange?"

"What is top dollar?" I asked.

"One thousand dollars for the both."

"Do you have the money?"

"I can have it first thing tomorrow morning."

We discussed the details and I told him that the mute kid could help me carry them, and thus a business partnership was born. One that would involve thousands of dollars over the next two months. He was sharp and quick with numbers and he never tried to cheat me or take advantage of my position. The MPs had their eyes out for people who constantly made big purchases. We avoided this by stationing the kid at the front of the PX with his shoeshining business as a cover. He kept an eye out for the MPs who were on duty and what their schedule was. He was instrumental in assuring a successful operation and I paid him handsomely for all the work he did. I personally made over $1,500 during the next two months of my tour doing business with Mr. Choi. I cut Hawks in on the money for the disposal of his helicopter. This made it possible for him to fly me in and out of Saigon, sometimes twice a week.

Back at Blackhorse the days were going by quickly. Before I knew it I had 62 days left in the Army. My friend Lance back home in Montebello had told me about a trip to Europe he was planning. Would I be interested in going? Hell, yes, I would. I had all this black-market money along with what Mercury Records owed me. I needed to find out when he was going. It just might help me to adjust to civilian life.

March 18, 1970

Dear Mom and Dad

I am fine and still in Bien Hoa. I have 62 days left and the time just drags on unless I keep myself busy. My friend Dizzy has about 16 days left. He got a two week drop. There is

*a chance that I might get one, too. If I do I'll leave on about the
6th of May. I went to Saigon two days ago and had a real nice
time. I got the money orders and the goodie box. Thank you.
Can you send me another hundred because everybody tells me
I am going to need more than the $250. When is Lance going
to go on his trip to Europe? I would like to go if it is after I had
been home for a few months. Tell him I'm interested and tell
him to write to me and let me know the details. I'm sending a
picture of me and some guys in the club I'm running. It's just
a big tent with a television, pool table, and a refrigerator. We
will be moving to Zion on the 21st so I hope there will be a little
more to do there. Well, this is all for now. I miss you very much
and send you all my love.*

    Fred

Capt. Clark had a policy of sending guys to the rear when they
had ten to fourteen days left. He didn't want to see a guy serve out
his entire tour under fire and then buy the farm when he got short. It
was a very popular policy with the men of C Troop. This allowed me
to spend ten wonderful days with my old pal Dizzy. When he rotated
through he was excited about the war finally coming to an end for
him. I told him how happy I was that he'd survived the invasion of
Cambodia. One night, as we were sitting around getting loaded, he
told me about it.

"When we first went in we had grunts from the 1st Infantry
Division with us."

"Yeah, the same guys we always worked with out of Lai Khe," I said.

"Right. Remember that captain you stopped to talk to when we
did that Thunder Run?"

"That guy with the tattoo?"

"He was with them. He must have been the company
commander. Dude, they ate it! I never saw so many guys get aced in
one day. And this was just on our first day in. The Dinks had concrete

bunkers and positions in the trees. They were dug in solid. Fuck, they had been there unmolested for all those years. We took the grunts to a drop point and the NVA .30-cals were popping. They had *beaucoup* RPGs and, Fred, they even had tanks. Fucking tanks! You're lucky you sat that one out," Dizzy exclaimed, almost losing his breath.

"Is that when Ernest and Jenkins were killed?" I asked.

Dizzy turned away and lit a cigarette. It was clear that he was uncomfortable talking about this, so I changed the subject. "What's the first thing you're going to do when you get home, Diz?"

He turned back around and looked me in the eye and simply said, "Sleep."

I enjoyed my friend those last days of his. We had gone through much together. We worked hard during the day and mostly hung around drinking beer and smoking dope at night. We exchanged addresses and phone numbers and one afternoon he was gone, and I had less than 50 days left.

Benson was the next old buddy to show up. He was on his way out, too. We worked hard those days preparing for the squadron to move the base camp to Zion. We were going to turn Blackhorse over to the South Vietnamese. The Vietnamization of the war continued as Nixon sued for peace in Paris.

My days clicked by.

After a month and a half of fucking around away from any action, word got to Lt. Chapman that there was a guy getting over in the rear. Now, I had never had the pleasure of knowing or serving with that man. He had no idea of what kind of soldier I was or what battles I had been in before he arrived. He was what we called a ninety-day wonder. He was a college graduate who attended a ninety-day program at Officers' Candidate School. They had a reputation of being completely untethered from reality and the ways of war. The stories I heard of his map-reading skills or lack thereof were legend. He once lost the platoon for a half a day as he struggled to meet up with the main force.

When he heard of me, he made it his mission in life to get me out to the field. Word came in daily for Sgt. Major to ship me out to the troop. He and I ignored the directives and I continued living it up in the rear. I was getting really short and I had a bad attitude toward the LT. I came to find out that blowing him off was a mistake. I underestimated the prick to the point that he made a special trip in the resupply chopper to drag my ass back out into the field with him.

On Thursday April 16, 1970 Lt. Carl Chapman arrived at the small LZ at Charlie Troop, Blackhorse. That evening he summoned me to his office and proceeded to call me a coward and every name in the book. His eyes bulged and he turned red as a beet as he swore up and down that I was to accompany him back out to the field in the morning. He stood five feet six inches tall in his combat boots and I swear he suffered from a Napoleon complex. His red hair and red complexion turned ever redder as he screamed.

Batty and Squires stood outside where he could not see them, and they were mocking him and cracking up. I tried not to smile. This guy meant nothing to me. When he was finished I asked him if I was excused.

"Sorry to cause you any problems, lieutenant," I said.

"We have no problems as long as you go back out with me in the morning," Chapman answered. "You better go pack your gear up."

I was totally in acceptance of the situation. I truly had been blessed to get out of combat these past few months. I felt like God had not carried me all this way just to drop me at the end of my tour. Call it karma or whatever you want, but I was feeling pretty fucking fortunate and if I needed to spend my last five weeks in the field, well, so be it.

That evening I got with Squires and collected up the equipment I would need. Flak jacket, helmet liner, steel pot, canteen, web belt and all the gear that went with it. Batty from personnel came by to wish me luck. I went to the armorer and picked out a brand-new M-16 and grenades. I made sure to include a .45 with black leather holster.

I was once again ready for war.

In the morning I found myself on the helipad wearing my flak jacket and steel helmet. It was only 9 a.m. but the heat was unbearable. The heaviness of the body armor crushed me and I could not find a way to evenly distribute the unbearable burden. I thought of the mud waiting for me out in the field. I had been without this load for a good four months and it seemed foreign to me now. Beads of sweat fell off my forehead only to evaporate on contact with the scorching pavement. I pushed back my helmet and looked at Chapman. Maybe I didn't put up a good enough fight.

"I'm going to put you on Three-Four," he said.

"I've got *beaucoup* history with that old bucket," I told him.

"So I understand. I put in your promotion orders last night after we talked. Congratulations. You are now a sergeant."

Shit. That's what I had feared. I felt a heat rash start itching underneath my flak jacket. Small boils were appearing on my arms.

Hawks had the chopper idling as we waited for clearance to take off. Every time the rotary blade would swoosh around, I felt the vibration deep within my chest. I was having trouble breathing. I was on the verge of a panic attack when all of a sudden I heard a voice, faint at first, but growing louder with every turn of the chopper blade.

"Rivera! Rivera!"

I looked over at the Troop Headquarters and saw Batty running with a hand full of papers.

"Fred Rivera!" Now louder. Chapman glanced over at Batty and raised a hand.

"Easy, trooper." He tried to calm Jim Batty down. "What is it?"

Batty didn't slow down one bit but came running full throttle at us waving the papers.

"It's Rivera, sir. He just received a 30-day drop. Rivera, you're going home!"

With those words I welled up. I was awash with emotion. At that very instant I knew I had won the war and the war was over. I looked at Lt. Chapman and said, "I have ten days left in the Army. You can court-martial me, hang me, put me in front of a firing squad but you're not getting me to go out with you today, lieutenant! I'm going home."

With the blades swooshing overhead he looked at me and I saw the anger return to him.

"You son of a bitch!" he said. He glared at the fistful of papers Batty was holding without bothering to read them. He slowly turned and mounted the helicopter and slammed his fist into the back of the seat as a signal for Hawks to take off. That was the last I ever saw of Chapman. I turned and looked at Batty.

"Let's get you out of that monkey suit," he said. Squires collected my war gear as I discarded it to the ground. I couldn't believe what had just happened.

"Is it really over?" I asked myself.

I looked at Herman's bootlaces braided so elaborately on my left wrist. His memory was strong in my heart. I thought of Dizzy, Benson, Olgovey and Teddy Jones. I could see Teddy's dead eyes staring at me. He was telling me, "Go home, Fred, you've done enough. Go back to the World and live a happy life."

Batty and Squires and all the rear-echelon guys were whooping and hollering that "Fred got over!" That's all we draftees thought about. How could we fuck the Army? What small actions could we take daily to throw a clog in the machine? I had been ripped out of a life of being a rock-and-roll star two years ago by the draft. I knew that I would become cannon fodder in a civil war that we had no business being in. Still, when ordered to, I had killed. I had burned villages when told to. For eight months I had been a good soldier, bold enough to go through *hundreds* of dead bodies without being squeamish or hesitating. What more did they want from me?

After I changed uniforms, Batty called me into his office. "I've got to prepare the letter."

"What letter?"

"The letter to your folks," he said.

"What the fuck you talking about, you crazy son of a bitch? I
ain't dead!" I told him.

"Just shut up and watch. Everyone gets one."

Batty was excited. He pulled out an 11th Cav. letterhead and put
it in his typewriter. He typed:

Dear Family, Friends, Civilians and Draft Dodgers,

*In the very near future Fred Rivera will once more be in
your midst, dehydrated and demoralized, to take his place
again as a human being, to enjoy the well-known forms of
freedom and justice for all and to engage in life, liberty and
the somewhat delayed pursuit of happiness. In making your
joyous preparations to welcome him back into organized
society, you might take certain steps to make allowances for the
crude environment which has been his miserable lot for the last
12 months. In other words, he might be a little Asiatic from
Vietnamese-itis and over-sea-itis and should be handled with
care. Do not be alarmed if he is infected with all forms of rare
tropical diseases. A little time in the "Land of the Big PX" will
cure this malady.*

*Therefore, show no alarm if he insists on carrying a weapon
to the dinner table, looks around for his steel pot when offered a
seat, or wakes you up in the middle of the night for guard duty.
Keep cool when he pours gravy on his dessert or mixes peaches
with his Seagram's VO. Pretend not to notice that he eats with
his fingers instead of silverware and prefers C-rations to steak.
Take it with a smile when he insists on digging up the garden to
fill sandbags for the bunker he is building. Be tolerant when he
takes a blanket off the bed (and leaves the sheets) and puts it on
the floor to sleep on.*

*Abstain from saying anything about powdered eggs,
dehydrated potatoes, fried rice or fresh milk or ice cream. Do*

not be alarmed if he should jump up from the dinner table, rush over to the garbage can to wash his dish with a brush. After all, this has been his standard. If it starts to rain, pay no attention to him if he takes off all his clothes grabs some soap and starts to shower.

When in daily conversation he should utter such things as "Xin loi" or "Choi oi", just be patient. Just leave quickly if he suddenly yells "di di" with an angry look on his face.

Above all, keep in mind that beneath that tanned and rugged face is a heart of gold. The only thing of value he has left. You will be able to rehabilitate what now is the hollow shell of the happy-go-lucky guy you once knew and loved.

Send no more mail, fill the refrigerator with beer, get the civvies' out of mothballs, get the women and children off the road: BECAUSE THE KID IS COMING HOME!!!!!!!

J. Batty, Captain

I read over the letter. "That's stupid. My folks are going to think I've been killed with an official-looking letter like that," I complained. I tried to grab the letter out of his hand but he ran around the desk laughing. I moved my hand down to where my holster was supposed to be but came up empty. I had turned in my weapons.

"Fuck it. Send it."

That desk jockey had put more truth than fiction in that damn letter. I was going for my weapon to settle a small dispute. This gave me pause. What kind of a monster had I become? I thought about what it really would be like to go home.

Batty stopped laughing and came up to my side. "You're going to have to be fitted for a Class-A uniform. Also, there are tons of paperwork for you to sign before I can book you on a bird."

Eventually, I picked up my new dress uniform, and Batty, knowing all the regulations and measurements, pinned all of my medals and badges on my chest. I looked down. How did I win all this shit?

I would have thought that my last night in camp would be full of drinking, smoking, and partying with the fellows. It was not. I lay in bed quiet as a mouse, reflecting on what lay ahead. Why was I more frightened about going home than I ever was before a battle? This place had been my home and I was afraid of leaving it. I spent a restless night.

At 10 a.m. the following morning I stepped onto an American Airlines commercial flight out of Tan Son Nhut and took the giant Freedom Bird to California.

I thought it was over.

XXII
Going Home

The flight took twenty hours to reach San Francisco. It was a rough trip. When we took off, the pilot raised the nose so high that I thought we were in a rocket ship. In fifteen years of this war no commercial airliner had ever been shot down but I suspected that these pilots liked to think that they were always in danger. We stopped to refuel in Alaska and I got off the plane to stretch my legs. I went behind a building and smoked some opium and swallowed four pain pills. The rest of the flight was uneventful. As I understood it, all crew members who made these flights were volunteers. It was nice to see long, sleek American legs merging with smooth white thighs that disappeared into mini-skirts. With their long blond hair flowing across their faces, they stood in direct contrast to the small, skinny Vietnamese women I had come to know on Tu Do Street. I was thankful that I had gotten to know Thieu. Our intense but all-too-brief relationship made me realize that some basic human trait remained in me, and I had not turned completely into an uncaring, empty monster as I had feared. I ordered a Jack Daniels on the rocks and sat content to smell the sweet fragrance of the stewardess who served it to me.

After twenty-three and a half hours of flight, the captain came on the intercom and announced that we had just entered the continental United States. A loud roar rose from the passengers as we cheered and yelled, screamed and cried at our arrival home. We deplaned as a group and quickly went to retrieve our duffel bags. Some contained contraband that went undetected. Some contained souvenirs and some, like mine, contained nothing but clothes.

I wondered if Clementi had brought home his ears.

Outside the terminal, four buses awaited us. We were not yet free. We needed to be taken to the processing center in Oakland. As I reached the automatic doors at the airport I heard chanting and yelling. A peace demonstration was taking place directly in our path to the buses.

It did not look that peaceful to me.

Long-haired protesters, mixed with a cross-section of the populace, carried signs and tried to intimidate us as we made our way to the buses. I stepped away from a Catholic priest and thought back to that scene in the jungle. I saw a handful of vets wearing their fatigue shirts. A girl looking no more than seventeen years old took two steps toward me, smiling, and spit in my face.

"Baby killer!" she screamed.

"Baby killer!" The unruly crowd took up the epithet.

I wiped the spittle from my face and tasted blood. I moved forward now, pushing my way to the bus. I would not let this clueless little girl ruin my homecoming. I was in the United States and that's all that mattered. Baby killer. The thought lingered, anyway.

It took two days to process out of the Army in Oakland. Clerk after clerk, line after line, paper after paper until finally I received my discharge papers.

"DD214: The most important document you will ever own!" a major repeatedly told us. "Is there anybody here who wants to re-up for another tour in country?" he was obligated to ask.

There were a few laughs and lots of smiles but what came as no surprise to me were the twenty or so guys who became so angry at this that they yelled, "Fuck you!" with no "sir" attached.

Having no takers, he quickly issued the last order I would ever receive from an officer of the United States Army: "Dismissed!"

Hats flew in the air. Men hugged total strangers. We were free. There would never again be anyone to report to. Never again jungles to bust, mud to sleep in. Somehow I had survived. We were now off to our homes: back to our families.

When I landed at LAX, more of the same was waiting for me.

Why did these people hate me so much?

The only welcome sight was my mother and father. My mother was overjoyed with such happiness as I had never seen. My father just kept staring at me as if he didn't believe that I was here. Their love was overwhelming. We drove the forty minutes to Montebello and I was sobbing as I gazed out the window. I thought about Herman. I thought about Teddy Jones. I looked at my mom sitting in front of me and how much she loved me. I thought of that girl that spat on me. How the country had changed while I was gone.

I received news of the family happenings: the births, the deaths; life had moved on while I was away. Yesterday I stood in the hot, humid air of a country at war. I took in a lungful of the Los Angeles basin smog and let my breath out slowly. I was home.

Finally we turned off of Beverly Boulevard on to 21st Street and drove up to the side of our house. A large, homemade banner flew across the fence with the words boldly written, "**WELCOME HOME FRED.**" I opened the back door of the car and walked right up to that sign and yanked it down. I was ashamed to be a soldier returning from such an unpopular war. I wanted to hide from my neighbors and passersby. My extended family of aunts and uncles, cousins and friends were waiting for me in the backyard. They were barbecuing *carne asada* and drinking beer. The yard was decorated with festive ribbons of red, white and blue. The children were playing games, waiting for me to break the *piñata*.

It was too much for me to take. I stormed into my bedroom and closed the door. I lay on my bed, eyes shut, unwilling to open the door for anyone. My mom started crying and my dad started picking up the pieces of the sign and throwing them in the trash. "Who put this stupid sign up anyway?" he scolded. He himself had done it, but that was my dad, trying to joke to lighten what had become a dark, uncomfortable mood. As I lay on my bed I could hear the cheerful noise of laughter and shouting of children diminish almost to a whisper.

He knocked lightly, and when I did not answer my dad walked into my room and sat on my bed. "Do you want me to send everyone away?" he said softly. I looked in his eyes and I could see they were red and moist. My father had been crying too.

"No, I'll be all right. I didn't expect this ... Dad, can you ever forgive me for the things I did over there?"

He grabbed my hand and squeezed it. "It was war. You did what you had to do."

"I'm no hero. Why is everyone here?"

"Your family is here because they all love you. They are happy that you are home. You can't stay here sulking. You're going to have to face up to the fact that you were in Vietnam. Lots of boys your age went and came back."

"Lots of them didn't."

"Your cousin is doing all right."

"He was in the *Air Force*," I said angrily.

"He seems settled. He is going to get married. You're just tired."

"Maybe. It was a long fucking trip. My bones are tired. My brain is tired."

"You have to take time to get used to being a civilian once again. We'll go to a ball game. You can start playing in a band again." I sat up in the bed.

"*Mijo*, let me be honest with you. When you first left for Vietnam I wasn't so sure that you would make it back."

"I know."

"Every day was hell for your mom and me. One day a government truck pulled up in front of our house and a man in uniform came up to the door carrying a letter. Your mother almost collapsed. It was the goddamn mailman!" He started laughing. This made me laugh too.

"Oh, Dad, I'm sorry I didn't write more often."

"We will have plenty of time to catch up," he said. "Now, go outside and enjoy your party."

When I stepped out the back door the silence was as deafening as my .50-cal. Everyone was gone. The cool afternoon breeze blew the red, white, and blue crepe paper banners gently against the lawn chairs and glass tables. The *piñata* hung unbroken from the giant tree near the garage. A wheelbarrow full of watery ice and beer sat on the side of the walkway near the still-smoking barbeque. My sister and brother-in-law were starting to put things away and clean up the paper plates and plastic cups left over from the day's celebration.

My sister looked up at me and asked, "Are you all right?"

I walked over to the wheelbarrow and grabbed a beer. "Yeah. Are you?" I popped open a Coors.

"We've just been worried about you. That's all."

"Sorry. I'm OK." I was getting pretty fucking tired of telling everybody I was sorry. What had I done? Oh, well, it didn't mean nothing. I had forgotten my Nam way of thinking. I had to harden myself again.

That night after my sister left, I told my parents about Herman, Dizzy and the guys I hung with over there. I did not mention Herman's death or the gruesome task of body-stripping that I did after every firefight. Like my letters, I gave them a sanitized version of my experience. They knew better than to ask a lot of questions.

When we were all talked out, I went to sleep in my own bed in my own bedroom. I looked around and in the dim light I saw my guitar sitting on its stand, begging to be played. I looked at my desk against the far wall with half-written songs stacked on top. I finally gazed at a large poster taped to my other wall showing a dirty GI in flak jacket and steel pot staring at the camera. Printed along the top was "Vietnam Veterans Against the War." I had put that up when I was home on leave before going to Nam. It had not meant much to me at the time other than being cool and half-heartedly opposing the war. I stared at the image for a long time before finally falling into a deep sleep. When I awoke, I vowed to visit the headquarters of the anti-war organization and join.

My war was *not* over.

I called my friend Lance and he came right over. We were happy to see each other and he gave me an accounting of all our friends. Reggie Rodriquez, James Kell and Mont Dives had been killed in the war while I was gone. The news of Mont hit me hard because when I first got to Nam, I had tried to transfer to his unit as a door-gunner. We got in Lance's car and lit a joint. We stopped at Sam's Liquor Store and bought a fifth of Jack Daniels and we headed to Vermont Avenue.

The headquarters of the Vietnam Veterans Against The War was in Hollywood. When we arrived, I stumbled out of the VW bug and walked in the front door. Various vets with different stages of hair growth manned the typewriters and the phones. A guy with a decent beard and shoulder-length blond hair walked up to me and asked, "When did you get back?"

"A few days," I slurred.

"Welcome home, brother. Who were you with?"

"Blackhorse." That was enough for the typewriters to go silent and the other guys to look up at me.

"We are going to have an action at Griffith Park this coming Sunday. You are welcome to attend. In fact, you are welcome to join our chapter and come to our meetings." He put his hand out and said, "I'm Jack."

"Fred," I said as we shook hands. He looked hard into my eyes, like he was studying a map and looking for landmarks.

He moved his hand up to my shoulder and said, "Look man, I know it hurts. I guarantee that the men in the VVAW will make you feel at home. You will have new comrades here and although we know we could never replace the ones you lost, we will always have your six." My eyes welled up. These were my people.

"And, Fred?"

"Yes?"

"Easy on the bottle. We are here to honor our fallen and we disgrace their memory if the public perceives us as a bunch of drunks. That's what the American Legion is for."

"Right on," I said.

"Bring your shit Sunday. We're throwing it all into a coffin as an act of defiance." I knew what he meant without asking.

"I'll see you there," I said over my shoulder, as I returned to Lance's car.

I arose early Sunday morning and donned my fatigue shirt with a pair of Levi's. I was surprised at how loose my pants fit me. I had to drill an extra notch in my belt. I pulled on my jungle boots and drove to Griffith Park. I arrived two hours early so I could check things out before committing myself to this peace thing. I was amazed at the number of people already there. They were setting up booths and refreshment stands. It was a wide mixture of people. I thought there would only be long-haired counter-culture people, but I saw Mothers for Peace, various church groups, and others. They were decorating their booths with banners and streamers. American and POW/MIA flags flew in the air. All the time in the Nam we were told that the peace demonstrators were anti-American, communist sympathizers and basically the scum of the earth.

I was looking at real Americans at this peace gathering.

I quickly found the booth for Vietnam Veterans Against the War. I looked around for Jack and found him directing fellow vets in various stages of set-up.

"Fred," he said as he looked up and saw me, "Welcome, brother." I was confused with all the action taking place around me and I had mixed feelings about taking part in an anti-war demonstration after just over a week of being back in the World.

But now that I was home, I could not see any good reason for the war and the killing to continue. When I was there, the only thing on my mind was surviving and making it home. Well, here I was.

"Did you bring your medals and ribbons?" Jack asked.

"Yes," I answered, as I fingered the leather pouch on my belt.

"We will be marching in formation to the gravesite about half an hour after the speeches." By now most of the booths were up and decorated. I saw Students for a Democratic Society, the Black Panther Party, the Quakers; I never realized how broad and inclusive the movement was. The last booth on the left was large and fully staffed by young men in brown shirts and brown berets. I was at once drawn to them. They were my people. A large banner blew slowly in the breeze and said: "National Chicano Moratorium Committee."

I was called over by a young Chicano about 18 years old.

"Are you a vet?"

"Yeah, I'm with the Vietnam Veterans Against the War."

"You need to be with us, *hermano. Somos gente. Esta es Aztlán, entiendes?*" I was taken aback. Of course I knew that we were brothers and together we were part of a long line of fierce warriors. Aztlán, the Chicano movement's paradise. My first impressions of this group were not very high but as he talked, I warmed up to them. He laid out reason upon reason as to why I should join their movement. I looked around at the other people in the booth. I found a fine-looking Chicana with long black flowing hair. I was struck with her Aztec beauty and the music they had playing on a tape machine took me back to my childhood.

The kid I was talking to moved forward and we shook hands. I was becoming interested in their movement, but I had come with the VVAW and needed to get back to them.

I said nothing else to him and returned to the VVAW booth and was greeted by my new friends. Jack stood up and for the first time, I noticed the prosthesis where his left leg used to be. He caught me staring.

"101st, A Shau Valley," was all he had to say. I knew the battle.

"Why don't you walk around and get to know the people," he said. "Most are cool, and in your fatigues you will be honored."

"That's what I've been doing. This is awesome. I thought it would be this way when I got off the plane," I ventured. "Some bitch at the airport spat in my face."

"That's the fucking SDS. They are the most militant and the most stupid. They don't separate the warrior from the war. Did you join or were you drafted?"

"Drafted."

"I have no respect for those fuckers at the SDS. They all got their student deferments and if that didn't work, Mommy and Daddy paid top-dollar to some fancy lawyers to get them out. They need to be taken and rubbed in the dirt."

"Or mud," I pictured in my mind. *Mud,* I pondered. I walked around the carnival atmosphere and saw families arriving with picnic baskets. I saw more and more vets arriving. Most wore their fatigues and many of them wore the brown berets I had seen before. They moved to the National Chicano Moratorium Committee's booth. By now it was the largest contingent on the fairway and I couldn't help but notice their discipline. I walked over to the stage and saw Tom Hayden and other anti-war luminaries taking their seats, getting ready to speak.

When the last speaker took the mike I scurried back to the VVAW encampment. By now the park was full of people and I found it difficult to maneuver my way back. Jack and a guy named Dave Portugal were hurriedly arranging the small army into a cohesive formation getting ready for us to march to the open coffin. It was pine and sat on two planks of wood raised about three feet in the air. The first to reach it tossed in the medals, badges, ribbons and other military decorations handed out for their individual achievements in Vietnam. Jack nudged his way through the crowd and stood behind me.

"What you got? Bronze Star? CMH? You know once they're gone, they're gone." I think he was enjoying playing with my mind.

"I don't know if I want to toss it all," I said.

"It's a commitment. You're either in or out," he said. When my time came, Jack, to his credit, looked away. I had no trouble tossing my

Campaign Ribbons or Presidential Unit Citations. I easily threw in my Sharp-Shooter Badge but when it came to my Combat Infantryman Badge, I hesitated. I valued this award. Only a small percentage of Nam vets received this special citation. Jack turned his head to look at me and I let it go.

Suddenly on my right flank a great commotion commenced. Police with riot gear marched toward us with batons and face shields held up over their heads.

Jack and Dave started yelling, "Pigs!" I ran for cover and was immediately sprayed with pepper spray and hit with a night stick over the head. The blow opened a seam over my right eye that started a flow of blood all over my face. *Jesus!* This shit never happened in Vietnam.

I was trained to identify the enemy. I saw them divided into three groups. The majority was LAPD in their blue uniforms. There was a small contingent of Park Police in their Boy Scout uniforms, but the cruelest by far were the Los Angeles County sheriffs. Dressed in their khaki and green, they seemed to take pleasure in their work. It was one of those bastards that attacked me.

I was trained to fight to the death with my attacker. I wiped the spray from my eyes and tackled the son of a bitch who assaulted me. I was immediately smothered by three of his comrades. I was hit again and again though I offered no resistance. I was kicked repeatedly in the ribs and back. As I was held down, feet and arms spread open, the motherfucker who started it all roughly cuffed me and picked me up by the wrists and shoved me in a van that already held six cats who were guilty of the same crime I had committed: exercising our First Amendment rights. I had no idea why the cops were attacking us. I leaned to the dirty window and could make out whole families receiving much the same treatment. I lost all respect for the law that day.

After eight hours of overcrowding and no food or drink, my father picked me up at the East Los Angeles Sheriff station on Beverly Boulevard, five miles from our house. I had never been so happy to see him. Even more so than when I got off the plane.

"What did you get yourself mixed up in?" he asked, without judgment. He kept his eyes on the road and did not turn to look at me. I think that would have made him cry. I could tell that he was hurt deep down inside at what I, his only son, had been through the previous year. And now this!

"Dad, there is a war going on right here, in this country, in this community. Until today, I never saw the strength of opposition to the war I just abdicated. I believe the American people can bring an end to this vicious war."

"Vicious?"

"I don't know if I ever could tell you the truth about what goes on there."

He finally looked at me. "Try me," he almost whispered. "I am your father and I love you more than you sometimes realize."

"I know, Dad."

I thought of my talks with Gordon, and although he helped me tremendously, he was not my father. There was nobody like Art Rivera. There was no doubt in my mind that I could tell my father what really happened in the Nam and why I felt so compelled now to protest and see that no more Herman Johnsons or even Joe Harveys died in that muddy mess of a country. I had traveled halfway around the world to get home; I now realized that what I had been searching for was the ear of Art Rivera, my father. I had it now, and once my mouth opened, I felt it would never shut. I told him about Herman. I told him everything and in doing so I felt cleansed. A tremendous weight was lifted from my heart.

Monday morning, after taking one look at my face, my mom wanted to take me to the hospital. My dad and I finally prevailed but she made me wear icepacks above my eye all morning.

That afternoon Lance came by and took me to the bank. I had $7,000 sitting in a trust account from my days with Mercury Records. Apparently, Jackie Coogan, the child star during the era of silent films, turned 21 to find that his mother had stolen $68 million from him.

The Coogan Act was passed and all entertainers had a percentage of their earnings placed in a trust until they turned 21. I hit that mark in the Nam and I was here to collect.

I bought a car and no longer had to rely on my buddy, Lance, to get me around town. I went and bought clothes and a new bass and amp. I started doing gigs around town and I was happy to be home, living with my parents and doing what I loved, playing music.

Still, something was tugging at me and I had cold sweats at night and was easily distracted during the day by cars backfiring, and especially the sound of helicopters. They all belonged to the Sheriff's Department, and they had many. They were East L.A.'s occupation army.

I was on the mailing list of the Chicano Anti-War Group. It was early August 1970 and I had been attending covert meetings in East Los Angeles. There was much paranoia among many of the members, and we shifted our meetings from location to location, avoiding anything that looked like a pattern. Sometimes we would meet in a church basement, sometimes in a living room with closed curtains. I felt like I was in the Vietcong; our enemy was the L.A. County Sheriff.

The key slogan of the movement was, "Our struggle is not in Vietnam but in the movement for social justice at home." I was in the Nam to fight a war supposedly to free a people from tyranny and social injustice. I fought shoulder-to-shoulder with guys who thought nothing of calling me a beaner or Herman Johnson a nigger. I was home now and I realized why the movement needed my presence to inspire the youngbloods.

We grew stronger every day. Carlos Salgado, Bobbie Padilla, Sal Alcazar and other well-read, natural-born leaders had organized marches in 1969 and early 1970. These actions had gone off without incident and this encouraged them to join the larger National Chicano Moratorium Committee, the one I had met up with at the Peace-In at Griffith Park when I first came home. The plan called for a march down Whittier Boulevard through East Los Angeles on August 29.

As the time approached, my family and my friend Lance begged me — *pleaded with me* — not to do it. There was talk of the largest sheriff's presence ever assembled in Los Angeles history and the press coverage predicted trouble beyond imagination. I remembered the helicopters spreading propaganda in Nam during my first weeks there. I believed Mayor Sam Yorty's propaganda machine was spewing fear among the citizens of L.A.

No matter how much my family beseeched and implored that I stay home that day, I knew it was my destiny to be there. Every patch of ground we took in Vietnam, every inch that we moved the NVA back was all leading me right here. Herman died, Bobby died, and even Teddy Jones died for my right to stand up for the injustices laid on our people. My dad, having to swim in the pool on the day before they cleaned it. My high school girlfriend's father insulting my dad at our front door. All this would be put to rest on the 29th.

I was made captain of a group of roughly fifty people who gathered around the sign I held high in the air. Our group was a mixture of students, families, hippies and veterans of World War II, Korea, and Vietnam. I was made captain because even though I was only twenty one, I was older than those great college students who organized our area.

At the early morning meeting, all captains were instructed to keep the peace at all costs. There was to be no provocation on the part of the marchers. We were to stay in the street. There were groups of people all over East Los Angeles: from Lincoln Park, City Terrace, Boyle Heights ... if it was in the *barrio*, it was represented.

A festive mood prevailed as the morning chill gave way to lush rays of sun beaming out of a clear blue sky. Laughter filled the air and the sweet scent of humanity hung low like a blissful cloud. We were ready. At exactly 8 a.m., more than 100 whistles were blown to signal the start of the march.

We moved out. We came down Whittier Boulevard toward Atlantic Boulevard, where we would turn left and make our way to

Belvedere Park. This was an extreme strategy born of much discussion and argument by the top organizers. The park sat right next to a sheriff's station. It was a bold move made to express our commitment to peace. We were following the paths laid down by Gandhi and Martin Luther King. If everything worked out, our march would end in joyous celebration *with* our tormenters. There was to be no talk or yelling out the word "Pig." The key word in the Peace Movement was forever to remain *Peace*.

On we marched, past storefronts full of shiny new shoes, past car dealerships displaying giant, long, slick cars. I looked at the middle-aged man marching on my left and felt a deep love and a great inner peace just for being human. That feeling had been stripped away from me in the war. I was just one in the beautiful flow of thousands of people.

It started out slowly as we made the wide turn onto Atlantic Boulevard. Screams and the all-too-familiar sounds of helicopters filled my ears. I knew the sound of panic. I knew the sounds of war. I thought I had left them behind in the jungle by the Cambodian border. I could hear the pop, pop of tear gas canisters being fired up ahead.

Suddenly, our peaceful walk turned into frenzied running and scattering. I looked up and saw the fucking choppers dropping tear gas from the sky. I had been sprayed with Agent Orange, I had seen the devastating destruction of napalm. I was witness to an airstrike so close that I could see the pilot give me the thumbs up from his cockpit. Where was I? *Americans* were dropping ruin from the sky upon us, and ranks of them were charging the crowd with a vengeance that I had never been witness to.

They made the Griffith Park incident look like child's play. They formed a line and a flanking maneuver that I was very familiar with. I was a trained soldier and I ran and outflanked those bastards.

I picked up a tear gas canister rolling in front of me and hurled it right back at them. They picked up on me and shot two more canisters at my feet. The gas was so intense that I could not breathe or see. My eyes teared up and instantly swelled shut.

I leaned against a brick building upwind of the gas and unzipped my fly and pissed into my joined palms. I spread my urine all over my face and my eyes and felt instant relief. This was a tactic I had learned from watching the Vietcong after we gassed them. I was now on the receiving end. I was once again in battle and my old instincts kicked in immediately. Of course, the first plan of action called on taking out the helicopters.

I laughed as I put my Johnson away. So far the only weapon I had to counter the attack was my dick, and as young and virile as I was, this would never do. What was called for was a hard charge to take possession of my enemy's weapon. This seemed to be impossible, but how could I think straight with piss all over my face?

I frantically searched for the smallest cop and ran as hard as I could into his chest. He was caught off guard and he relaxed his grip of the shotgun just barely enough for me to wrestle it away. In truth, that was the last thing I remembered. It was later relayed to me that I was at once taken down by four pigs who took all their fears and frustrations out on my insensible body. I was kicked in the head with sufficient intensity to suffer a concussion. They put their boots into the side of my torso enough to break three of my ribs and puncture my lung. I lay on the ground in front of the Silver Dollar Café bleeding, motionless, and as broken as those bodies that I used to have to go though in Nam after a firefight.

Somebody did go through *my* pockets and found my VA card. I was barely conscious as they loaded me into the ambulance. As dangerous as I was, I was no longer a threat and everyone's attention was focused on the events transpiring in the bar. A pig, and what else could we call them, apparently had put a round of tear gas directly into the head of a reporter. The smoke was thick and the air that started that day as the sweet scent of humanity hanging low like a blissful cloud was now the all-too-familiar smell of war and death. I slipped in and out of wakefulness as we took the 710 to Long Beach. I had vague visions of the emergency room and the welcome shot of Demerol that dulled the extreme pain I was in and settled my mind.

When I was finally established in my room with my ribs wrapped, I looked around and thought I was back at the Third Field Hospital in Saigon. The dull green walls and black and white linoleum floors shouted out, "The war is not over! It will never end!"

That night, my family arrived and I was thrilled to see my mom, dad and sister with her husband, Bob. I realized that my mother was the cord that held us all together. Her strength was amazing, and as she looked down at me I could only imagine the pure pain and suffering she had gone through while I was in the Nam. I thought of my letters home and how I had tried to shield her from the brutality of war.

There was no hiding the truth from her now. Here I was, head bandaged and ribs wrapped, her only son writhing in pain. It was at that moment that I came to understand that she had known the truth all along. My dad and sister knew it too. All that mattered was that we were all together as a family. I vowed never to shut my door on them again.

The next morning bright and early, my father came to visit me on his way to work. He brought me the newspaper and a cup of hot coffee. I read that Ruben Salazar, a reporter for the Times, was the one who was killed inside of the Silver Dollar Café.

The mayor was calling it a riot.

The public was calling it a police riot.

It was indeed a riot, instigated by those fucking cowards, the L.A. County sheriffs. I had seen the hatred in their eyes, felt the brutality in the way they swung those nightsticks and felt the cruelty when they kicked me with such pleasure.

My dad got up to go to the bathroom and the paper was left strewn about on the table open to the crossword page. I glanced over at 8 down; an eleven-letter word for *enduring through all time*. I saw it immediately, **Everlasting**.

Epilogue

On August 2, 1964, I was a sophomore at Montebello High School, driving over the old wooden bridge on Bluff Road to visit my best friend, Scott. As I reached the center of the bridge, a newsflash came over the car radio that the North Vietnamese had just attacked the USS Maddox in the Gulf of Tonkin. The first thought that entered my mind was: *I'm going to war.* I forgot about it by the time I pulled into Scott's driveway.

Five years later I found myself a soldier in the United States Army in the jungles of Vietnam. What came out of that experience defined my existence. I went there a boy and came back a raw man. Aged beyond my 21 years and unprepared for the troubled years to come. I was witness to death, cruelty, and a war so brutal that I was scarred from the time I first searched a dead body to the day I discovered that our military managed to kill 430,000 South Vietnamese civilians.

In 1970, it was no surprise that 65 percent of American servicemen abused drugs. We were sent there alone, and returned home alone, 58,000 of us in body bags. Those of us who survived carried back a collective shame to a nation that hated us. Yes, it is true: I was spat upon and called a baby killer at the San Francisco Airport.

After my mother passed away, my sister and I were going through Mom's possessions as people do when closing a home. We were trying to figure out what to keep, what to give away, and what belongings were personal to each of us. My sister, Barbara, came across a shoebox filled with letters. We discovered that Mom had kept every letter I had ever written to my family from Vietnam. Chronologically arranged, covered in that red dirt of Vietnam, the letters gave us a few hours of distraction from our grief. When we finished reading them, I took them home and they sat on my shelf for years.

A friend suggested that I type them onto my computer so I could better preserve them. As I typed out each letter, memories flooded my mind as I recalled the truth of every incident that I wrote home about. I realized that I was always trying to shield my parents from the horrors of my existence. The letters are the genesis of the book you are holding in your hands, and they were purposely left unedited with misspellings and grammatical mistakes. They were written by the twenty-year-old Fred, sometimes by torchlight, almost always under duress.

The names have been changed except for a handful of men that I loved. For my surviving brothers: I am happy that you may see your name in this book and not on a marble slab in Washington, D.C.

All the battle scenes are as true as my 66-year-old mind can remember them. Because some events and characters are composites, it is more accurate to call Raw Man a novel, rather than a memoir, but most of the things I write about happened in front of my eyes ... seared into my heart and for me, 44 years later, are still real.

My time in the field left me with deep, chronic back pain and PTSD so severe that I have had episodes where I have actually felt like I was back in the Nam. Like so many combat veterans, I found myself continuing to self-medicate upon my return to civilian life. There was nobody that I felt I could talk to about my experiences. Who could possibly understand? I found my way back into the music business and none of my new or old friends ever heard me speak a word about Vietnam. It was a shameful secret that I kept to myself. I became a Winter Warrior. First came the heavy drinking and eventually the hard drugs arrived. I sank lower and lower into the depths of alcoholism.

In 1974 I was given my first miracle. I met and married the most beautiful, caring, and sympathetic woman, Lynda Gomez, without whose unconditional love and support, I doubt that I would be alive today. She breathed fresh hope into me and stood by my side through the darkest days of my life, always doing her best to love a broken man. She gave me the precious gift of three wonderful children. Always running through my mind was the thought that God would take one back to settle the debt of taking that boy's life in the Nam. After years of replaying the events of that fateful day in my mind, I am certain it was me, and not Benson, who fired that fatal round.

There were problems with all three births. We lost a fourth. Did God collect my toll? My daughter was born with a 50 percent chance of survival. A doctor asked me if I was ever exposed to Agent Orange. I thought of that old crop duster flying over us and nodded my head. Our youngest son, Nathan, was in neo-natal intensive care for close to two months. He fought for his little life and still, I could not get sober. At the time of this writing, he is a healthy young man of 27.

Twenty-seven is a big number for me. Having thrown all of my medals, ribbons, and awards into that coffin at the peace rally in Griffith Park in 1970, I realized that the war was over for me and now I had children. I wanted to have something to leave them to remember me by. The year was 1987. I was driving down Beverly Boulevard with a beer between my legs when I saw a building with a sign that said: "Vet Center." I had driven on that road hundreds of times and never noticed it before. The thought crossed my mind that maybe they could help me recover my medals.

I walked in the front door and was greeted by a friendly woman. I explained my dilemma and she straightaway told me that yes, yes she could get them from St. Louis. I was pleased and slightly buzzed. She searched my face and saw right through me.

"I have no problem helping you with your wish, but are you willing to do something for me?" she asked.

"Anything."

"We are a separate entity from the VA. We receive our funding solely on the amount of traffic we can generate. We are an outreach program and as long as you're here, would you mind filling out a small questionnaire?" she maintained that trusty smile and I told her I would be happy to do it.

What could it hurt? I asked myself. We sat across from each other at her desk, and she pulled a form from her top drawer. She handed it to me along with a pen. I opened it up and saw the standard questions: Name, rank, years served, marital status, all innocuous questions that I quickly answered and turned the page. The first question on the next page made me break into a cold sweat.

"Did you ever kill anyone?"

I started trembling softly. The questions were all along the same line and when I reached question seven, my heart stopped and a tremendous force screamed within me and I felt the dam about to break.

"DID ANYONE EVER DIE IN YOUR ARMS?" The dam burst with such incredible power that I almost knocked her off her chair. I broke down crying like I had never cried before. Before long I was telling her that I was an alcoholic and cocaine addict. I had never uttered those truthful words before. She stood up and embraced me and I cried some more. All the hurt, guilt, shame, and remorse that I had carried around for the last seventeen years came to the surface simultaneously and like a mass jail break, they broke free together and laid siege to my soul.

Her name is Natalie Matson and on that day in May, she saved my life. She told me that I was suffering from post-traumatic stress disorder. She called it PTSD. The words meant nothing to me for I had never heard of such a thing. I just knew that I carried a deep hurt within me and I had been stuffing it back down inside with Jack Daniels for so many years. I wanted to be a good husband. I desperately wanted to be a good father. Some force was holding me down in chains. I have heard that you hit your bottom when you throw the shovel down and quit digging. I threw that shovel all the way back to An Loc.

She told me that the only way I could deal with Vietnam was sober. I had no idea of what she was talking about. We sat and talked for over an hour. I told her of Herman. I told her about Teddy Jones.

She listened. We made an appointment for the following week and asked me if I could go that long without a drink or a drug.

"I don't know," I answered honestly. She told me to try it one day at a time. Today I have close to ten thousand one-days-at-a-time clean and sober. I got hooked into the Vet Center and all of the programs that they offer. I spent all of 1988 and most of 1989 attending debriefing groups. I did this group and that group and any sponsored event. I found my new platoon in that group of Vietnam Veterans attempting to stay sober and work through PTSD. There were no secrets among us. Some of us made it. Some of us did not. As in Vietnam, some of us died. Our team leader was himself a combat veteran. Ed Carrillo guided us through our trauma. Gradually the demons were replaced with thoughts of hope. We found that in helping each other, we helped ourselves. Within my first three weeks out of the Army, I became a life member of Vietnam Veterans Against the War. I remain active in VVAW to this day.

I was driving down the street one day and I saw my buddy, Tim, a former medic with the 101st Airborne, walking out of a gun shop with his six-year-old son. I made a U-turn and pulled up next to him and we slapped hands and smiled, and Tim looked like he didn't have a problem to his name. I left him standing on the curb smiling with his boy and went on my way. The next day they told me that he went straight home and blew his brains out right in front of his son. This is PTSD.

Twenty-two veterans commit suicide every day in this country. If this book helps touch one life, it has done its job.

Fred Rivera

Raw Man

Publishing Raw Man

Fred returned from a distant battlefield only to discover that the enemy had stowed away, infiltrating his psyche through a breach in his battered spirit, where it continues to wage war, one ambush at a time. PTSD is an insidious foe, but not invincible. Publishing Raw Man *will be a battle won, and a personal triumph for Fred. Be part of his victory.*

Funding for the publication of *Raw Man* was made possible by all of you listed here, who accepted our invitation on Kickstarter to be part of his victory.

M.M. Cranston
> *I dedicate this on behalf of my father, James R. Cranston, Lt. Col. USAF (Ret.), 7th Air Force HQ, Tan Son Nhut Air Base, Vietnam.*

Lauren Marie Salcido

Steve McDonald

Dante Puccetti
> *I dedicate this to SP/4 Don Poirior, who ran down the hill with the M-60 machine-gun and saved my life during my ambush in Nam.*

Sally Pla

John Westfall

Eva Westfall

Renee Nicole Whitfield

Lisa Ramirez

Victoria Starr

Elizabeth Sloan
I dedicate this on behalf of Chester W. Sloan, WWII veteran.

Cathy Sempol

Mike Wall

Andrea Travers

Helene Leonard

Miceal Kelly

Dick Cummins

Chris Anderson

Connie Nguyen
I dedicate this on behalf of all the innocent civilian war casualties and all the mistreated veterans who are overlooked and forgotten after the war. And on behalf of my mother, I am obliged to dedicate this to her father who served in the Viet Nam War, Charles E. Auge. I don't know his rank, but I do know, if he never served in the war, I would not be here today.

Carin Johnson-Kragler

Alma Delacruz Gossman

Ronald Sandate

Margaret Southern

Amanda Mullens

Kenneth Weene

Lynn Buettner
I donate on behalf of all of our men and women who serve our country.

Sue Wong

Michael L Sawyer
I dedicate this donation to All who have served.

Austin Storm

Pamella M. Bowen

Raymond and Christi Lacoste

Amanda Byzak

Jeannie Meador Chandler

Don Maker
I donate on behalf of Spec. 4 Harry Maker.

Rob Swofford

Michelle Bushner Wise

Nicholas Fortuna

Kimberly Stanphill
I donate on behalf of all the veterans that I've worked with and my grandfather, a veteran from WWII.

Jeffrey D. Urbina

Nancy Milby

Robert Hill

Thornton Sully
I donate on behalf of my father, Artillery Capt. Langdon Sully, US Army, WWII, Solomon Islands.

Harry Caldwell

Jesse Smith

Deanna Paige Uranga

Sable Jordan

Kim Hoedeman

Jess Cotton

Jeff Semones

Brian Meredith
I dedicate this on behalf of Major General Smedley Butler, who, by the time of his death, had become not only the most decorated Marine in U.S. history, but also this nation's most important 'whistleblower' regarding the true business objectives driving its bloody wars, occupations and interventions.

Chynna Barron

Jay Nomura

Patricia Oppelt

Bunnie Rivera
I dedicate this on behalf of all those who serve.

Therese Pontrelli

Patricia C. Lowery

Russell Shor

Richard Urick

Jasper Langedijk
Dedicated to this Raw Man project and to the people the book is about.

Sgt. Michael Whitfield and Cpl. Renee Whitfield

James Williams
I donate in honor of Edward James Olmos - aka Admiral Adama.

Jill Anfinson

Annie Drake

Wendy Joseph

Marie Therese Stone

Frank and Cathy Merickel

Courtney Janes
I donate on behalf of John Janes.

Kimberly Persiani

Tom McDermond

Ryan Rivera
I contribute on behalf of Jake, Grace, and Julia Rivera.

Lisa Southwick

Alexander Franco

Cheryl Davis
I donate on behalf of our son-in-law, Chad Folds, currently serving.

Holly Ryno

Judy Olmos

Michael J. Martin

Thomas Dahl

Cynthis Lazaris
I donate on behalf of George Paul Lazaris.

Brian Fiala

Kaija Keel

Bernd Kistenmacher
I donate with best wishes for Fred Rivera.

Helene Leonard

Jonathan Trujillo

Cameron Hamilton
I donate on behalf of all veterans and Shovel Head Ed, the guy who carries around a ball peen hammer to tune up nuts!

Barry Drucker

I cannot thank you enough for your sacrifices for our abundant freedoms, and I wish you, Fred, and your family, good health and happiness.

Kristine Tsatsakos-Starr

I donate on behalf of Murray Gentile.

James Caouette

Vivian Alvarez

I donate in honor of Frank Alvarez, Red Bull Battalion, 34th Infantry, WWII.

Kayla Roth

I donate on behalf of PFC Michael Roth, USMC, Vietnam War 1970-71.

John Hager, SSgt., Air Force Viet Nam 69-70 & 71-72.

This is to all of us that suffer in silence, God Bless all of us!

Tony & Tiffany Vakilian

Jason Lawrence

In honor of my father John E. Lawrence, USN, who enlisted at age 17 and is sole living survivor of the USS Henley that was torpedoed by the Japanese. He served and fought in WWII, Korea and Vietnam. Now residing in Vista, CA and just celebrated his 90th birthday January this year.

Freddy Rivera (Fred Jr.)

Alfredo Ballesteros

Robert & Paula Gomez

J. Dow Covey, Cpt., US Army

Sharon Johnson

Frank S. Herrara

Chris Davis

I donate in honor of Dan Chadwick, CMSgt., US Air Force, Korea

Lisa Ramirez

Amanda Mullens

I donate on behalf of my father, 1ˢᵗ Sgt. John H. Mullens, Jr. (Ret.) and the 2-70th Armor "Aces of Death".

Wendy Manning

In honor of my Uncle Fred Rivera - so proud of you.

Mike Casper

I donate in honor of cabin crew of UA 93.

Scott Travers

I donate on behalf of Evert Raymond Curtis Sr., Evert Raymond Curtis Jr., Charles Travers, Walter Ray Travers.

Nico Loeff

Thank you to all veterans and men and women currently serving in our country's military. God bless you all.

Gerald Arriloa

John Salcido

Thank you, Fred, and all of you have served in our armed forces!

Wayne Bosna

Dedicated to vets everywhere.

Jim St. John

I donate to honor vets everywhere.

Niles Nicholson

Peace to the veterans who served our country.

Craig Albert

In loving memory of Leonard R. Albert, 1ˢᵗ Lieutenant, US Air Force ('52 to '56).

William Rodriguez

I donate in honor of vets everywhere.

Josie Noriega

Lance Goto
To current and past vets.

Barbara Briones
With pride, in honor of my brother Fred Rivera, U.S. Army, Blackhorse Cavalry Division.

Jerry Clark
Thanks to my brother Gary Clark, a member of the USAF during the Vietnam era. He has helped me and other veterans through his personal counseling as well as his writing. He has encouraged me to be my best after war. Thanks, brother!
(Editor's note: Gary Clark was a true friend to all veterans, and a member of our staff at A Word with You Press. Gary died of cancer as "Raw Man" was in the final stages of editing before going to press. At Fred's heartfelt suggestion, a true character in the book was given Gary's name so that Gary will remain with us all in spirit, and wink at us when we come across his name.)

Catherine Kelly Baird
For my amazing husband Monty Baird "the Sarge" – a true brother to Fred and all Vietnam vets.

Lee Mentley
Peace

John Fortuna
Dedicated to vets everywhere.

Robert L Brieda
In memory of Sgt. Eric Williams, US Army Medic, KIA Afghanistan, July 23, 2012, Operation Freedom - Dustoff.

Tom Noriega, USCG 1984-1988.
Thanks to all the men and women who have served and sacrificed.

Alex B/Loretta Pellem
Dedicated to William Watkins, US Army Rangers (Ret.) & Anthony Sink, US Army (Ret.)

John Westfall
To all who have served.

Eva Westfall, USN (Ret.)

Wheeler Backer
Dedicated to my father, my brother and to all other veterans who have sacrificed so much for our country and our freedom.

Edward James Olmos

Anthony Salcido

Parisianne Modert
Dedicated to my Father - Dr. Alson W. Modert, MD - Navy Hospital Apprentice First Class USNR - WWII – Deceased.

Kyle Katz

Michael Stang
Dedication: Marian C. Spaulding, Yeoman Second Class, 1942-1944.

Stephanie Allison

Marie Panlilio

Laura Girardeau
I donate in honor of Fred Rivera's fallen comrade, Herman Johnson.

Albert Foster

Walter Savell
I donate on behalf of myself, my father, and my grandfather: PO2 Walter L. Savell III USN (Ret.), LCDR Walter L. Savell Jr. USNR WWII Arlington, COL Walter L. Savell Sr. USA,WWII Arlington.

Lynda Rivera
In honor of my husband Fred Rivera, who served our country in Vietnam. I am proud to watch as he continues to serve by helping veterans who live with the effects of PTSD, that they, too, may have a better life.

Several of our donors chose to remain anonymous.

Thank you all from Fred Rivera, Lynda Rivera, and the entire staff at *A Word with You Press*:

Tiffany Monique, Diana Diehl, Derek Thompson, Morgan Sully, Gary Clark, Teri Rider, Billy Holder, Kristine Tsatsakos-Starr, Thornton Sully, and project associates Robert Kahn and Scott Siedman

"There it is."

–Fred Rivera

Fred Rivera was born in East Los Angeles, raised in Montebello, and currently lives in Murrieta, California, with his wife of over forty years, Lynda. Together they have raised raised three wonderful children, Andrew, Marissa and Nathan. Writing and publishing Raw Man is a natural extension of his volunteer work with the sober community of Temecula, and with various organizations nationwide focused on supporting veterans and their families grappling with the lingering effects of war, PTSD. Despite living in constant pain, Fred is devoted to living a creative, joyful life, counting on the other constant in his life ... the loving support of his friends and family.

Join Fred on Facebook @ Fred Snowball Rivera or log on to rawmanthebook.com

Full circle, Author's note:
As every veteran knows, the bonds we form with our comrades-in-arms at time of war are unbreakable. John Fortuna, who you met inside these covers, not only took the initial photo that Scott Siedman used to create our cover, but also took this recent photo of me. Proof that I get better looking as I age!
F.R.

A word about *A Word with You Press*

Publishers and Purveyors of Fine Stories

In addition to being a full service publishing house founded in 2009, *A Word with You Press* is a playful, passionate, and prolific consortium of writers connected by our collective love of the written word. We are, as well, devoted readers drawn to the notion that there is nothing more beautiful or powerful than a well-told story.

We realize that great writers and artists don't just happen. They are created by nurturing, mentoring, and by inspiration. We provide this literary triad through our interactive website, www. awordwithyoupress.com.

Visit us here to enter our writing contests and to become part of a broad but highly personal writing community. Improve your skills with what has become a significant, *de facto* writers' workshop, and approach us with your own publishing dreams and ambitions. We are always looking for new talent. Visit our store to buy from a distinguished list of our books, which include the work of a Pulitzer Prize winner, an award-winning poet, and first rate literary fiction. Attend our seminars and retreats, and consider joining our growing list of published authors.

A writer is among the lucky few who discovers that art is not a diversion or distraction from everyday life; rather, art is an essential expression of the human spirit.

If you are such a writer, join us on our website and help us save the alphabet one letter at a time!

Available or coming soon from

A Word with You Press

Almost Avalon

by Thornton Sully

A young couple struggles with love and life on the island
frontier just twenty-six miles west of Los Angeles.

The Mason Key
Volume One
A John Mason Adventure

by David Folz

A street urchin in England about the time the Colonies declare
independence cheats the hangman to begin this historical
adventure series. He discovers that his father's death may not
have been an accident at all, but part of a broader conspiracy.

The Mason Key II
Aloft and Alow
A John Mason Adventure

by David Folz

The historical saga continues as young Mason becomes
a mid-shipman on the very ship on which he was as
stow-away at the conclusion of *Mason Key, Volume One*.

Angus MacDream and the Roktopus Rogue
by Isabelle Rooney-Freedman

Young adults on a mythical Scottish island save the world.

The Wanderer
by Derek Thompson

A stranger wakes up on a deserted beach and
embarks on a journey of discovery.

The Coffee Shop Chronicles, Vol. I,
Oh, the Places I Have Bean!

An anthology of award-winning stories inspired by
events that occurred over a cup of coffee.

Visiting Angels and Home Devils
by Dr. Don Hanley, Ph.D.

A discussion guide for couples.

The Courtesans of God
by Thornton Sully

A novel based on the real life of a temple priestess
in the palace of the King of Malaysia.

Bounce

by Pulitzer Prize winner Jonathan Freedman

A nutty watermelon man, a spurned she-lawyer, a frustrated carioca journalist and a misanthropic parrot set out to Brazil to change the world.

Left Unlatched
in the hopes that you'll come in...
A Book of Poetry

by R.T. Sedgwick

Winner of the 2012 San Diego Book Awards – Poetry.

The Boy with a Torn Hat

by Thornton Sully
Debut novel was a finalist in the 2010 USA
Book Awards for Literary Fiction

"Henry Miller meets Bob Dylan in this coming of age romp played out in the twisted alleyways and smoky beer halls of Heidelberg. Sully is a cunning wordsmith and master of bringing music to art and art to language. Excessive, expressive, lusty, and once in a blue metaphor—profound. Here is what I mean: 'Some women are imprisoned like a tongue in a bell—they swing violently but unnoticed until the moment of contact with the bronze perimeter of their existence—and then the sound they make astonishes us its power and pain and beauty, and its immediacy'—Wunderbar"

—Jonathan Freedman, Pulitzer Prize winner

CPSIA information can be obtained at www.ICGtesting.com
Printed in the USA
BVOW04s0414101014

370282BV00001B/40/P